THE POWER OF THE PAST

Emily knew now that her errant mother's specter would follow her everywhere. She could see it in the insufferable Colonel Rogers' mocking, calculating gaze, even after she had vehemently denied his infuriating insinuations.

"Althea Wyndham's daughter virtuous? Impossible!" the colonel said. He took her arm in his and squeezed her hand intimately. "But whoever your lover is, he does not do you justice, child. You should be decked out in jewels and satins. I should treat you better. Perhaps we can come to some arrangement of profit to us both—as well as pleasure."

This man, like every other, seemed so sure of his mastery over her—even as she was becoming increasingly unsure of her strength.

How then could Emily accept the impetuous proposal of the Duke of Wrotherham, the man she loved despite herself—and expect him to trust her when she could not trust herself. . . ?

THE EMERALD DUCHESS

The Emerald Duchess

Barbara Hazard

A SIGNET BOOK

NEW AMERICAN LIBRARY

NAL BOOKS ARE AVAILABLE AT QUANTITY DISCOUNTS
WHEN USED TO PROMOTE PRODUCTS OR SERVICES.
FOR INFORMATION PLEASE WRITE TO PREMIUM MARKETING DIVISION,
NEW AMERICAN LIBRARY, 1633 BROADWAY,
NEW YORK, NEW YORK 10019.

SIGNET, SIGNET CLASSIC, MENTOR, ONYX, PLUME, MERIDIAN
and NAL BOOKS are published by NAL PENGUIN INC.,
1633 Broadway, New York, New York 10019

First Printing, January, 1985

3 4 5 6 7 8 9 10 11

PRINTED IN THE UNITED STATES OF AMERICA

For my friend Olga
With love and thanks

Prologue

∽

It had been over two years since her mother's death, but Emily Wyndham could still remember that brilliant September afternoon with a clarity that refused to fade. Indeed, she knew she would remember it all her life, for how could she ever forget the day when she had changed so suddenly from a highborn lady of quality to a disgraced girl with a tarnished name, so poor she was forced to earn her bread to survive?

Sometimes there were only fragments of memory, like pieces of dreams spinning in her mind: her aunt's dislike, her uncle's lechery, the sneers of the maid and barely concealed contempt of the housekeeper, the elderly lawyer reciting in a dry, unemotional voice the nonexistence of any inheritance. Or she would see those letters she had found from her mother's lovers, and her stomach would churn anew in horror and revulsion.

And then she would remember how innocent she had been, how insulated and protected by the knowledge that she was a Wyndham from Berks, the daughter of the late Captain Thomas Wyndham of the Royal Navy and the niece of Lord Gregory Wyndham. How little she had known that her mother's indiscretions had brought such infamy to the name of Wyndham that she would never be able to use it again.

But sometimes, instead of fragments, she would remember in detail the afternoon of her mother's funeral.

She remembered how quiet and empty the cottage had seemed after the carriages of the few mourners had driven away, and how she had gone to her mother's room, where she had spent so many hours, hoping to feel close to her still. She had opened the curtains and the windows as well, for the

7

room was dim and stuffy. As she did so, the bright sunlight streamed in as if to mock her sadness. The room was neat and impersonal, with all signs of illness and death removed. Now the table near the bed was almost empty, instead of being crowded with pills, medicines, and cordials. She stared at the smooth counterpane of the bed with its primly aligned pillows, and clasped her hands together tightly, trying not to give in to her grief.

It had taken Althea Wyndham a long time to die, and her daughter felt it was almost more than she could bear, to see her beautiful mother fade away, getting thinner and thinner, but still with the bright complexion of the consumptive that seemed such a mockery next to the faded blond of her hair. Her uncle had brought baskets of delicacies to tempt the invalid's appetite, and flowers to cheer her, but outside of his visits and those of the doctor, the rest of the village left them strictly alone. They had arrived here from London only a year before, when her mother could no longer ignore her illness, although she claimed the country air would cure her faster than any smart city doctor could.

Her daughter had wondered then why she had chosen this little cottage, with only a housekeeper-cook and a raw country maid as staff, but Althea Wyndham had offered no explanation, and somehow her daughter had not liked to question her. They had always had plenty of money in the past, even though her father had died in the Battle of the First of June, serving with Howe in the Royal Navy, when his only child was two years old. From the time she could remember, her mother had been a gay widow, always going to this party and that, beautifully dressed and coiffed and jeweled. They had lived in an elegant town house surrounded by servants, and although Mrs. Wyndham had not married again, her daughter knew it was not for lack of opportunity, for she had been much sought after. As a little girl, Emily had often been dazzled by the sight of her mother dressed for a rout or a ball, and one evening had exclaimed as Mrs. Wyndham whirled to show off her new gown of white satin spangled all over with tiny beads. "Oh, Mama, how beautiful you are! Just like an angel!"

Her mother had laughed gaily and replied, "Hardly an angel, but thank you kindly, Miss Emily Margaret Wyndham.

Someday, my dear, you shall look like an angel, too, and break all the young men's hearts."

"I shall?" Emily had asked doubtfully, her eyes wide, but then she had looked in the pier glass and compared herself to her mother, and had shaken her head. She was twelve then, and thin and pale with fine, flyaway blond hair. "Never to compare to you, Mama," she had said sadly, and her mother had kissed her for the compliment.

She had been a lonely child, although she was unaware of it. There were no young relatives or friends to play with, and so she lived in a world of her own devising, a world of fantasies made up from the books she read. There had been some talk of sending her to school, and Emily had looked forward to it with a delicious sense of dread for the unknown, but it had not come to pass. Mrs. Wyndham had come back from inspecting one excellent school for the daughters of gentlemen in such a temper that she had frightened her daughter with her wild talk of silly old maids and jealous cats. Somehow Emily had stayed at home, and various masters came and went, teaching her to dance, to play the pianoforte and to sing. She had begged to be allowed to learn French and Latin, and her mother had agreed reluctantly. "For it would be fatal to turn you into a bluestocking, my dear," she had said.

Emily had no idea what a bluestocking was, but she wished to be able to read and understand her father's books. Fortunately, the elderly tutor who was engaged saw nothing amiss in the girl with an acquiring mind and taught her languages, science, and history.

She was happiest when she was with her mother, but of course, Althea Wyndham was so busy with all her engagements that Emily often found herself alone with the servants. Of them all, after her nanny, Darty, left, she liked her mother's dresser best, for Miss Witherspoon was always happy to talk to her while she ironed or mended Mrs. Wyndham's gowns. And when she was off duty or out on an errand, Emily had her books. Indeed, they became her closest friends, for how could anyone be lonely when they could open a page and be transported to ancient Greece, or the Alps, or the excitement of the colonies?

And then, as the years passed, Mrs. Wyndham stopped going to so many brilliant parties, and there were fewer new gowns resplendent with spangles and lace. Emily enjoyed the quiet evenings together, but it was obvious that her mother was bored and impatient. Besides an expression of petulance, there was often a worried look on her face, but when Emily asked if anything were wrong, Mrs. Wyndham always changed the subject.

And then, when Emily was sixteen, Miss Witherspoon left. As a most superior dresser, it was due to her skill that Mrs. Wyndham remained a reigning beauty long after she could lay any claim to youth. Emily was bewildered when Withers left without even saying good-bye, and watched with concern as her mother sat at her dressing table, trying to brush her hair.

Mrs. Wyndham caught sight of her expression in the glass and shook her head impatiently. "Try not to look so glum, Emily," she said. "We shall manage very well without her. She has a better position now, and to tell the truth, I was growing tired of her anyway."

She caught the brush in a snarl and threw it down in a temper, and Emily picked it up. She began to brush with the long, smooth strokes she had seen Withers use.

Mrs. Wyndham smiled. "How good that feels. Why, you are as accomplished as Withers any day."

And somehow the dresser had not been replaced, and it was Emily who took over her mother's hair arrangements and facials, and the care of her clothes.

And now, after barely a year in Wantage, Althea Wyndham lay dead, and never again would Emily lay out a gown, or apply lotion to that still-beautiful face, assuring her mother that the wrinkles were hardly noticeable, or hear again that gay, lilting laugh of disbelief. Her mother may have been flighty and frivolous, but Emily had loved her. Now, remembering her former gaiety, she felt the tears welling up in her eyes, and she turned away from that empty bed and went to sit down at her mother's dressing table.

Idly, she opened the drawers, one by one. There were her mother's combs and hairpins, and here the preparation she had used on her hair. Emily had always hated the pungent odor, and protested, but her mother had said sharply, "Believe me, it is necessary when you get to be my age. How did you think the color stayed so bright?"

Emily shook her head and opened another drawer filled

with handkerchiefs and gossamer stockings. The lavender sachet her mother always used sweetened the air, and Emily was quick to close it. She opened the deep bottom drawer. On top was her mother's jewelry box, and she lifted it out. There had been no occasion for Mrs. Wyndham to wear her jewels this past year, and Emily was anxious to see her favorites again, the emerald and diamond set given by her father on their first wedding anniversary. The box seemed oddly light, and when she had the lock undone and had raised the lid, she saw why. She gasped as she realized it was practically empty and only a few fripperies remained: a necklet of coral, some amber earrings, a broken pearl bracelet, and a small cameo. But where were the emeralds? And, yes, the ruby pendant? And those creamy ropes of pearls? She sat perplexed, a tiny frown between her eyes, and then she shrugged and set the box on the dressing table. She would ask her uncle tomorrow; perhaps Mama had given him the jewelry to have it cleaned.

Left in the drawer were a few fans, old loo masks, and party favors, and Emily ruffled through them casually. She was about to close the drawer when she spotted the heavy leather case at the bottom and drew it out. She remembered the dark-red moroccan leather from years ago when it had been placed on the library table of the house in London. Once in a great while, her mother would take out one of her father's letters and read it to her. She tried the clasp, but the case was locked, and although she searched the drawer impatiently, no key came to light. It was then she remembered the little china heart on her mother's bedside table. There was a secret rosebud you pressed, and the box flew open, disclosing a tiny hiding place. She went to the table, opened the heart, and as she had hoped, found the key inside. Taking it and the case, she went to the chair by the window and sat down to explore the contents.

On top, she found a great many unreceipted bills, and she frowned. Careless Mama, to leave them hidden away, instead of paying them, she thought as she put them to one side to give the lawyer. Under the bills were piles and piles of notes and letters. They did not look like her father's handwriting; indeed, they were all in different hands. She turned one over, wondering if she should read the contents, but then, remembering her mother's death, she withdrew the note from its vellum envelope and began to read. Her face grew pale, and she threw it away from her after only a few sentences and picked up another. Her hands were shaking, but she continued until she had read them all, and then she dropped them to the carpet and stared out the window, fighting a wave of nausea at what she had discovered.

Putting her hands to her hot cheeks, she began to sob. Suddenly all the events of the past that she had tried so hard to ignore were made plain, for here was indisputable evidence. They were love letters, all of them. And not from her father, but from any number of men, even including her Uncle Gregory. Why, Mama had been the mistress of all these men! No wonder her aunt had stiffened whenever they met, and stared at them both with cold hatred. And she, in her innocence, had never guessed. She had thought her mother's comings and goings were because she was so beautiful and popular. She squirmed, remembering all the "uncles" she had had over the years. Emily shuddered. She had never known because her mother had not lived with them openly, but now she remembered all the house parties her mother had gone to, all the three- and four-day excursions that she had always been excluded from.

"This is not the kind of party for a little girl, pet," her mother would say as she put on her furs and a dashing hat before she ran downstairs, leaving her daughter alone with the maids. Obviously they were not parties for little girls, Emily thought bitterly. But how *could* Mama? Hadn't she realized that if Emily were to make her come-out, everyone would remember the gay widow who passed so quickly from one member of the *haut ton* to the next, with never the tiniest regret for her lack of morals in her pretty head? Hadn't she cared? Had she been that selfish?

Wearily, Emily picked up the letters and began to arrange them in piles, one for each correspondent. When she was done, there were twelve, some larger than the others. Her uncle's was very thick. What a foolish man, she thought, to write so often and in such a revealing way. She did not know how she was to meet him on the morrow with any composure. At least she never had to see any of the others again: the Duke of Wrotherham, Count Philippe d'Aubrey, Lord Andrews, the Earl of Jarrett, Sir Percival Gunther.

She restored the letters to the case, and one bold handwriting leapt up and made the bile rise in her throat again. It was from a Colonel Rogers of the Coldstream Guards, suggesting he might be willing to part with a large sum of money in return for her—*Emily's*—favors. Emily remembered him. He had been a stern, forbidding-looking man who had stared at her one evening when she ran down the stairs with a handkerchief her mother had forgotten. How horrible men are, she thought as she put the case away and restored the key to its hiding place. She wished now she had never seen her mother opening the china heart one morning as she was laying out a clean nightgown in the dressing room; she wished she had destroyed all those horrible letters without reading them, for then she would still believe that her mother had been a good woman, faithful to her husband and careful of her daughter's name.

Suddenly she remembered the first time she should have realized that her mother was not like other women. She had been reading in the library, curled up in the window seat and hidden by a large wing chair, when her mother and her Great-aunt Bess had come in. She would have run to join them, but their voices were so angry she pressed back against the window and remained silent.

"And who is this new one, Althea?" her great-aunt asked sharply. "I have heard such tales, even in Berks, that I could hardly credit it—Althea Wyndham, a common demirep!"

Her mother had laughed an angry, disagreeable laugh. "Dear Aunt, if you please! I may be a demirep, but I can assure you no one would call me 'common.' You may ask anyone you like."

"I am sure I may," came the swift rejoinder, "for your reputation appears to be known throughout England. How could you, Althea?"

Mrs. Wyndham threw down her gloves and reticule and went to stand before the fire. "How could I not?" she asked. "How else was I to live when Tom died and left me a young widow with a baby? A practically penniless widow, as I am sure you know."

"You could have come to me. I would have taken you and Emily gladly."

"I thank you, but burying myself in genteel poverty in the country was never my intention."

"Better to be a common doxy? Oh, very well, an *uncommon* doxy? You should be ashamed of yourself, Althea."

"But I am not. I have had a lovely life, and if I did not marry again just to acquire respectability and an assured income, that was my choice."

There was a short silence, and then Aunt Bess asked in a severe voice, "And what kind of life do you think your daughter will have? What kind of marriage can she possibly contract with such a notorious mother? Who will overlook her background as well as her poverty, no matter how beautiful she is? Unless, of course, you have sunk so low that you contemplate having her follow in *your* footsteps."

Peeping around the corner of the chair, Emily was afraid that her mother would strike Aunt Bess, she looked so fierce. "That was unworthy of you, Aunt," she said finally, her face white. "When the time comes, Emily will be well taken care of, for I shall see to it. She is only nine, there is plenty of time to think of her future. Perhaps I shall marry, after all; I tell you it is not impossible even now, for there have been offers . . . Why, you would be amazed!"

Aunt Bess sniffed. "Most men are fools, that comes as no surprise. Is it this latest lover that makes you so sure of yourself?"

"Lord Burr? No, he is too conventional. But there are others . . ."

Just then a footman knocked with a note for Mrs. Wyndham, and the two women left the room. The memory of that afternoon came flooding back, and Emily called herself every kind of fool that she should have forgotten it. Perhaps she had put it in the back of her mind because she did not understand what the words meant, and her great-aunt had been so cross, her mother so angry.

The day Aunt Bess left them, she stood in the front hall and said, "Yes, you will go your own way, Althea, but you will regret it someday. And poor Emily!" Here she had stooped and drawn the little girl into her arms to kiss. "You may always come to me, my dear," she had whispered . . . but of course, Great-aunt Bess had been dead these past five years.

Emily shook her head and sighed, memories of the cottage at Wantage and the interview with her uncle and the lawyer coming again to her mind. She had worn her hastily made black dress, her blond hair pulled back into a severe knot. She had tried not to look at herself in the mirror as she did up her hair, although for years she had searched every day for signs she was growing up to look like her mother. Now she wished that, instead of her blond hair and delicate rose-tinted complexion and graceful figure, she were ugly and commonplace. She steeled herself as she entered the parlor and both men rose.

"My dear child," her uncle said. "I trust you slept well?" He made as if to embrace her, and for the first time she stiffened and drew away. Lord Wyndham looked at her searchingly, but he made no comment as he introduced her to the lawyer, Mr. Brown.

The interview was just as difficult as she had imagined, and made more so by the searing realization after not too many moments that outside of the cottage, heavily mortgaged to Lord Wyndham, and the empty jewel case, she was penniless.

Lord Wyndham begged her to forget the mortgage, and Emily, sure the lawyer knew why he was so generous, felt her color rise. Thinking quickly, she asked Mr. Brown to sell the cottage so she could pay the servant's wages and have some money of her own, and he agreed to do so.

At last, everything was settled, and the lawyer bowed himself away. Her uncle saw him out, and then he returned to the parlor where Emily had retreated to the window in some confusion. Somehow she had thought he would go as well; now it appeared he intended to speak to her alone.

"Emily, I must talk to you, my dear. I wish with all my heart that I could take you up to the hall with me this very afternoon, and assure you you will never have to worry about money, or a roof over your head ever again, but . . . but it is not possible." He glanced at her stern profile and continued more slowly. "I am sure you are aware, puss, that your aunt took an unreasonable dislike to your mother and yourself as well, and there is nothing I can do to change that, I am afraid. Besides, and although I should not be telling you this, she is in what you ladies call 'an interesting condition.' You see, I am sure, how I cannot upset her at this time."

He paused, and Emily swallowed. She could not speak, but she nodded her head a little, and taking that as a sign of her acquiescence, he continued, eager now to be done. "There is no need to be precipitate, however. Probably it will be some time before the cottage can be sold, and you will need some money. Here, take this . . .''

Emily turned and stared at him unsmilingly as he held out a heavy purse, and for a moment, there was a deathly silence in the parlor. His good-looking florid face, framed with thick gray hair, turned pale. Then he whispered, ''You know, don't you? How did you find out?''

''Yes, I know,'' Emily said quietly. ''I found your letters to Mama last evening.'' She moved to a chair by the fireplace, wondering why, in spite of the cheerful blaze, she felt so cold. ''There is no need to offer me money. I could not accept it, especially from you.''

He had the goodness to flush. ''Emily, my dear, do not be hasty. You must have something to live on until the cottage is sold—and then what will you do? Where will you go? I demand to know, for the love I had for your mother.''

Emily stiffened, but as she looked into his anguished face, she felt a sudden pity for the man. He looked years older than he was, his face twisted with feeling. He had loved her mother through all the years, and he had not deserted her in her final illness, when many another man would have looked conveniently the other way.

''Sit down, Uncle,'' she said calmly. ''Very well, I will accept this money, but it must be the last, and it will be repaid somehow, as well as the mortgage on the cottage. As to what I am going to do, I do not know. I only found out about my mother yesterday. It is still a shock to me, but you may be sure that I will not ask you for any more help.''

He shook his head. ''I could not offer it, in any case. My wife, well—''

Emily put out her hand. ''I understand, and I do thank you for your kindness. Your letters shall be returned; no one else will see them. But if I had only known! All those needless lessons in deportment, the piano and dancing masters—what a waste!''

Her uncle thought for a moment, and then he said, ''You are right, of course. It would be useless for you to make your bow to society. Too many fathers would remember the ravishing Mrs. Wyndham to permit their sons to court her daughter, she was much too well known. But what else can you possibly do? As a young lady of quality, marriage is the only thing you are trained for.''

"I do not know, but I shall think of something," Emily said with more assurance than she felt. She rose, to terminate this painful interview, and her uncle followed her reluctantly to the hall.

As he stood at the door, he said with regret, "I wish so much that I could do more for you, my dear. You are so like your mother when I first fell in love with her—those same beautiful emerald-green eyes, her lovely mouth . . .''

Suddenly he dropped the hat and cane she had given him, and before she knew what he was about, he drew her into his arms. "Dearest Emily, little sweetheart," he said in a husky voice, and she felt a great faintness come over her as he bent his head and kissed her. Did he think he could exchange Althea Wyndham for the younger version? she wondered. Perhaps he thought she was like her mother and would welcome his attentions. She felt a roaring in her ears, and with a strength she did not know she possessed, she pulled away from him.

"Get out of this house," she said in a shaken whisper. "Do not ever let me see your face again."

"But . . . but, I did not mean . . .'' he stammered.

"Did you not, sir?" she asked, looking at him with cold loathing, and he could not restrain a guilty flush as he picked up his hat and cane and almost ran past her stern, accusing face, her rigid back.

When he was gone, she closed the door quickly and leaned against it until she could control her trembling. She wished she might return his money immediately, but a small voice in her head advised caution. "You may need that money, m'dear,'' it said, and she nodded.

"Beggin' your pardon, I'm sure," came the maid's voice from the back of the hall, and Emily looked up, astounded by her sarcasm.

"Yes?" she asked coolly. "Was there something you wanted, Betty?"

"Only two's due me, that's all, but wot I wants to know is am I goin' to get it?" She advanced toward Emily, folding her arms insolently. Lounging against the stairs, she added, "Wot's that lawyer chappie to say about me wages? I tells you clear, if there's no pay, I leave. You can wait on yourself, for you ain't no better than me now, no, you ain't, me foine lady.''

"You forget yourself." Emily was horrified that a servant should take that disrespectful tone with her, especially Betty, who had always been so meek, waiting on her with downcast eyes and many a dropped curtsy, and always with a "Yes, miss, right away, miss," in her soft voice. Before she could go on, Mrs. Abbott spoke up behind the maid.

" 'Tis only to be expected, Miss Wyndham. And what did Mr. Brown have to say? I have as much interest as Betty here."

Emily was stunned. Betty, after all, was only a common scullery maid, but here was the housekeeper questioning her as well.

"As soon as the cottage has been sold, you shall be paid in full," she managed to get out before she turned and almost ran up the stairs. It was too much, first the scene with her uncle and now the servants. She had planned to order hot water so she might scrub away his hateful embrace, but she did not dare. The maid might refuse to bring it. All the evils of her situation burst upon her as suddenly as if she had been struck a mighty blow, and it was all she could do not to wail in agony.

For the next few days, she seemed to move in a vacuum, almost as if she stood outside herself and observed the behavior of a stranger. She received the few lady callers with dignity, but although she was polite, they were made aware by her stern direct gaze that their false sympathy and eagerness for gossip were clearly understood, and no one ever called back again.

In the evenings, she sat by the fire in her mother's room, and as coldly as possible tried to think what she might do and where she might go. She was too young to be a governess, even with such education as she had, and the thought of dealing with a large number of unruly, mischievous children filled her with terror. As an only child, she had no experience with them. No, that would not do at all.

Neither did the possibility that she might find a post as a companion to some sick, cross old lady interest her. She was only twenty-two and she had had enough of sickness for a while.

But what other possibilities were there for a girl in 1812?

Since she could not marry, she could only become a governess, a companion, or a servant, or she could sell herself as her mother had.

She jumped to her feet and began to pace the room. "I will never follow Mama's example, never," she exclaimed aloud. "No, not even if I starve."

"Well, starve you may, dearie," the little voice in her head said. "How will you get on? The money Lord Wyndham left you will not last long."

"I don't know," Emily said crossly. Suddenly she caught sight of herself in the glass over the dressing table. In the black dress, with her hair pulled back so severely, she did not look at all like Althea Wyndham. Why, she thought, I look almost like Withers did when she was Mama's maid. All I need is an apron and cap!

Abruptly, she sat down on the little satin stool and stared at her reflection, her eyes wide. The answer to her problem stared back at her. With growing excitement she thought of this new solution. Was she not, by training, a most superior dresser, experienced in all matters to do with caring for a lady of quality? Had she not learned all the tricks of presenting her mother at her best, from creating her elaborate hairdos to coordinating her outfits and jewels, as well as mending and laundering her clothes? And then, because she had been such a solitary child, there had been all those hours spent watching Withers: the way she spoke and acted and conducted herself with the other servants. Of course it was ridiculous that a Wyndham of Berks should ever lower herself by going into service, but there was nothing else she could do. And surely even being a servant was more comfortable than starving and less demeaning than becoming a Cyprian like her mother.

Emily got up to pace the room again. I shall not *be* Emily Wyndham, she thought, for that would never do. As her uncle had pointed out, there were too many people who would remember the dashing bark of frailty who had brought to the name of Wyndham such infamy and shame. No, not a Wyndham at all. She would take her mother's maiden name and her own middle name as well. Yes, Margaret Nelson, that sounded prosaic enough. Or should she be Maggie or Meg? She reminded herself she was about to become the most-sought-after, most superior dresser in all London: Margaret it would be, or perhaps just Nelson.

Suddenly she bent and stared at her reflection in the glass again. She knew it was the perfect solution, so why did she feel this terrible sense of unease, of doubt? She did not think it was because she was afraid of hard work, although she knew that she had never really done much of it until the last few months of her mother's life, and even then she had always summoned Betty to carry the slops and chamberpots and change the soiled sheets. And she knew that taking care of her mother had not really prepared her for serving as a stranger's maid, forced to live in close proximity and involved in all the intimate details of her life. She would have to help her mistress from her bath, dry her, clip her toenails, and pluck her eyebrows, as well as wash her soiled linen and care for her when she was ill. And perhaps her mistress would have rotting teeth and bad breath, or a foul body odor. Ladies of quality were not all sweet young things, not all beautiful, fastidious Lady Wyndhams. She shook her head and swallowed. She would just have to adjust, she had no other choice, and if a situation became too unpleasant, she could always hand in her notice. Besides, this was the only solution that made any sense at all; the days when Miss Emily Wyndham could pick and choose were gone forever. No, Margaret Nelson it would have to be.

"I don't think it's that easy, m'dear," the little voice warned. "How will you get a position? You can't just knock on imposing doors and bid the butler present you to the lady of the house."

Emily sank down before the fire and pondered this new problem. Of course, she would need references, very, very good references. But where on earth could she get them? She supposed she could write them herself, but what if her employer checked up and discovered that Lady So-and-So and Countess Such-and-Such did not exist? What, then?

Suddenly, a picture of Lady Wyndham's fat, disagreeable face came to mind, and she knew she had her answer. Interesting condition or no, Aunt Mathilda was going to come to her aid by fair means or foul. Somehow she knew instinctively that the lady would be delighted to assist in whatever was necessary to remove her, and the memory of her mother, from Berks forever.

As if fate had relented at last, everything went smoothly from then on. With a great deal of relief, Lady Wyndham wrote a glowing reference, and to it Emily added another she wrote herself from a fictional Mrs. Salisbury-Jones, who, she claimed, was about to sail to India.

As she waited to hear from the lawyer, Emily kept busy making over some of her mother's more sober clothes, and stitching aprons and caps from some white muslin gowns.

The news that the cottage had been sold came at last, and Emily went to the churchyard one showery October afternoon to say a final good-bye to her mother. Already the pain of her death and the betrayal she had felt at first at her mother's way of life had faded: now she just felt sadness that such a beautiful woman had had to resort to such tactics in order to live in luxury, and regret that she had not been strong enough to try to survive some other way.

As she stared down at the grave with its simple headstone, Emily made a silent promise, clenching her hands in the pockets of her cape. "No matter what it takes, I will survive, Mama, you may be sure of that. And I will do it without stooping to the role you played."

She raised her chin and stared with unseeing eyes at the rooks who were circling the stone church tower, crying to each other. She did not feel the chill wind that rustled the dying grass and stirred the leaves at her feet. Somehow, from somewhere, she felt a deep sense of peace, almost as if what she had planned was the right path for her, after all.

1

In November, in the year 1814, as Margaret Nelson, lady's maid, made her way to Number Twelve Charles Street, Mayfair, she suddenly recalled the promise she had made to herself in the churchyard by her mother's grave, and her lips twisted in a wry smile.

It was true she had survived, but at a cost it was just as well she had not known would be required of her at the time. As she recalled the young innocent she had been, so sure of herself and so determined to make her own way in the world, she had to shake her head. Since that day she had been hungry, overworked, reviled by her employers, and ridiculed by her fellow servants. She had also been pursued, and it had taken more character than she had known she possessed not to give in to despair and take the easy way out.

Heaven knows she had had plenty of opportunities. She had expected that she might have trouble with the male servants she encountered, but she had not thought the nobility— the sons and brothers and even the husbands of her mistresses— might also consider her fair game. Indeed, it was because of the younger son of the family in Yorkshire that she had left her latest post. Not, she told herself as she avoided a crossing sweeper, that she was sorry to leave Oak Park. Her attic room, shared with three other maids, had been unheated in winter and stifling in summer, and the poor, scanty food left her constantly hungry. Her mistress, a young lady about to make her bow to society, had been spoiled and ill-tempered, and given to temper tantrums if she had to wait even a minute for her maid's services. The nights Emily had dragged herself up to bed, her feet and ankles so swollen from fourteen or fifteen hours of work that she could barely remove her shoes, were more than she cared to remember.

Emily paused in a doorway to consult the piece of paper in her hand. She hoped that this Lady Quentin she was going to be interviewed by was a kinder woman, and that she would get the job. She had made too many trips to the Free Registry for the Placement of Faithful Servants already, and her money was running low. If she did not get the position, she would have to look for cheaper lodgings. Bradley's Hotel on Davies Street would be far from her touch.

At Number Twelve, an elderly butler showed her into a cheerful morning room to wait until Lady Quentin was ready to see her. It seemed a very long time before he reappeared to take her upstairs, a time Emily spent in fervent prayer.

She curtsied to the lady still reclining in bed, sipping her morning chocolate, and tried to take her measure in the brief second that was all she had before she had to lower her eyes in servility.

What she saw was a young woman with a slight, immature figure. She had light-brown hair that curled charmingly under her cap and a pretty if not a beautiful face. You would never have called her an Incomparable, and in the company of other more dashing ladies, she was sure to go unnoticed, but there was a great deal of sweetness in her expression and her large gray eyes were kind.

"How young you are," she exclaimed, although she was not far from girlhood herself. "I am not perfectly sure—but then, of course—well, you may sit down. I do not have much time. How could I forget?"

After presenting her references, Emily took a straight chair near the fireplace, realizing that the question was not addressed to her. She hoped that the lady did not always speak in fragments, for it made it difficult to follow her. As Lady Quentin read her letters, Emily had a chance to inspect the dainty bedroom. It was decorated in shades of pink and rose, with deeper rose accents, from the hangings of the large four-poster, to the draperies and rug, the ruffled pillows and the striped upholstery of the chairs. Idly, she wondered what the lady's husband was like. She could not imagine a man in this powder puff of a room.

Lady Quentin reread the letters before she put them down, then, with a slight smile, she asked Emily how old she was.

"For, Miss Nelson, you seem very young to have so many accomplishments. And I am used to an older maid—dear, dear Daffy!"

Before Emily could answer, a knock came at the door, and it was opened immediately by a large, handsome gentleman dressed in full regimentals. "There you are, sleepyhead, awake at last," he said, striding quickly to the bed and sitting down to plant a careless kiss on Lady Quentin's cheek. She smiled up at him, her eyes glowing, and Emily realized that she was much more attractive than she had at first appeared.

As for her husband, Emily saw with a sense of foreboding that he was one of the handsomest men she had ever seen. She prayed he was very much in love with his wife. In the delicate, feminine room, he appeared very tall and masculine. He was powerfully built from his broad shoulders to his long, muscular legs, and he sported a head of jet-black hair, a mustache to match, and the fresh complexion of the confirmed outdoorsman that complimented his soldierly bearing.

As he turned away from his wife, he caught sight of Emily, who rose and curtsied. "And who have we here, Alicia?" he asked.

"This is Miss Nelson. She has applied for the position as my maid to replace Daffy," Lady Quentin said in her girlish voice, clasping his arm tightly and cuddling closer.

"Indeed? She is much better-looking than Daffy, pet. Have you engaged her?" the captain asked idly, little knowing he was striking fear into Emily's heart.

"Not yet—I do not know—well, what do you think? I mean, she is so young, and even though her references are excellent—well, what does that prove? Besides, Daffy was a dear. I was so sorry she had to leave me because of her sister's illness, for you know she has been with me ever since Mama decided it was time for me to have a maid."

The captain put a large hand over his wife's mouth. "Enough! I shall be late to headquarters if I stay to disentangle and answer all of that statement." He unclasped her clinging hands and added as he rose, "I must be off, my love. Do what you think best, but you know the Racklin ball is only a week away, and you will certainly need a smart dresser for that. It is most important for me to stand well with Sir Reginald, especially now."

"But, Tony," Lady Quentin interrupted, "you have not

told me why he is of such importance, and I do not understand—''

"It is nothing for you to worry your pretty head about, my dear. If you would please me, just be sure you look your most entrancing. Perhaps you should ask Bella to help you engage a maid; yes, that's the ticket,'' he added as Emily's heart sank. "Bella will be glad to tell you what you should do.''

With a wave and a blown kiss he was gone, even as the lady frowned at his last words and called after him, "But, Tony, when will you be home?''

But the captain did not reply, for both of them could hear him running downstairs and the sound of the front door slamming behind him.

All the light went out of Lady Quentin's face as she sank back on her pillows with a little sigh. Catching sight of the letters of reference again, she returned her gaze to Emily's face. "Bella, indeed! I suppose Tony is right, but somehow . . .'' She frowned a little and added, "I cannot call you Nelson or Margaret, what shall I call you?''

Emily said nothing as the lady threw back her bedclothes. "Very well, never mind that now. Bring me my peignoir and we shall see how you dress me for luncheon with Lady Wilcox. She sets fashion: let us see if you can make me her equal. Not that I care especially what she thinks, but Tony insists I cultivate her.''

Emily quickly removed her pelisse and bonnet, wishing she had thought to bring her apron and cap with her as she helped Lady Quentin into the soft pink robe that lay across the foot of the bed. She followed the lady to her dressing room, noticing how very short she was. Emily herself was only of medium height, but Lady Quentin lacked several of her inches. She could not repress a gasp when she saw the dressing room, and the lady turned around, her eyes twinkling.

"Yes, it is unusual, is it not? Tony had his sister Bella design it for me as a wedding present. We have only been married six months, and I myself am not quite accustomed to it as yet.'' She paused as if she were going to say more, and then she shrugged.

Emily gazed at the gilded tub, shaped like a shell and set on delicate clawed feet, the mirrored walls, and the velvet chaise and matching chairs. Even the ceiling was painted with a soft mural depicting the sky and some rosy clouds.

Lady Quentin threw open the doors of the wardrobe and selected an afternoon dress of dusty rose. "I shall wear this, I think, for it is new."

Emily restrained another gasp, for she had never seen so many clothes. Row after row of morning dresses, afternoon ensembles, ball gowns, riding habits, and beautiful furs. Although every color of the rainbow was represented, pink and rose predominated.

"Tony likes me to wear pink, Nelly," Lady Quentin explained, and Emily, her heart sinking at the thought of being addressed as Nelly, nodded her head. It appeared the lady called everyone by a diminutive, from her husband, Tony, right down to her lady's maid. As she helped her to dress, Lady Quentin continued to chat. In spite of having to decipher some of her more tangled statements, Emily found herself warming to the young lady. She was just like a kitten, so open and playful, and when she squeezed Emily's hand and declared she was more than pleased with her turnout, Emily was bold enough to ask the salary.

"I paid Daffy twenty-five guineas, and you shall have the same," Lady Quentin said in a businesslike way. "And any time off whenever I do not need you, as well as every other Sunday afternoon, and a full day once a month."

"That will be satisfactory, m'lady," Emily agreed in relief, and as Lady Quentin was pulling on her gloves, she asked what other activities she was engaged in for today. At her look of surprise, Emily explained. "If I know what gowns you will require, I can be sure to have them ready for you. Then, too, I should like to fetch my baggage from my hotel in Davies Street and unpack at such a time as you do not need me."

Lady Quentin nodded. "Come with me now, Nelly. The hotel is on my way, and you shall ride in my carriage so I can tell you my plans for the day. What a good idea! I am sure we will deal extremely together, and to think I imagined—well, I am just the silly goose that Tony calls me—and Bella," she added, somewhat more tartly as she led the way downstairs.

Instructing the butler to have a room prepared for her new maid, she took the time to introduce them. "Nelly, this is Goody. He is a pet, and he has been with me since I was a child," she said, smiling at the old man. As she swept by him to the front door, the butler looked at Emily and raised his eyes heavenward. Emily smiled in return.

The carriage was modern, and although the seats were cushioned in rose velvet, Emily was glad to see the exterior was painted buff and the two footmen were dressed in somber livery. All the way to Davies Street, Lady Quentin chattered without stopping. By the time Emily was set down at the hotel, her head was ringing. As near as she could make out, her new mistress would be home to change her clothes for a drive in the park with some friends of Captain Quentin, and then there was an evening reception at the Lovelaces'.

"Oh, and Tony promised to be home for dinner before that—the deep-rose satin, Nelly, and my diamonds, I think, and I do hope you have some cheerful gowns, I hate depressing colors. I absolutely forbid black, such a horrible color, don't you think? It quite gives me the megrims to have anyone dressed in black near me."

And then tomorrow she would require Nelly to attend her while she shopped. She had a fitting at Mme. Pauline's, some perfume to be chosen at Croxton's, a pair of sandals to be purchased at the Pantheon Bazaar, and a special gift for her husband that she wished to select at Dudley's. He had mentioned how much he admired Lord Grant's dress sword; she had determined that he should have one just as magnificent. Interspersed in this conversation were questions about Nelly's former mistresses, where she had lived, and how she had learned her trade.

"Whew," Emily said to herself as she reached her hotel room. This was going to be quite a change from her last job in Yorkshire, that was clear. In an hour she had packed, settled her bill, and hiring a hackney, was once again on her way to Charles Street.

The butler, who was quick to tell her his name was Mr. Goodwell, "not Mr. Goody, miss," had a footman bring in her portmanteaus. Her trunk would come by carter later. He himself took her to the fourth floor, where the servants had their rooms. Emily was glad to see that her room already had a warming fire burning in the fireplace and the bed was covered with a cheerful quilt. The room was small, but there was a rug and, luxury of luxuries, a mirror over her dresser. Her spirits brightened considerably as she thanked him, and he offered to introduce her to his wife when she had unpacked.

"Mrs. Goodwell is the housekeeper. Of course, we keep a French chef." Here Mr. Goodwell sniffed, letting Emily know he did not approve of employing foreigners, not when England had been at war with France for so long. "There's the bell to call Nancy, the upstairs maid; she will fetch your water and tend the fire, miss."

He bowed, with a dignity belying his nickname, and departed, leaving Emily to unpack and think how lucky she had been to get a position in this household. She had not finished when the bell rang to summon her, and stopping only to tie on her apron and cap, she went to attend her new mistress.

When Lady Quentin was safely bestowed on her gentlemen escorts and had left the house with one last lilting laugh, Emily went to seek out Mrs. Goodwell in hopes of a cup of tea. That lady was much more unbending than her husband, even introducing herself as Mrs. Goody, and over a good tea, she lost no time in telling Emily all about the household.

"Lady Quentin, now, she's a new bride, and it's a good thing she has me, I can tell you, Miss Nelson," Mrs. Goodwell said, rocking comfortably. "No more sense than a baby, she has, although a sweeter young lady I never hope to see. The captain now, he knows what's what, but he's not home often."

"Is he on duty a great deal?" Emily asked.

Mrs. Goodwell nodded. "You'd think, now that that nasty Napoleon has been exiled to that island—whatever is the name of it, I can't recollect—the captain would have more time to spend with his wife, but Lady Quentin goes about without him. Of course, his sister, Miss Arabella, is here more often than not, but that's not my idea of how to treat a bride. But there, I do hope she'll be happy."

Just then Mr. Goodwell came in, and his wife abruptly stopped gossiping. Emily thanked her for the tea and went back upstairs to lay out the deep-rose satin gown Lady Quentin planned to wear to dinner. Emily was busy in the dressing room when the bedroom door was thrown open and an authorative voice cried out, "Don't fuss, Goodwell! I shall just leave a note for Lady Quentin before I go, there is no need for you to escort me. Heaven knows I have been up here often enough."

Emily came around the corner to see a dark-haired lady firmly shutting the door in the butler's face.

"Old fussbudget," she muttered, and then, catching sight of Emily, she said, " 'Pon my soul, who are you?"

"I am Margaret Nelson, Lady Quentin's new dresser, ma'am," Emily replied with a curtsy.

"Indeed?" the lady asked as she removed her gloves, looking her up and down intently. "Now, why didn't Alicia consult me before she took such a step? You are much too young—and much too pretty! But there, Alicia is such an unworldly baby, she probably never even considered that. By the way, I am Arabella Quentin, her sister-in-law."

Emily curtsied again as the lady continued, "I suppose you had good references? I must assume you have all the necessary skills: hairdressing, sewing, cleaning clothes of stains and candle wax, and painting the face. However, to be sure, I give you a small test. What is virgin's milk made from?"

Emily was indignant to be quizzed by an outsider, but since she was not sure of Miss Quentin's role in the household, she thought it best to answer her as humbly as she could. "Tincture of benzoin mixed with water, miss," she said. Emily had often prepared this mixture for her mother, for it gave a lovely rosy coloring to the complexion. "But if I may say so"—she waited until Miss Quentin inclined her head an inch—"I do not hold with the use of such cosmetics for a young lady. At Lady Quentin's age such preparations are unnecessary, and to begin their use too early is to risk the most dangerous consequences: loose teeth, swollen eyes, and coarsened skin texture, to name but a few. I would never employ them on any one but an older lady well past her prime. The young need very little in the way of artifice to show them at their best."

She stopped, for Miss Quentin was sputtering, and two bright-red spots burned high on her cheekbones under what Emily now saw was a heavy *maquillage*.

"That will be quite enough! I am not interested in your insolent opinions," the lady managed to get out as she went to sit down at a small writing table set against the wall. She then proceeded to ask several more questions about Emily's past—where she was from and for whom she had worked—and Emily made herself answer in an even voice.

"Very well," Miss Quentin said at last. "If you are not

satisfactory, we can always discharge you. By the way, stay well away from my brother or you will be back in the street before you know it."

Emily's eyes flashed her indignation before she lowered them. Miss Quentin sneered, "Hoity-toity, girl! I am well aware of the morals of the lower classes. No better than animals, the lot of you." She turned to the desk and then asked suddenly. "What salary is Alicia paying you?"

"Twenty-five guineas, miss."

Miss Quentin snorted. "Just as I thought. I could have found her someone much more suitable, and with a more civil tongue in her head, for only fifteen." She shook her head and drew a sheet of paper from the desk. "I shall write Lady Quentin a note. She has forgotten that we had an engagement to walk this afternoon. I take it she has gone to drive?"

"Yes, miss," Emily said, setting her lips firmly.

"Well, speak up, girl. Was it with Lord Andrews?"

"And Mr. Ashe," Emily admitted.

"I shall roast her for that," the lady said, her grim tones at odds with the light statement as she began to pen a few lines.

Emily studied her carefully. She was above medium height and had her brother's dark hair, high complexion, and aquiline features, but whereas these attributes made him such a handsome man, they did not become her as well. Indeed, besides being so determined and self-satisfied, she had a rigid cast to her features that was most unpleasant. She was older than her brother and seemed to have set her girlhood firmly behind her, along with any thought of matrimony.

"See that she gets this the minute she returns, girl," the lady commanded, walking briskly to the door. "Does Lady Quentin still plan to attend the Lovelace reception tonight?"

"I believe so, miss," Emily replied, curtsying as she accepted the note, and although she could have added that the captain planned to dine with his wife, she refused to volunteer any information to this unpleasant woman.

After Miss Quentin left, Emily went back to her work, thinking about her. Besides being rude and abrupt and prying into Emily's past, there had been a forcefulness about her, an air of always knowing what was best, that put up Emily's back. She was glad Miss Quentin was not an inmate of the house.

As soon as she heard Lady Quentin in the hall below, she

rang for Nancy to bring some hot water and went out to greet her mistress, who was standing on the bottom step questioning Mr. Goodwell.

"You say the captain has not returned home, Goody? Well, no matter, I guess. I really did not expect . . ." She laughed a little and came lightly up the stairs to her room. As she undressed, she chatted gaily to her maid about her drive: whom she had seen, what her escorts had had to say, and whom she might expect to see at the evening's reception. It was some time later, just as she was lying down and Emily was closing the drapes so she might rest before dressing for dinner, that she remembered the note from Miss Quentin.

"Oh, dear! How angry Bella must be with me," Lady Quentin said in a failing voice. "I promised faithfully that this time I would not fail."

Emily left her, wondering if such fluff-headed behavior was common to the lady. She began to think it would drive any husband mad to have to deal with it, to say nothing of her long-suffering friends . . . and servants.

It was very late before Lady Quentin returned from the Lovelace reception and called Emily to undress her. Promising to wake her mistress at eleven the following morning, Emily softly let herself out. Of the captain there was no sign, but she did not know if this was normal or not. It is none of my business, she told herself as she climbed the stairs to her room wearily. At least he had been present at dinner, along with two of his fellow officers, and Emily had heard from Mrs. Goody that Lady Quentin had been delighted with her husband and her guests. But when Emily brought down the lady's sarcenet stole, Lady Quentin was just discovering that the captain was not going to accompany her to the reception. Emily thought her face shaded a little at this news, but she laughed gaily as the others thanked her for the delicious meal before they all went off to Brooks. Lady Quentin was left to ride in solitary state to her evening's entertainment.

Emily herself had had a pleasant evening, meeting the rest of the servants at dinner. The food was excellent, thanks to the despised French chef. She noticed that Mr. Goodwell's scruples did not extend to refusing a second helping of everything. Everyone chatted happily during their meal, from Nancy, the upstairs maid, to Perry, the youngest footman. Even the chef tried a few words in English as he pressed

Emily to try the turbot in wine sauce. She answered him in his own tongue, and his face lit up, loosening a torrent of French. As Emily looked around the table, she saw she had made a mistake, for the others were all staring at her. She hurried to tell them she had only a few words she had learned from a French *émigrée* who was the dressmaker at her last employment, and promised herself to be more careful in the future. A lady's maid had little education and certainly did not speak a foreign language, and Mrs. Goody had already remarked on her refined accent.

The days sped by, for Lady Quentin never seemed to be still. If she were not shopping or meeting friends, she was riding or attending a party. Emily wondered at this feverish activity, but she supposed it was preferable to sitting at home waiting for the captain to return. It certainly kept Emily busy, for sometimes Lady Quentin changed her clothes five or six times a day, and as Emily was seldom in bed before two in the morning, she was often weary. Lady Quentin might be a sweet-natured lady, but she was no more aware of her maid's long hours than any other lady of fashion. Emily knew she would stare if it were brought to her attention. After all, she would reason, that was why she was paying her maid twenty-five guineas a year, was it not?

On her first full day off, Emily slept very late, luxuriating in her brief day of freedom. It was a beautiful late-fall day, and in high spirits she bathed and dressed in one of her best dark-green gowns and matching pelisse, deciding to go for a stroll in the park and enjoy the sunshine, the brisk air, and the throngs of people.

She was about to return to Charles Street late in the afternoon when she was accosted by a young Corinthian on the strut. Since she was unaccompanied, he assumed she was one of the muslin set, and he took her arm and began to murmur of the delights they could share.

Emily insisted he release her and tried to pull away, but before she succeeded, a gentleman on horseback reined in and intervened. Emily looked up from her struggles into a pair of cold black eyes that seemed somehow familiar. But perhaps it was the eyelids drooping with boredom, or the sardonic twist to that well-shaped mouth that reminded her of someone she had once known, she thought. He was a stranger, for she knew she would never forget such aristocratic good looks, such a well-tailored, powerful frame.

"I am sure I am correct in assuming that you do not care for the gentleman's attention, miss," he drawled in a deep, harsh voice. "Why it is not as obvious to him, I cannot say. You there, release the lady at once or be off with you before I lay about your worthless back with my whip."

The beau complied immediately, backing away and apologizing, for there had been a quality to the order that told him the gentleman was used to command and expected instant obedience to his wishes. Emily was about to thank him, but before she could speak, he touched his hat and said, "Next time, bring your maid. It does not do for ladies of your quality to walk alone."

He was gone on that statement, digging in his heels and cantering away, and Emily was left to smile a little ruefully at his instructions. Her maid, indeed!

2

In December, the Quentins began to make plans to go out of town. They had been invited to a Christmas house party by the captain's cousin, the Countess of Gault. This lady and her elderly husband, the earl, had an estate in Lincolnshire, and it was their custom to ask several of the *ton*, as well as various relatives, to stay for a few weeks. From what Emily could gather from Lady Quentin's disclosures, the countess was a dashing figure, adored by her husband, whom she had firmly under the cat's foot. She went her own way most of the year, but each Christmas returned with him to the ancestral acres, well attended by the most amusing people she could assemble to make the visit bearable. The countess hated the country and she could not stand to be bored. Lady Quentin could hardly wait to join the fun, for at Hartley Hall there was always something going on: an impromptu ball, a riding expedition, or a masquerade.

Emily herself was dreading the experience. She hated to leave her comfortable room for a strange household, full to bursting with guests and their numerous servants. She knew she would have to share a room with another lady's maid, or perhaps even more than one, and once again she would be pitchforked into the company of strange valets, footmen, and grooms. And then there was the journey itself; the different inns and the other travelers and their servants to be encountered in the halls and on the stairs. She would be fondled and pinched, and there was nothing she could do about it but try to remain as aloof as possible. Pretty servants were fair game to every male in sight, from noble lords to common coachmen. As she fastened her hair in its customary tight bun one morning, Emily sighed. The only good thing about the trip was that Miss Arabella Quentin had not been included. Emily wondered whether she or her mistress was the more pleased to escape her constant attention and criticism.

The Quentins, with Emily and Perry, the youngest footman, who would serve as the captain's valet in the absence of his batman, left London the morning of December 16. It was several days' journey to Hartley Hall, for it was located a few miles from Leadenham. Lady Quentin beguiled the trip with breathless chatter. She was so pleased to have her husband's undivided attention, she did not even seem to notice the tedious journey. Emily and Perry, sitting facing back and holding various parcels and dressing cases, could not agree.

They spent the last night on the road in an inn in Stamford. The captain wished to make an early start, and so it was barely light when they ate a hurried breakfast the following morning. Emily stood in the posting yard, busy even at this hour with carriages and drays, horses and ostlers as the captain helped Lady Quentin to her seat in the coach. Emily could see her breath in the cold air and she envied her mistress her sable-lined cloak.

Suddenly she was aware she was being stared at, and she looked up to see the gentleman who had rescued her in the park observing her with interest. He was standing beside a smart curricle attended by his tiger, but when he saw the company she was in, and the bags and parcels she was holding, he raised his eyebrows and strolled over to her side.

Now that he was standing, Emily could see he was about six feet in height and slimly built in spite of a pair of powerful shoulders. As he smiled at her, his air of boredom disappeared and she realized he was nowhere near as old as she had thought, perhaps only in his late twenties. It was obvious that he was an aristocrat from the top of his arrogantly tilted beaver set on shining black hair, to his well-polished boots. The devil that gleamed in his dark eyes and his slashing white grin all cried out, "Danger here, beware!" as clearly as if the little voice in her head had spoken aloud. He was obviously a man who got what he wanted, and without a moment's delay. Emily was glad there was no possibility of his ever giving her a command.

"I see I was in error that day in the park, m'dear," he drawled, looking her up and down in open appraisal. "How strange that I mistook you for a lady. I am so seldom wrong."

Emily was angry at his insolent words and those probing eyes, which seemed to see right through her clothes; and she forgot her station to say in a cold voice, "I have never heard, sir, that being a lady is reserved only for the upper classes. Indeed, I have often found that there are several of the *haut ton* who are sadly lacking in common courtesy and good manners."

She raised her chin and gave him a sparkling look of scorn. At the expression of arrested surprise on his arrogant face, she remembered her situation and lowered her eyes in confusion.

"Come, Nelly," Lady Quentin called from the coach window, "we must be off. Have a care for my dressing case, mind!"

Emily turned to do her bidding without another word, being careful not to look into those cold black eyes again. As she moved toward the coach, she heard the stranger muse, "I cannot recall being treated to such a severe setdown in my entire life—and from such an unexpected quarter as well. My congratulations, ma'am."

Somehow, for the remainder of the ride, Emily found her thoughts returning again and again to the arrogant stranger. He looked so familiar, and yet she was sure she had never known him, even though his type was familiar to her after her two years of servitude. He had all the insolence of the well-born and even more pronounced than most, and the sneering disregard for the feelings of inferior people she had grown accustomed to. She stared out at the bleak countryside they were passing through. It looked so cold and forbidding under its thin blanket of snow that it reminded her of the expression on his haughty face. Clasping Lady Quentin's jewel case tightly, she could only hope that their paths would not cross again.

At last, some hours later, they drove up the long drive to Hartley Hall, a huge pile of ivy-covered gray stone with narrow windows, whose turrets and towers proclaimed its age. For the next several hours, Emily was too busy to think of the stranger again. She barely had time to glance at the small room up under the roof that she was to share with another maid, or even to unpack her bags, for she was summoned by Lady Quentin to help her change for tea. And then, of course, she had to unpack the lady's trunks and portmanteaus. Several of her gowns had become sadly crushed; she set them aside to be ironed.

At dinner in the servant's hall, she made the acquaintance of the dresser who would share her room. Miss Hentershee was a middle-aged woman with sandy hair, very slim and neat, but somehow she seemed worn and fragile. They sat next to each other at the table, and Emily was amused at the rigid protocol that was followed; the upper servants at the head and foot of the table, and all the others in ranks down the sides, according to their jobs. Next to her on the other side was an older upstairs maid who stared at her dark-blue gown with envy, but spoke not a word.

The butler said grace and the plates were served. There was no general conversation; grooms spoke to grooms while valets and dressers exchanged a few words. Emily discovered that there were some twenty guests expected, with more to attend a gala ball to be given shortly after Boxing Day. These additional guests would spend the night as well, and since each guest had at least two servants, and in some cases as many as four, the servant's hall would be crowded.

After the meat course, the butler gave the signal for the upper servants to retire to the housekeeper's room for their pudding and cheese. Emily was glad that the food had been plentiful, if somewhat plainly cooked. She would need her strength, for this was not a compact, modern house. There were miles of passageways and stairs to travel, and she knew Lady Quentin would demand the same instant attention she had become used to in town.

In the days that followed, Emily was glad she was young, but even so she was often weary when she fell into bed late at night. Miss Hentershee grew even paler and more frail, and it was not long before Emily discovered that she was troubled by an arthritic complaint, a condition she hid carefully from her mistress.

"She would discharge me in a moment, you know, if she even suspected," the older dresser confided one morning as she struggled into her clothes. "She's a hard one, is Lady Williams. And if I lose my place and my salary, I do not know how I shall live. In a few years I will have saved enough to retire, but it is difficult on fifteen guineas a year to put anything aside.''

Emily was horrified, especially when she learned Miss Hentershee had been with Lady Williams for twelve years, and from then on she tried to help the older woman as much as she could by taking over some of her chores. This was difficult, for Lady Quentin, entering into all the amusements of the party, changed her clothes several times a day, and when she dropped so much as a handkerchief, never thought of picking it up herself. She might be having a wonderful time with all the dances and teas and card parties, but her maid worked harder than she ever had in town. She could hardly wait to return. Besides, the countess did not believe in indulging the servants. There was no heat in the attics where they slept, and when Emily asked a housemaid to make up the fire in her room, the girl jeered at her.

''And 'oo do you think you are? A princess or summat? We ain't allowed no fires.''

Emily winced. She had been called ''princess'' once before in an earlier situation, and the servants there had made her life a misery.

Now Emily could not help muttering, ''Spoiled brat!'' as she picked up a discarded stole from the floor after Lady Quentin had gone down to dinner on her husband's arm, laughing gaily as she did so. The dressing table was covered with powder and hairpins and jewelry, and there were slops to carry away and fire to be made up again. Emily knew she could have no respite until she had the room in perfect order. She had been up since six, and her back ached and her feet were swollen. Besides, she did not care to linger on this floor alone. Lord Hunter, the Marquess of Benterfield, had rooms opposite the Quentins', and Emily had seen him watching her as she went about her duties. She thought he was one of the most unattractive men she had ever seen. Of no more than medium height, with an undistinguished lined face and thinning gray hair, only his great air of consequence told you he was someone of importance. In repose, his face had a hint of cruelty in it; Emily could easily imagine him abusing a servant or beating his horses without a second thought.

But all thoughts of the marquess faded from her mind the afternoon of the long-awaited ball. As she was leaving Lady Quentin's room with some mending, she saw the arrogant stranger again. He was a little way down the corridor and in the process of entering the bedchamber next to Lord Hunter's, and his eyebrows rose when he recognized her. Emily lowered her eyes and dropped a hasty curtsy before she hurried away, her heart pounding. She was almost sure she heard a deep chuckle, and she shivered. At least he will be here only overnight, she told herself as she went up the long flight of stone stairs to the sewing room. I wonder who he is?

That evening, Emily hooked her mistress into a new gown of pale-pink silk and dressed her soft brown hair in shining curls on which she set the ruby tiara that had been the captain's Christmas gift.

She does look lovely, she thought as she knelt to arrange the lady's skirts, a task made more difficult as Lady Quentin whirled before the pier glass to admire her gown. When she had gone, Emily straightened the room and went to join Miss Hentershee. As she gained the hall, she could hear the strains of a waltz from the ballroom on the floor below. For a moment she lingered, unable to stop herself from taking a few steps in time to the music, her skirts and apron swinging as gracefully as Lady Quentin's expensive ball gown had done. Emily felt a longing in her breast and such a sudden misery that it was all she could do not to cry out in her pain. It wasn't fair! Just one flight below the ladies and gentlemen who should have been her peers were dancing and amusing themselves with light flirtations and sparkling conversation, but she, Emily Wyndham, could not join them. She put a trembling hand to her mouth. I must remember that I am Margaret Nelson now, she told herself. There will be no balls, no parties for me. No, before me is only a life of constant toil, and someday I will be like Miss Hentershee, a middle-aged, worn spinster.

Emily stifled a sob and ran to the stairs and her attic room. It would be hours before she would be summoned to put Lady Quentin to bed, but at least she did not have to remain here and torment herself listening to festivities that she would never know.

It was very late indeed before her mistress retired and Emily was able to blow out the candles and take herself to bed. As she closed the door softly and started down the hall, she realized she was not alone. From a dimly lighted alcove nearby, the Marquess of Benterfield rose from a sofa where he had obviously been waiting for her, and came toward her with a leer. From his uneven gait and flushed face, Emily could see he was drunk and her heart sank.

She tried to scurry past him, but he reached out and slid his arm around her waist and pulled her harshly into his arms.

"Pretty little thing," he crooned, and then one hand forced her chin up and he bent his head to kiss her.

Emily twisted her head, unable to restrain a whimper of panic as she pushed him as hard as she could, causing him to stagger backward. She was very frightened, for she knew she must not cry out for help; to raise an alarm among the sleeping guests would mean instant dismissal.

The marquess came back to her and grasped her arms in a tight hold. "You must not fight me, dear child," he said. "You cannot get away."

"Let me go, sir. Oh, please, let me go," she pleaded, and he laughed, his bad breath washing over her and making her feel faint. She noticed that he was perspiring and his mouth was wet and loose.

"Let you go? When I have just captured such a prize? No, no! Come now, no more of this innocent cringing. I know you maids, and I want my share. Why, you should be honored that I ask you into my bed."

He laughed again as Emily cried out, "No, no!" She thought she had never hated anyone so much in her entire life as he pressed his body against hers and forced her hard against the wall. Suddenly, behind him, she heard a soft but forceful voice.

"Do you really find rape that amusing, m'lord?"

The marquess dropped his hands and whirled, and Emily saw the arrogant stranger leaning casually against the opposite wall.

"Your Grace!" the marquess sputtered as he attempted a low bow.

"Now, I myself prefer a willing partner," the stranger said in a conversational way as he straightened up. "And this girl does not appear at all willing Bad *ton*, Richard, bad *ton*. Besides, I am surprised you would lower yourself to make love to a common maid. Can it be the highborn ladies all despise your suit?"

His voice was scornful, and the marquess flushed. "Oh, I am sure the mighty Duke of Wrotherham has never had any need to seek any lady under the rank of countess,'' he sneered as Emily gasped. The Duke of Wrotherham? Why, his father had been one of her mother's lovers! No wonder he had looked so familiar.

The duke nodded in acknowledgment of the compliment. "You should emulate my fastidious example, m'lord. Come now, off to bed with you. I doubt that in your condition you would find the encounter at all, er, fulfilling.''

The marquess sneaked a sideways glance at Emily and licked his lips, but when he looked back at the duke, it was to see him advancing purposefully, rolling up the sleeves of the open shirt he wore above a tight pair of evening breeches as he did so.

"I should hate to rouse the house, for then everyone would learn of your indiscretion,'' the duke pointed out in a deep-voiced whisper.

The marquess tugged at his collar and turned away without another word.

As his bedroom door closed, Emily looked up to see the duke regarding her closely.

"But one must commend the marquess on his excellent taste,'' he said softly, and Emily, her hands going to her cap, discovered that her hair had escaped its severe bun and was falling down in disarray. She flushed but spoke up bravely.

"I must thank you, your Grace, for coming to my rescue,'' she said as she curtsied, trying to control her uneven breathing. She did not miss the way his eyes traveled so insolently up and down her figure in its neat gown and lace-trimmed apron. She wished it did not fit so well.

"What is your name, girl?'' the duke asked, stepping closer.

"Nelson—Margaret Nelson, your Grace.''

He reached out a careless finger and tilted her chin, and Emily did not realize how her emerald-green eyes flashed at the intimacy. Suddenly, the duke laughed softly. "Go to bed, Margaret Nelson. It is very late. And I would advise you to eschew dark hallways until the marquess has left the hall.''

Emily curtsied again and ran to the stairs to the attic. Her heart was pounding in earnest now, for she knew the duke was infinitely more dangerous than the marquess. And why had she had such an urge to tell him she was Emily Wyndham? It had almost slipped out before she could stop herself. He was an alarming man—thank heavens he would be leaving on the morrow with the other guests invited especially for the ball.

Emily was careful to avoid the Marquess of Benterfield for the remaining days of the house party, and she sighed a heartfelt sigh of relief on the morning they took coach again for London. She had not seen the duke again, and although her thoughts often strayed to him, she told herself she was glad that their encounter had been limited to that one meeting in the dark hall.

Life in London resumed its usual pace, and then, toward the end of February, Lady Quentin's mother, the Countess of Ridgely, arrived for a visit. With this lady came her maid, her own footman, and her coachman, and a vast amount of baggage.

Emily saw the lady the next afternoon when she was drying and curling Lady Quentin's hair. The countess settled herself in a straight chair and began to talk. It was difficult to see any resemblance between mother and daughter except for their slimness. Indeed, the countess was thin to the point of gauntness. She had a cold, dignified manner that became evident after she had stared at Emily and then promptly forgot her as she told her daughter the news of home.

"Your father sends his remembrances, Alicia," she began, "and of course your brothers. I am delighted to inform you that your sister Agatha is about to make a most satisfactory match—Lord Dale, so well-to-do and of such a good family. Even though he is several years older than Agatha, we are extremely pleased. Well! I have also to tell you that your grandmother has succumbed to the gout once again and has retired to her own estates."

"Oh, Mama, how fortunate! I do hope you will make a long stay with us in that case."

Her mother stared. "Can I have heard you correctly? To be pleased when your grandmother is suffering? As for making a long stay, I am sure your husband will have something to say to that. With a new bride he will be wishing me away in a week."

"Not Tony, Mama," Lady Quentin protested. "He is so busy now we are back in town that I scarcely see him. I did so hope that now the war is over he would be able to be with me more often.'' She sighed and the countess looked at her shrewdly.

"You will remember what I told you when you were married, Alicia,'' she said firmly. "It is fatal to hang on a man's sleeve, even as a bride, for there is nothing that gives a husband such a disgust of a female as her constant begging for his attention.''

"I know, Mama, indeed I remember,'' Lady Quentin said, hanging her head and making it difficult for Emily to continue to brush her hair. "I have done just as you told me. In fact, in the beginning, it was often Tony who begged for my company, but I kept your precepts in mind and did not allow him to see me more than once or twice a week.''

"Good! That is the only way to keep a marriage happy.''

"I do wish Tony would talk to me more, Mama. He never tells me why it is important for me to attend this party or that, or be sure to talk to certain people in my most charming manner, and he never tells me what he is doing at the War Office, or why—''

The countess interrupted. "That is none of your concern, daughter. That is man's business, and of course beyond your understanding. You must not pry.'' Then in a lower voice, she added, "I am sure you remember what I told you about gentlemen and their lady friends. It is especially important for you to bear in mind, for the captain is such a handsome man, and you, my dear, are not at all beautiful or captivating, nor do you have much of a . . . of a shape. So if you see him in attendance on one of the demireps of the town, you must look the other way and never show him that you think his behavior disgusting.'' She sighed and added repressively, "Men are different from women. Their amusements are such that no decent woman would indulge in them. Besides, you must keep your own reputation above reproach. What is sauce for the gander is most definitely not sauce for the goose.''

"How very unfair, Mama,'' Alicia exclaimed, but at the sight of her mother's horrified face, she added, "Not that I have any desire for a lover. My dear Tony is everything a woman could want.''

"It is of course gratifying that you feel that way, Alicia,'' the countess said dryly. "But on no account must you let him know it. No silly raptures, no languishing looks—you know the form. You will submit to your husband, Alicia—I am sure I do not need to tell you your duty—but there is no need to pretend any enjoyment in the act. That is why men go with women of loose character; from their wives they expect only a dignified passivity. If you would be a good wife, heed me.''

"But . . . but Mama! Is a woman never to enjoy—I mean, well—sometimes it is so beautiful and overwhelming—''

"*That* is quite enough! To think I should ever hear one of *my* daughters make such a disgusting statement! You seem to forget the captain only married you for your money. He does not love you.''

Lady Quentin paled at her sarcasm and nodded her head. "I know you must be right, Mama, but Arabella says I should stop going about town on my own and be with Tony more often.''

"Hmmph!'' Lady Kinsley sniffed. "I did not realize Miss Quentin was still in town. When does she plan to retire to Burton-Latimer?''

"I have no idea; never, I imagine, as long as Tony is in London,'' Lady Quentin said tartly, shaking her head.

Lady Kinsley rose. "I can see it is a very good thing that I have come to town, Alicia. I did not expect to hear you speak so of one of your husband's relations, who has, after all, done everything in her power to assure your happiness. Why, Miss Quentin, if she has any weakness, it is that she does not perfectly understand the married state, never having been so blessed herself. But in other matters''—she shook a bony finger at her daughter—"do not be setting yourself up as an authority, Alicia, it ill becomes you: rather, listen and obey when older and wiser heads take the trouble to advise you. I shall go and rest now before dinner. It has been a fatiguing day, and I see I have quite a task before me to bring you to a correct state of mind.''

"Yes, Mama,'' Lady Quentin murmured in a soft, discouraged voice as her mother went majestically to the door.

Emily tightened her lips. She was horrified, for never had she thought to hear a mother speak so to her daughter. It was obvious now why Lady Quentin behaved as she did. No wonder she ran around town, filling her days with shopping and parties. Emily wanted to put her arms around the bride and tell her her mother was wrong, for she was a very pretty girl and in a few years, with more experience, would be a lovely woman. As she took some mending away with her and left her mistress to write a few notes, she shook her head. Between Lady Kinsley and Miss Quentin, they were in a fair way of ruining the girl, for she had little self-confidence and no way of standing up to her elders. Emily wondered what Lord Kinsley was like, and what he thought of his wife's ideas of marriage, poor man.

Now that Lady Kinsley was visiting, Captain Quentin was seen even less than before. He left early for Headquarters, he played cards with his friends, he had engagements at his club. Through it all, Emily watched Lady Quentin fade into a meek submission, as her mother nodded at each new instance of her son-in-law's indifference.

She was also privileged to see both the countess and Miss Quentin taking her mistress to task one morning in the drawing room. Miss Quentin had called to welcome the countess to town. When Emily came in with the handkerchief Lady Quentin had dropped in her room, they were deep in a lecture on the responsibilities of the modern wife.

"I must tell you, dear Lady Kinsley," Miss Quentin was saying in what she considered a playful tone, "that Alicia has been very naughty. Indeed, she is fast gaining a reputation as a gadabout, care-for-nobody!"

"Indeed?" Lady Kinsley asked frigidly. "I find it hard to believe of one of *my* daughters. Perhaps you exaggerate?"

"I can assure you that I do not," Miss Quentin replied, her high color even more prominent. "I wish it were not so, for you must know it is repugnant for me to find fault and have to report such behavior to Alicia's mother."

The two older ladies glared at each other as Emily handed Lady Quentin her handkerchief and could not resist pressing her hand warmly as she did so. Lady Quentin looked up to see her maid smiling at her in complete understanding of her predicament, and her expression brightened a little and she sat up straighter on the sofa.

"This is all a farradiddle and you know it, Bella," she said. "I am very disappointed that you would repeat such untruths to my mother. I am not a gadabout. I attend the parties of the *beau monde* with my husband's friends when he cannot escort me himself, and as for being a care-for-nobody, that is also untrue. I care very much for my husband. Thank you, Nelly, that will be all."

Emily curtsied, but as she left the room, she heard Miss Quentin say, "Well, I see I have been put firmly in my place." Her tone was disbelieving and a little stunned. As Emily shut the door, Lady Kinsley said, "I knew I could not be mistaken in my own child, but on the other hand, Alicia, it is the outside of enough . . ."

Emily frowned as she made her way upstairs. Lady Quentin's independence was not to last long, by all accounts.

Two weeks later, as Emily was putting away some clean laundry in the dressing room while Lady Quentin enjoyed her usual breakfast in bed, the captain threw open the bedroom door and rushed in, throwing his gloves and sword stick down before he approached the bed.

"My darling Alicia, I came at once to you. I have the most exciting news, just wait till you hear."

"Do you, Tony?" Emily heard her mistress ask. "Whatever can it be?"

Emily put down the pile of chemises and petticoats that she was holding and prepared to slip out the dressing room door to give them some privacy when she heard the captain exclaim, "It is famous, pet! Napoleon has escaped from Elba."

Emily froze, her eyes widening as she heard Lady Quentin put down her cup with a snap.

"Napoleon has escaped, Tony?" she asked. "And that is famous? Why—why, we will be at war before the cat has time to lick her ear."

"That is what is so famous, Alicia. Don't you see, I will be sent abroad again; the battle is not over, as I feared."

"Oh, Tony," his wife wailed. "How can you wish to leave me—to go where your life will be in danger?"

There was a pause, and then Emily heard the captain say, in slightly less-excited tones, "Now, my dear, you married a soldier, and a soldier is never happy unless he is fighting. Nothing will happen to me, and this may well be the means to advancement. It is not that I wish to leave you, but that I must. Besides, you will be so busy with all your parties, I vow you won't even know I'm gone."

"Tony, how can you say so," Lady Quentin asked, her voice injured. "I shall miss you quite dreadfully."

She began to cry and there was another pause, and then the captain asked in a strained voice. "Do you love me so much, then? I did not know. Do not cry, my love. Perhaps you would like to go to your father's estate until I return? Or if you want to remain in town so as to be near the news, I am sure Bella would be delighted to bear you company."

"No! Not my mother, and *never* Bella!"

Emily heard the captain rise from the side of the bed and begin to pace the room, bewildered at his wife's vehement weeping. "But I do not understand. Come, my dear, be calm. There is no need to make any hasty decision, for I have to get an appointment to Wellington's army. No one knows if the Guards will be included.

"You mean there is a chance your regiment will not be called?"

"Well, it is nowhere certain, which is why I shall have to bustle about, for if they are to remain here, I must get myself appointed an aide-de-camp to some general. I have it in mind to ask General Raklin this very day, just in case. All this disbanding of the army after Napoleon was exiled last year, and now we see the result. There is no army left, no *real* army ready to fight."

Completely ignoring this diversion, Lady Quentin said crossly, "So that is why I had to be nice to him and his wife. No wonder you did not tell me what was in your mind, for I would surely have given the general a disgust of you if I had known to what purpose I was being used. Help you to the fighting, indeed."

The captain laughed at her. "Be glad for me, Alicia. It is what I am trained for and the only way for me to make my way in the world. If I get a promotion, I shall not have to live in your pocket anymore."

"And what does that mean?" she asked.

"Only that I have not liked being dependent on you, my love. I did not marry you for your money, you know, but in spite of it."

"Really, Tony?" Lady Quentin asked eagerly. "I am sure I never knew. Well, what I mean is— But truly, it does not bother me, and I am so glad you told me, I cannot say."

He laughed again. "That sounds more like the wife I know." Emily heard the bed creak as he sat down again, and then there was silence. In a few minutes, the captain was on his way, calling cheerfully over his shoulder, "I shall return as soon as I have news, love. Pray for my success."

The door of the bedroom banged, and when Emily heard Lady Quentin begin to cry as if her heart would break, she slipped out of the dressing room and went away until her mistress should summon her again.

3

The days sped by, and for a while it seemed that the captain was to be frustrated in his desire to make his way to Belgium so as to be ready when the summons came for battle. Every evening that he returned home with a dark frown on his face, his wife was sure to be all smiles, although she tried to restrain her relief. Most unexpectedly, she was joined in all her feelings by her sister-in-law. Miss Quentin was not slow to learn the news, for all London buzzed with it, and there was very little else discussed no matter where you went. From the balls to the parks to the circulating libraries and the shops, the news was all of Boney and what Old Nosey would do to him this time for having the temerity to escape his exile. Not that anyone was at all sure that the duke would be appointed head of the army, for he had been in Vienna for the Congress since early February, and if Napoleon chose to march at once, there would be no time for him to travel north and assemble his army.

Napoleon had arrived in France on March the first, and the allies waited breathlessly for the news that the king's troops had stopped his march on Paris, but it never came. Even Marshal Ney deserted the king in favor of throwing in his lot with his newly returned former master. And then, on the twentieth, Napoleon entered Paris, and King Louis XVIII fled.

Now, as Captain Quentin tried desperately to get himself reassigned, all England waited to hear that Napoleon was on the way north, and Bella told Alicia that they must both pray that Anthony would be unsuccessful and remain in London.

"But we must not let him know we feel this way, Alicia," she warned. "He would be most displeased."

Lady Quentin was quick to agree, but then Miss Quentin ruined this budding camaraderie by adding coldly, "You, of course, did not even know my brother when he was wounded at Talavera in the Peninsula campaign; I was out of my mind with worry before he returned to recuperate. There was some talk that he might lose his arm; indeed, he was lucky to escape with his life, and until now there was no thought of his returning to the war. His wound was so slow in healing. I felt sure he would remain here in London, where he is a most valuable asset to the War Office."

The Countess of Ridgely was making plans to return to her home. She had had a letter from her husband, and it appeared that there was some delay in Agatha's accepting the suitable Lord Dale, and so she did not feel she could remain. She confided coldly to Alicia that Agatha was being very silly, but she was sure she would be able to put her in a more amenable frame of mind. Lady Quentin spared a sympathetic thought for her sister as she waved her mama good-bye.

Emily was glad the countess had departed and fervently wished there was some way that Miss Arabella Quentin could also be banished. The young couple were so much happier on their own, without her interference. Emily had a premonition that the captain was going to be successful in being sent abroad and she wished they might have this time to themselves. There was, after all, a distinct possibility that it would be their last.

All through April, the captain fretted and fumed, and Lady Quentin smiled. He was gone from morning to night seeing this colonel, that general; trying in every way he knew to convince his superiors that the wounds he had received in Portugal had in no way incapacitated him from the fight that everyone was sure would come. No one of the military expected Napoleon to remain quietly content in France, even though the days passed and he made no move to renew the fighting. Wellington had left the Congress at Vienna on March 20, and when Captain Quentin learned he had arrived at headquarters in Brussels on April 4, he renewed his efforts. With Wellington in position, surely the action could not be far off.

In between his efforts to get himself ordered overseas, the

captain was often with Lady Quentin. He escorted her himself to any party she wished to attend, and no more was heard of her *cicisbeos*.

One afternoon he arrived home early to find his sister and his wife in the drawing room having tea. He kissed them both before he called the butler to bring up the best Madeira and three glasses.

"I do not feel it is wise, dear Tony, to be indulging in spirits at this time of day," Miss Quentin remarked. "Let me give you a cup of tea."

Emily heard all this from Lady Quentin that evening, for she was indignant that Bella should take over as hostess in her own drawing room. Evidentally the captain agreed, for he was swift to refuse. "If I wanted tea, dear Bella, I would ask my wife for it, for she is sitting behind the tea tray as mistress here." As Miss Quentin colored up, he added, "But come, we have a toast to drink. The Guards have been called up." He did not appear to notice that both women paled.

"Indeed, Nelly," Lady Quentin told her maid, "I thought I should have to call you to bring my salts, I felt so faint. It was only that Bella was there that enabled me to control myself."

The toast was drunk—"To Wellington, and to success!" —without much enthusiasm by anyone but Captain Quentin. Alicia asked when he had to leave, wishing with all her heart that the two of them were alone so she might run into his arms and be comforted, and he told them that he expected to embark within the week. "So soon!" she mourned, holding tight to his hand.

On the sofa, Miss Quentin frowned. "But, Tony, how can you be ready? That is surely much too soon. Perhaps it would be wise to plan for a later departure."

"I have been ready for weeks, to tell you the truth. And my batman, Sergeant Boothby, goes with me, of course. That should reassure you, Bella, for you know that I would never have come through the Peninsula Campaign if he had not been with me to care for me. So you see, there is nothing to worry about. I have no doubt that we shall rout Napoleon in short order; perhaps we might plan on spending the rest of the summer in Burton Latimer, just the three of us."

At this, Lady Quentin told her maid, she wanted to cry out that she wished it might be the two of them, not the three.

She thought Bella would never take her leave, busy as she was issuing orders for his equipment and what medical supplies he must be sure to take with him, until even Captain Quentin had had enough.

"Bella, I am not a raw recruit, you know. Have done! And that reminds me, are we not engaged to dine with the Biddleslys this evening, Alicia?" At her nod, he put down his glass and went to escort his sister to the front hall. "In that case, we must bustle about. How I look forward to telling Percy my good news! Such a stir there will be! Poor fellow, since he lost his leg at Badajoz, there can be no question of his going."

Bella said dryly. "In that case, Tony, perhaps you should not gloat too much? To think that he will miss such a treat! It does not bear thinking about, does it, Alicia?"

Even in Lady Quentin's dressing room, Emily heard the shout of laughter that accompanied this sally, and Lady Quentin was able, as she came upstairs on her husband's arm, to smile a little as well, in spite of all her fears.

The days rushed by. One afternoon Lady Quentin insisted the captain take her to Tattersalls so she might buy him the finest horse there, to carry him safely through the battles. He called his new black charger, Dane, in honor of the Duke of Wellington's famous horse, Copenhagen.

By the first of May he was gone, leaving very early one morning for the coast and the ship that would carry him to Belgium. Lady Quentin wanted to get up to see him off, but the captain intercepted Emily in the gray dawn light as she was coming to wake her mistress, and told her she was on no account to do so.

"I shall slip in and wake her just before I leave," he told the maid, for the first time looking a little unhappy. "There is no need for her to bestir herself so early."

Emily was glad to agree, for she did not feel her mistress would be able to contain her tears through a long leavetaking.

"I have a special charge for you, Miss Nelson," he added, his dark eyes somber and his handsome face serious. "You must take the greatest care of your mistress while I am gone. True, there is my sister to watch over her, but she and Alicia do not get on as I had hoped. I have noticed that my wife is fond of you and depends on you a great deal. You will see to her, is that understood?"

Emily dropped him a curtsy. "You may rely on me, sir," she said, and then added, "May I wish you good fortune, sir? We shall all be praying for your safe return."

"Thank you, Miss Nelson! And now I shall speak to my wife before I must leave."

He did not remain in Lady Quentin's bedroom long, and Emily heard him close the door behind him and stand quietly for a moment before he ran down the stairs. Mr. Goodwell had had all the servants assembled there to bid him good-bye, but Emily was not among their number. She had gone without being summoned to Lady Quentin's room to comfort her. She was surprised to discover her mistress standing at the window, a smile on her face as she held the drapes aside and peered down into the street.

"There he goes! How splendid he looks on Dane," she said as she waved and blew a kiss. In a few moments, she dropped the curtains and turned blindly away. The tears she had held back so valiantly now streamed down her cheeks. Quickly, Emily went to help her back to bed. Lady Quentin collapsed in her arms. "Oh, Nellie, what shall I do without my Tony?"

Emily soothed her as best she could. A minute later, Mrs. Goodwell tapped on the door and handed her a cup of steaming liquid. "Get her to drink this, Miss Nelson," the good woman whispered. " 'Twill help her sleep, and sleep is the best thing in the world for her right now."

When Lady Quentin woke again, she was subdued, but very calm. She allowed Emily to dress her and followed her regular daily routine. She was seated at the desk in her room writing to her husband when Miss Quentin was announced. Emily was in the dressing room and she made no move to leave, for she decided she would interrupt if she felt the call was distressing her mistress. There was no need for such vigilance, however, for Lady Quentin was very much in command of herself. Emily was as surprised as Miss Quentin must have been at her dignity and self-control.

She began by bemoaning her brother's departure; Lady Quentin agreed it was very sad. Then Miss Quentin mentioned that she was sure the captain expected her to take care of his wife and she considered it her duty to do so while he was away.

"How much better, my dear Alicia," she said in her cool,

authoritative way, "if I were to move in with you for the duration. It would be so much easier for you if I were here all the time to take over the running of the household and bear you company, for I fear you will be very lonely with Anthony away. Of course there can be no thought of your continuing to rattle about town with all the Corinthian set, now your husband is gone. Then, too, you are very young. Even as a married woman, I cannot feel easy to have you live alone. It will cause gossip. Do say you agree. I am sure it would be Anthony's wish."

Emily held her breath, but Lady Quentin was more than equal to the task before her. "How very kind of you to offer, Bella, when I know how comfortably situated you are with Miss Twitchell and her mother. I would not think of inconveniencing you."

When Miss Quentin would have spoken, she continued quickly. "Besides, I am hardly alone with a houseful of servants to take care of me. And I must point out, dear Bella, that no matter what my age, I am a married woman. There can be no gossip about what I do, not as Tony's wife. No, I thank you, I prefer to keep house by myself."

Miss Quentin argued the point again and again in the hour she remained. Lady Quentin denied her each time in a light pleasant voice before she adroitly changed the subject. Did not Bella think the weather very pleasant? Surely Tony would have a good crossing. And what did she think of her new afternoon gown? She had worried when she ordered it that it was too ornate, but perhaps she was wrong? It was the third row of ruffles that bothered her; what did her sister-in-law think? Miss Quentin's voice grew more and more aggravated as Lady Quentin's grew lighter. At last she broke into the inconsequential chitchat and said, "Come, Alicia, it ill becomes you to think so much of an afternoon dress with your beloved husband on his way to war. I beg you to reconsider my proposal. I can move my things today, for I am sure Anthony would wish to see us together."

"Do you, Bella?" Lady Quentin asked idly. "But in that case, he would have been sure to mention it before he left, would he not? And since he did not, I assume he knew I would prefer to remain alone. And now, my dear, I must ask you to excuse me. I have a letter I wish to finish to Tony. Do you have his direction? I am sure he will be delighted to hear from you. Oh, do not forget your reticule, Bella.''

Miss Quentin lost no time taking her departure, and Emily had to smile when she heard her slam the bedroom door behind her. Then she heard her mistress sigh, but when she peeked around the door, she was once again at her writing desk, quill in hand.

The following day, Lady Quentin told Emily that she was to accompany her shopping. ''I have a book I wish to return to Fancourt's Library as well,'' she said.

Emily was delighted at this sign of normalcy, but when they reached the library, Lady Quentin made no move to take out another book, not even when Mr. Fancourt himself presented her with the second volume of the book she had just returned. She smiled at him as she said, ''Thank you, but I do not believe I will have much time for reading in the future.'' She was bowed to the door, her puzzled maid in her wake. Not have time? What else was there to do? She could not write letters all the time.

On the sidewalk, just as she was about to step into her carriage, Lady Quentin was hailed by a young blond gentleman, who was strolling along in the bright sunshine.

''Alicia! Humble servant, m'lady,'' he said, sweeping her a most elegant bow while he removed the jaunty beaver from his carefully arranged locks. His glance slid over to Emily and his eyes narrowed. She was carrying Lady Quentin's reticule, and standing as she was a few paces behind her mistress as was correct, it was obvious that she was a maid, in spite of her air of breeding and fashionable clothes.

Well, well, what have we here? Lord Andrew thought to himself. What a little beauty, and what a waste that she is nothing but a lady's maid!

Emily felt his eyes and looked up, and the expression she saw in those intent blue eyes made her lower her own in haste.

He began speaking again. ''Sorry to hear that Tony has hopped the Channel, m'dear, leavin' you all alone. But do not fear; we are all eager to keep you company. Least we can do, friends of Tony that we are.'' He smiled slyly, and Lady Quentin smiled back at this obvious ploy. ''Do you attend Lady Jersey's reception tonight? I would consider it an honor to escort you.

The lady thanked him, but said she did not plan to attend, and Lord Andrews was quick to remonstrate with her, pointing out all the reasons why she should not bury herself in a nunnery while her husband was gone.

"If I might pass?" a deep, harsh voice said behind Emily, and she jumped a little and turned to one side. The gentleman trying to pass stared at her and checked his stride. It was the Duke of Wrotherham, and as Lady Quentin continued to chat, he murmured, "Can it be possible that you do not need to be rescued this afternoon, Miss Nelson? Behold me, at your service."

He smiled at her, and Emily clasped her hands together tightly. She had no idea how she was supposed to answer this sally, so she only shook her head, in her confusion, forgetting to curtsy.

"I see you have managed to keep the same mistress, girl," the duke continued. "Is her husband blind?"

At this Emily's eyes darkened, and the duke admired their emerald fire. "Not all men are philanderers, sir. The captain loves his wife," she admonished him.

"He certainly must, how refreshing! But, then, he is a bridegroom, is he not? I think it safe to prophecy that you will not remain in the Quentins' employ for more than a year. Do you care to wager on it?" His dark eyes were warm, and yet they taunted her with the dare, and Emily put up her chin and turned her back, seemingly fascinated with a high-perch phaeton that was passing by. The duke chuckled, and Lord Andrews caught sight of him.

"Your Grace, well met! I have just been trying to convince Lady Quentin that she must not fall into the megrims now that Tony has gone to the wars. Do add your entreaty to mine, if you please! Lady Jersey's reception will be a desert this evening if she does not grace it."

Lady Quentin curtsied to the duke, who swept her a graceful bow, removing his beaver from his shining black hair as he did so. Emily thought it looked just like a crow's wing, dark and smooth. "I am afraid I cannot do so in a convincing manner, m'lord," he remarked. "I am sailing myself in a few days and have no more time for balls and receptions."

"Are you indeed, your Grace?" Lady Quentin asked in real interest. "It seems all England is removing abroad. So, you go to see Napoleon beaten as well."

"Hardly that," the duke replied. "I do not hold with sighseers at the battlefield. I travel on a small commission for the Foreign Office. And now you must excuse me, Lady Quentin, Lord Andrews . . ." He bowed, and replacing his beaver while he stared at Emily, he nodded to her before he strode away.

Emily barely noticed his stare. So this was Lord Andrews! She shivered a little, remembering his father's love letters to Althea Wyndham, and she was glad there was no possibility that the young peer could know her real identity.

Lady Quentin continued firm in her refusal to attend the evening's party and before long was driving away, leaving a puzzled young man staring after her carriage. Lord Andrews did not do so for long, however, but turned his thoughts to the lady's maid as he resumed his stroll. She was so beautiful— with those unusual emerald-green eyes, and silvery blond hair that gleamed in the sunlight like the finest satin, and her trim, high-bosomed figure—that he could not remember when he had been so struck. He promised himself he would be most assiduous in attending Alicia while Tony was away. Perhaps if he did so, he would be able to convince her lovely servant that she was wasting her talents maiding Lady Quentin.

The Duke of Wrotherham was also thinking of Lady Quentin's maid, and with much the same admiration for her beauty, but unlike Lord Andrews, he was not planning to seduce her if he could. Servants, no matter how lovely and curvaceous, were not his style.

Meanwhile, Lady Quentin was asking Emily where she had met the duke, her voice a little stiff. "For it was obvious, Nelly, that he knew you. My, the Duke of Wrotherham! He has barely condescended to speak to me all the time I have been in town, but he had a smile for you."

Emily could see she was suspicious, and was quick to tell her how the duke had rescued her in the park, omitting any mention of his second rescue at Hartley Hall. She was glad when Lady Quentin turned the subject to the shopping she intended to do.

What on earth is the matter with me? she wondered as Lady Quentin continued to chat. Why had her heart pounded and her mouth grown dry when the duke stood so close to her, and why had her breath been so shallow and unsteady?

Was she attracted to him, even as arrogant and unattainable as he was? She determined to put him from her mind.

Lady Quentin made some rather unusual purchases that afternoon that had Emily in a quandary. Why did the lady feel the need for a most severe waterproof cape? And what on earth possessed her to buy such stout boots? She had never put anything but the flimsiest sandals on her little feet. But Lady Quentin did not explain, so Emily accompanied her home none the wiser.

The next day, Lady Quentin received a Lord and Lady Daggleston for tea. They remained together in the drawing room for some time, and as Lady Quentin went with them to the front hall as they were leaving, Emily heard the end of the conversation.

"What fun it will be, Alicia," Lady Daggleston said gaily. The lady was a plump, breathless redhead whom Emily had often heard her mistress castigate as having more hair than wit, and her husband, Lord Daggleston, as not much better. "I am so glad you are coming with us. So touching!"

"Happy to have your company, m'lady," her husband agreed. "Perfectly safe, y'know. And, of course, everything will be first-class, for a Daggleston knows what's what. To think we will hear the glorious news before anyone else. A hit! A palpable hit!"

Emily was confused, but as Miss Quentin arrived shortly thereafter and went upstairs with Lady Quentin so she might change her clothes for a drive in the park with Lady Racklin, she did not discover what was gong on. Lady Quentin did not mention the Daggleston's visit to her sister-in-law. Miss Quentin was annoyed that she had arrived just as Alicia was going out.

"I see you are still flitting about, Sister," she said as she sat and watched Emily adjust a stunning bonnet of white straw covered with tiny pink flowers on Lady Quentin's soft brown curls. "You will become known as a here-and-thereian! And that bonnet looks monstrous expensive, as well as being much too gay!"

"It is becoming, is it not?" Lady Quentin agreed, turning her head so she might admire the effect. Miss Quentin sniffed, and she turned to her. "Do you think I should dress in sober gray, Bella, because Tony is in Belgium? I am sure he would wish me to carry on as usual. And how absurd when Napoleon has made no move to engage our forces.'' She laughed and took up a matching pink parasol. "Come, what good would it do?''

Miss Quentin drew in her breath sharply. "Of course there is no need for you to be forever weeping into your handkerchief, Alicia,'' she said coldly. "But there is also no need for you to flit about as if you didn't have a care in the world. Such behavior ill becomes Tony's wife.''

Lady Quentin walked to the door. "You will allow me to know what becomes me, if you please,'' she said in quite the sharpest tone Emily had ever heard her use. "And now you must excuse me, Bella. If you continue to drop in without notice, you will very often find me out, I'm afraid. And really, Bella, it is the outside of enough for you to claim that I am flitting about. Going for a sedate drive in the park with General Racklin's wife? She must be sixty if she's a day.''

She left the room, forcing her sister-in-law to follow. There was a bewildered look in those hard brown eyes and a tiny frown between her brows as she was forced to take her leave.

Still Lady Quentin did not take her maid into her confidence, but one evening she called Emily much earlier than she usually did. Emily discovered her sitting before the fire in her bedroom. As she curtsied and would have gone to fetch her nightgown, Lady Quentin said, "Sit down with me, Nelly. I have something of great importance to discuss with you.''

Emily took the seat opposite, feeling confused. It was in no way usual for Lady Quentin to ask her maid to sit and chat, but she composed herself and waited quietly.

Lady Quentin stared into the flames for a moment before she began to speak. "I have made up my mind to follow Tony,'' she said finally. "Half of England is already in Belgium. Why should I not be too?''

"But, m'lady,'' Emily protested, "can it be wise?''

"Perhaps not, but I am going to my husband regardless.'' Here Lady Quentin rose to pace the room, and Emily was so astonished at her firm tones and air of decision that she forgot to rise as well. "I have been thinking a great deal since Tony left,'' Lady Quentin went on. "And I see now that I should never have allowed my mother's instructions on wifely behavior to rule my actions. I was wrong to have listened to her and pretended this stupid indifference to Tony. And I should have taken steps as soon as we were married to gently but firmly remove Bella's talons from our lives.''

She paused and came to sit down again, adding, "Now Tony is gone and I may never see him again. I cannot bear to remain here, letting the precious moments that we might be together slip away.''

Emily's head was reeling, for she had promised the captain to care for his wife, now it appeared she was to help her into danger. But her heart leapt at the news, for in her mind the little voice was saying, "And the duke is there too, isn't he, dearie?''

"I have quite made up my mind. And you shall come with me,'' Lady Quentin was saying.

She paused until Emily nodded, and then she confided, "I have made arrangements to travel with Lord and Lady Daggleston. We leave in three days' time, so you see we will have to bustle about to be ready.''

"But . . . but what about Miss Quentin?'' Emily could not help asking. "You know how angry she will be—''

"But I will not tell her anything until the evening before our departure. I know Bella will try to stop me, although it is none of her business. And if I tell her before, she will insist on coming with me. She should, of course, be delighted to have me remove from Hubert Andrews' vicinity. He has been forever on the doorstep lately, and Bella has remarked it. Besides, I am traveling with the Dagglestons.''

"But she will object even so,'' Emily could not help pointing out.

"Oh, I know that. But I am more than a match for her in this case,'' Lady Quentin assured her maid. And looking at her determined gray eyes and firm mouth, Emily had to admit she was probably right.

She had certainly handled Lord Andrews very well. Emily knew of his constant visiting, but she herself had only seen him once, one afternoon when he called just as Lady Quentin was preparing to leave the house. Emily had retreated to the back hall at once, much to the young peer's regret, but she had heard Lady Quentin scolding him and asking him, in exactly the same determined voice she had just used, to moderate his visits.

Now she knew why Lady Quentin had bought such strange things, and in the following days she was very busy packing them, as well as the rest of her mistress's clothes, and her own besides. Lady Quentin told her there were just as many amusements in Brussels as there were in London, so along with the waterproof and the stout shoes, fragile ball gowns and delicate morning dresses, satin sandals, cosmetics, and jewels went into the trunks and cases as well.

The evening before their departure, Emily eased her aching back as she stood up after packing the last gown and checked her list to make sure she had not forgotten anything, especially the medicines Lady Quentin had purchased.

Downstairs in the dining room she was entertaining her sister-in-law and the Dagglestons at dinner, and informing Bella of her plans at the same time. Emily, eating her own dinner in the kitchen, heard from Perry the footman what transpired every time he returned from the dining room with another tray.

"Whew!" he said, wiping his brow. "Not 'alf 'appy, she ain't I *don't* think. If looks could kill! 'Ere's milady and those other two drinking to their journey, and there sits Miss, a black look on her face and not a word out of her!"

"There will be," Mrs. Goodwell said. "There will be!"

And of course she was right. The Dagglestons took their leave early, and they were to begin their journey at eight the next morning. Emily was waiting at the top of the stairs, and she was surprised to hear her mistress invite Miss Quentin to come up to her room.

"I see you wish to speak to me Bella. Let us be private," she said calmly as she led the way up the winding stairs, and from what Emily could see of Miss Quentin's pinched face and stern expression, she could tell the interview was not going to be at all pleasant. She retired to the dressing room and shamelessly eavesdropped.

"How could you, Alicia?" Miss Quentin began before she was even seated. She stared around the room at the traveling bags and trunks. "If Tony wanted you with him, he would have taken you along. How can you be so harebrained, and to go with the Dagglestons, too? I do not consider either of them suitable chaperons."

"Once more I have to remind you, Bella, that I am a married woman, and it would be perfectly in order if I decided to travel with only Nelly as my companion. In going with the Dagglestons I merely mean to ease my journey."

"But to tear off like this, with never a word to *me*! Why did you not tell me of your intentions? I would have done my best to stop you—"

"And that is why I did not tell you, Bella," Lady Quentin interrupted. "I did not wish to argue the matter. It is my decision, not yours."

"But if your mind is quite made up, I consider it my duty to go with you," Miss Quentin argued. "In fact, I insist you stay until I can be ready to accompany you."

"You insist?" Lady Quentin asked in a calm little voice. "But it is not your place to insist. You have no jurisdiction over me, Bella. I think you forget yourself."

"How dare you?" Miss Quentin hissed. "I am Tony's nearest relative, and if it were not for me, he would not be where he is today."

"We have all heard time out of mind of your generosity and concern for Tony," Lady Quentin agreed. "And how it was your portion that bought him his commission, and how you have never married so you might remain by his side to help him. But there is no need for that now, Bella, for Tony is a married man, and as his wife *and* nearest relation, I am here to help him. Furthermore, I should be most happy to give you a draft on my bank and repay you for the money you so nobly advanced for my husband's benefit. That would release us from the obligation and allow you to fashion a life of your own as well."

"How dare you," Miss Quentin said again in a failing voice. "I did what I did freely out of love. And Tony depended on me long before *you* came along." She tittered angrily. "In fact, I am sure he depends on me first even now, for you have so little sense."

Lady Quentin was silent for a moment, and then she said, "I cannot tell you, Bella, how tired I am of your continued interference. In fact, since we are finishing this bout with the gloves off, I must tell you I have often resented your constant attendance, your never-ending advice, and your sure assumption that both Tony and I would be helpless if you were not here to steer us right. Has it never occurred to you, Bella, that as newlyweds we would have preferred to be left alone?"

"I did not think that I would ever hear such insults! You forget yourself, Alicia! Just wait till I tell Tony . . ."

"I shall tell Tony myself, and what I shall tell him is that from now on I do not want to have you constantly living in our pockets. And now I must ask you to leave, for I have to get up very early. I shall give Tony your love, of course. Do you wish to pen him a few lines so I can carry your letter with me?"

Emily waited breathlessly for Miss Quentin's frigid reply. "There is no need, for I shall be writing to my brother tomorrow. And you, you ungrateful, ignorant little snip, will find out whose advice he follows."

Emily was amazed to hear Lady Quentin laugh. "Now, Bella, do not let us part in anger. May I give *you* some good advice for a change? Do not always be trying to come between Tony and me. I assure you you there are weapons in my arsenal that will vanquish you most thoroughly. But come! I have no desire to cause a rift in the family."

Miss Quentin did not deign to reply, and Emily heard her calling Mr. Goodwell to fetch the carriage as she went down the stairs. As she went in to Lady Quentin, she heard her muttering, "And I hate pink bedrooms, *and* crocodile legs, *and* seashell baths! And as soon as I return, I shall do this room over myself, without any help from you, *dear* sister. Ungrateful, ignorant little snip that I am!"

5

The following morning, May 15, was pleasantly warm and sunny. The Dagglestons had brought their maid and valet, as well as an equerry to assist them on the voyage, so there were two carriages to travel to the coast. Emily was glad the weather was fine, for she was nervous about Lady Quentin's possible reaction to the crossing. As it turned out, it was Emily who succumbed to seasickness. She had eyed the whitecaps with trepidation when they finally reached Dover and the ship that was to carry them to Ostend. Even in harbor, the boat rose and fell in a sickening manner.

"I don't like the looks of it," Lady Daggleston's dresser murmured to Emily. "M'lady has such a delicate stomach." She sniffed and added, "What a mad do, racing over to the war as if it were a raree show."

Emily nodded. At least Lady Quentin had a better purpose in traveling abroad.

As long as they remained on deck, Emily was able to control herself by breathing deeply, but when she tried to unpack, the sailors began to thump about on the deck above her head. Looking out the porthole, she saw the quay sliding by. She held on grimly as the boat rounded the jetty and set sail for Belgium, but before many minutes, she knew it was no use. Lady Quentin, who had been calmly reading a book, took one look at her white face and insisted she lie down on the bunk while she went to call Miss Berry.

And so they came to Ostend. Because of the fair wind, it had not been a long crossing, although it seemed endless to both Emily and Lady Daggleston. After a few minutes on dry land, however, Emily felt much better and firmly put from her mind the thought that sooner or later she would have to return the same sickening way.

Even with the equerry's help, the accommodations and the food they were served, as well as the old barge that was to carry them to Ghent, were not in the least what they expected. Emily heard Lord Daggleston taking the innkeeper to task, but the man did not seem to realize his great good fortune in having members of the English nobility grace his establishment. Most Belgians, uneasily aware that Napoleon might be in command of their country again before long, resented the presence of the English, come to fight a war on their soil.

"Never saw the like of it," Lord Daggleston complained. "Don't seem to understand what's required, silly sod! *And* he expects me to speak his barbarous language, too! Sorry we came!"

"Oh, John, it does not signify," his wife assured him. "We will soon be in Brussels. Think of the stories we will have to tell on our return. Why, you shall dine out for months on them, and everyone will clamor for your attendance so they may hear you firsthand."

Lord Daggleston brightened considerably. Up to this point, he had not been in the least sought-after, and the dream of finding himself the center of an admiring group of peers did much to smooth the way to Brussels.

They arrived late in the evening, and as the equerry, Bertin, had ridden on before them, they found their rooms waiting in a small inn on the outskirts of the city. Mr. Bertin told Lord Daggleston that he was lucky to have found even these poor accommodations, for the capital was crowded with the army men of all the allies, as well as the lords and ladies of the nobility. "In the morning, m'lord," he added, "I shall of course try to procure you a house in the best part of town."

Lord Daggleston had to be content, although he pouted all through the poor meal they were served in their private parlor.

Lady Quentin remained cheerful through all adversity. "Every minute brings me closer to Tony," she told her maid. "How could I not be happy? But these absurd Dagglestons! To be fussing about a small room, a simple meal. I do hope we shall find Tony without delay, however, for I have no idea how to go about acquiring a house. Brussels is an ant heap!"

Emily agreed. From the little she had seen in the lamp-lights as they drove into town, there did not appear to be room for even one more visitor. She was up very early to ask the equerry to leave a message for Captain Quentin at the Guards' headquarters when he should locate it, telling him of his wife's arrival and present lodging.

Unfortunately, Captain Quentin was in Antwerp, having ridden there with dispatches from his commanding officer, and so it was a long three days later before he appeared at the door of Lady Quentin's room. They were still quartered at the poor inn, for Lord Daggleston had flatly refused to consider moving into a mean little house his equerry found.

Emily was with her mistress, hanging up the dress she had worn that afternoon, and she had no time to excuse herself before the captain was in the door in two mighty strides, lifting Lady Quentin from her chair and clear off her feet to enfold her in his arms and kiss her soundly. She smiled up at him and held his face between her two hands as she exclaimed, "My darling, how glad I am to see you!"

The captain kissed her again before he put her firmly back on the ground and asked, "And I you, Alicia. But what are you doing here, dear girl? I expected you to remain in London until my return."

"Now, why should I want to do that when half of London is here, from what I can gather? Why should I not be here, too? After all, I have a very good reason—you!"

He smiled, but Emily saw that he was tired and disheveled, as if he had been riding hard all day.

Lady Quentin noticed it too. "Come and sit down, my dear. Nelly, get the captain wine and some bread, meat, and cheese, if you please."

"Nelly here too?" he asked, staring with tired eyes at the maid. "And is Bella with you as well?"

"No, she is not. But I will tell you about that shortly, after you have had something to eat. You look tired. Well, I will take care of you."

As Emily hurried to fetch the food, she saw Lady Quentin settle down happily on her husband's lap. The captain looked bemused, for this new wife who so calmly crossed the Channel to be with him and gave such firm orders to both her maid and himself was a new come-out indeed. As Emily closed the door, she saw the captain's red-uniformed arms reach out to pull his wife close.

The Dagglestons departed the next day. They implored Lady Quentin to come with them, but she laughed and refused.

"But I have just arrived. And Tony will take care of me. Thank you for your kindness in letting me travel with you."

"I shall never go abroad again," Lord Daggleston said firmly. "It is not at all what I am used to, and not one of these foreigners seems to have the least idea of my consequence. Peasants, bloody peasants!"

Lady Quentin took Emily with her and the captain to inspect the house that Lord Daggleston had scorned, and declared herself perfectly satisfied with it, much to her husband's relief. The rooms were small and plainly furnished, and he had expected her to be as horrified as the Dagglestons. Instead, she pointed out how near it was to his headquarters, so that he would be able to come home whenever he was not on duty, and she promised to have a hot meal waiting for him whenever he wished, and for his fellow officers as well. He engaged a cook and a maid to do the scrubbing, and soon Emily felt as at home as she had in Charles Street.

It was not so different, after all. Lady Quentin had calls to make on acquaintances, receptions and picnics to attend, as well as race meets and cricket matches, and she looked forward to many gala balls. It was very difficult to remember that just over the horizon that French army might be massing, and as May drew to a close and there was no sign of Napoleon, many people began to believe that he would never dare to leave Paris to take the field against Wellington again. The captain was not one of their number, and he worked long, hard hours, although he spent all his free time with his wife. Lady Quentin glowed with happiness whenever he was able to take her for a drive in the park, or a leisurely stroll through the crowded streets, to admire the steep slanted roofs and fat chimney pots, and the flowers that bloomed in every window box.

Emily saw the Duke of Wrotherham one day when she and Lady Quentin were out shopping, but he was some distance away with a group of gentlemen, and he did not see them. She told herself she was glad. It was very strange, but she often found herself thinking of him, wondering if he had come to Brussels as he had planned, and if he were here still.

Then she would ask herself why it was so easy to conjure up his handsome, aristocratic face with its black eyes and bored sneer, and the wide shoulders of his trim, masculine figure, which was always so beautifully attired. She knew that if he were anything like his father, he was a dangerous man, and what had Margaret Nelson, lady's maid, to do with the Duke of Wrotherham, in any case? At these thoughts she would shake her head at her folly and resolve to put him from her mind . . . until the next time he invaded it.

She also saw another duke, the Duke of Wellington, riding with some of his aides. Lady Quentin had given her the afternoon off, since she was attending a cricket match at Enghien with Lady Caroline Capel. As Emily was strolling in the park, the duke cantered by. All the English cheered him roundly, and he raised a casual hand in acknowledgment. Emily thought him most impressive in his uniform, and a very handsome man, even if his nose was a trifle too long.

Emily was standing by a fountain, watching the play of the water, when she felt someone's eyes on her and looked up quickly. In shock, she stood frozen while an officer inspected her carefully from head to foot, and then, with a little nod, came to her side and took her arm. "I am sure I am not mistaken," he said smoothly. "It is Miss Wyndham, is it not? Yes, you have a great look of your mother, although you have indeed grown since last I saw you." He sneered a little as he ran his eyes up and down her figure, and Emily flushed as she pulled her arm out of his grasp. "How is dear lovely Althea, m'dear? Whose, hm, protection is she under now?"

"My mother is dead," Emily whispered through stiff lips, wishing she had the courage to walk away, for this was indeed that selfsame Colonel Rogers of the Coldstream Guards who had offered to pay her mother for her favors ten years ago.

"How very unfortunate. But I am sure *you* were not bereft for long," the colonel said. "Following the drum, are you? Who is the lucky man, Miss Wyndham?"

"I am not following the drum. There is no man," Emily blurted out, her face white with shock that he should think her like her mother.

"I am afraid I do not believe you, my dear. Althea Wyndham's daughter virtuous? Impossible! And there is no wedding ring on that little hand. Come, I insist you accompany me to the nearest café for some refreshment.'' He took her arm in his again and squeezed her hand intimately. ''You must tell me how you come to be here, and why you dress so plainly and with such a severe hairdo. Whoever your lover is, he does not do you justice, child. You should be decked out in jewels and satins, with blond curls dressed high to tempt a man to let 'em down and run his hands through them. I should treat you better, you know. Perhaps we can come to some agreement of profit to us both—as well as pleasure. My, ten years is a long time for such old acquaintances to be separated. You do remember me, do you not?''

Emily stood very still, her head high. ''I remember you very well, Colonel Rogers, and I have no desire to accompany you anywhere, or make any arrangements with you, ever! Let go of my arm. You may be sure I shall make a scene if I am not immediately released.''

She stared into those cold, hooded eyes until he dropped her arm, and then she spun on her heel and hurried away, sick to be discovered. Although she took a circuitous route home and often looked over her shoulder, she did not see him following her, and it was with relief that she shut the door of the house the Quentins had hired, and leaned against it, panting.

She would not have had such a sense of deliverance if she could have seen the urchin who scurried away with her address for the tall Englishman who had promised to pay him so well for the information.

Because of the crowded conditions in the small, rented house, Emily slept in a little room next to Lady Quentin's, and the walls were so thin that she soon had a very good understanding of what marriage was all about. No matter what she had thought after reading her mother's letters, it was obviously pleasurable, not only for the captain, but for his wife as well. Emily could not help comparing the love the Quentins shared with the cold lechery that Colonel Rogers offered her, and she thought it very sad that she would never have that kind of happiness.

One morning in Lady Quentin's dressing room, she heard the captain say from the bedroom, ''That is enough! Why, Alicia, I do believe you have turned into a witch. Do you know how many times I find myself thinking of you when I should be concentrating on my duty? You were not like this in London, pet.''

''That is because my mother told me that decent married ladies do not enjoy making love. But I can go back to my former indifferent state if you wish, Tony.''

''You must know I do not. Your mother, with all due respect, is an idiot. You are breathtaking—and I adore you! But I must keep my wits about me, for, unless I miss my guess, it cannot be much longer before the battle.''

''Are you sure, Tony? Why, I have heard that the Duchess of Richmond asked the duke if she might hold a ball next week on June fourteenth, and he assured her he saw no reason not to. In fact, he told her he is planning to give a ball himself on the twenty-first of June, to celebrate the second anniversary of the battle of Vittoria. Surely if Wellington does not expect trouble before then, there can be nothing to fear. Or have you heard differently, Tony?''

''No,'' the captain said slowly. ''But I think the duke speaks as he does to reassure the civilians, and to tell the truth, we have not the slightest idea where Napoleon's army is. Since we are not officially at war as yet—although no one could say we were at peace—we are not allowed to send out cavalry scouts as we did in the Peninsula War to investigate French-held territory. Napoleon *may* be in Paris still—or just over the next hill. Curse all politicians! It is just a feeling I have, as do many of my fellow officers, that the time is ripe. Do you realize it is almost a hundred days since Napoleon reached Paris? He will not delay much longer, not now when he knows Wellington is here with his army. And that's another thing. Such a rag-bag, grab-bag army it is. Germans and Dutch and Russians and Austrians and I don't know what all, all milling about and squabbling about command. Thank heavens we have Wellington at the head.''

Emily heard him stamping his feet into his boots and then there was a discreet knock on the door. Sergeant Boothby had an urgent dispatch for the captain, and in a moment, he was gone.

Emily, of course, was interested in the captain's assessment of the situation, but to be truthful, she was much more concerned with any possible confrontation she might have with Colonel Rogers.

For several days after their meeting in the park, she had started up every time the knocker sounded on the front door, and she remained inside the house whenever she could. Lady Quentin had found some friends to go about with, and if Lady Caroline Capel or the Misses Ord were about, there was no need for her to take her maid. Lady Quentin did not notice that her Nelly did not take any more walks in the park, or that when she asked her to purchase some small item, Emily sent the scullery maid or Sergeant Boothby on the errand.

On the few occasions when she was forced to accompany her mistress, there had been no sign of the colonel, and so she relaxed. Perhaps he had been sent away; perhaps he had taken her at her word and intended to leave her alone.

But Colonel Rogers had no intention of leaving her alone. Instead, he had the Quentin's house watched, and one evening learned that the captain and his wife had left in a carriage, accompanied by his sergeant. The urchin who brought the information said the lady and gent was dressed very fine, and since Colonel Rogers was well aware that Lord Uxbridge was gving an evening reception and that the duke was among the invited guests, he could be almost positive that the Quentins were even now on their way to attend, with the rest of the *haut ton* who were still in Brussels.

He made his way to their house and, marching up to the front door, gave the knocker a mighty swing. The maid answered and he asked for Miss Nelson, for he had investigated the inmates thoroughly while he waited for his opportunity. The maid nodded and led him to the door of the small salon. Emily had taken over tidying the lower rooms, for the housekeeper did as little as possible and left for her own home after dinner each evening, and the maid was slow and a little dim-witted.

"Good evening, Miss Wyndham—or should I say Miss Nelson?" Colonel Rogers asked, coming in and stripping off his gloves and shako. He turned and handed them to the maid and gestured toward the door. "Out!" he ordered, and the maid was not so slow-witted that she did not understand the brusque command, for she scurried away. The colonel closed the door.

Emily rose from the carpet where she had knelt to pick up some paper the captain had let fall, and backed away, her heart pounding.

"Come, my dear, such shyness," the colonel said, advancing into the room and going toward the fireplace, where there was a small blaze. He rubbed his hands together, his eyes bright with satisfaction.

"But who would have imagined it?" he asked. "Althea Wyndham's daughter a common maid. What a waste!" And scornfully he pointed to her apron and cap.

"I—I must ask you to leave immediately, sir," Emily said, trying to keep her voice from shaking. "My mistress will be home at any moment."

"Not unless she or her husband has forgotten something on their way to the Uxbridge reception," Colonel Rogers said blandly. "Come, aren't you going to ask me to sit down? Althea would never have been so unwelcoming." As if it were his own home, he went to pour two glasses of wine from the decanter kept on a side table.

"You had better sit down yourself. And you look as if you could use this," he said as he came toward her, and rather than have him make her do so, Emily obeyed. Their fingers touched as he handed her the glass, and she would have dropped it if he had not fastened her fingers around the stem, smiling a little when he felt her tremble at his touch. "Drink it up. You will soon feel more the thing."

Emily stared up at him, waiting until he had moved away to a chair opposite. Indeed, she did need the wine, for his appearance had been such a shock. And, she thought desperately, there is no one to call for help, for the housekeeper had left not two minutes after the Quentins' departure, and Sergeant Boothby had gone with them. By now, the little maid would either be finishing the dinner dishes or dragging herself up to her attic pallet. There was no help there.

After a few sips, she put the glass down on a table beside her and folded her hands in her lap, trying not to clench them.

Colonel Rogers stared at her over the rim of his wineglass. The years had not been kind to him. He must now be in his fifties, she thought, and his face showed only too plainly the life of dissipation he had led since last they met.

"Feeling better?" he asked, his courteous question at odds with the intent leer he gave her. "I had no wish to frighten you, my dear, but you see, I really could not allow myself to be so abruptly dismissed—and by a slut's daughter, as well."

Emily stiffened.

"Oh, yes," he said, nodding to her and saying in a conversational tone, "your mother was a slut. A very desirable, fascinating, and beautiful woman—but a slut, nevertheless. And here you are, her daughter. Did you know, Miss Wyndham, that I once asked your mother for you? She was not at all amused. In fact, it signaled the end of our relationship. I did miss her—for about a week!"

"My mother was not—not what you said! She was forced by circumstances to behave as she did," Emily could not help crying.

"I have no intention of arguing with you about such an unimportant point. I will say, however, that no decent woman would ever have enjoyed herself so much in her, hmm, chosen profession. But who am I to sneer at her, after all? There is a need for women of your mother's persuasion in this world. Bless me, what would we men do without them?"

He laughed at his pleasantry, and Emily wished she could kill him.

"But I am much more concerned about *your* profession, my dear. Oh yes, very concerned. It is not at all fitting for such a lovely thing to be carrying slops and changing m'lady's gown, and kneeling to put on her slippers. So much better to have you kneeling at my feet, and not to put on my slippers either!" He laughed, a hoarse, throaty chuckle. "As I said just now, what a waste. Now, I am here to remove you from such drudgery, and you may count yourself lucky that I will do so. In fact, after I have the schooling for you for a few weeks, I am sure you will change your mind about which is preferable as an occupation. And if I cannot, small loss. There is always another lovely girl to be had. Tell me, m'dear," he said, leaning closer, "can I be so fortunate as to be your first? Somehow I cannot imagine Althea Wyndham's daughter reaching your current age without losing her virginity. And yet there is an air about you of purity, as if no man has touched you. What a lucky plus if it were so."

Emily thought she would have to strike him if he did not keep his filthy mouth off her mother's name, and something of her feelings must have shown in her face and her blazing emerald eyes, for he stood up abruptly and came to her, pulling her roughly out of the chair and into his arms. At once she began to struggle and beat him with her fists as he ran his hands up and down her back, cupping her buttocks and digging his fingernails into her flesh.

He laughed at her efforts, for, fifty and dissolute or not, he was very strong. The long years in the service had given him iron-hard muscles, and he easily captured both her hands in one, and with the other pushed her head back by the hair and kissed her. It was a brutal kiss. He forced her mouth open and thrust his tongue inside, and if Emily had not been so angry at his description of her mother, she might have fainted. As it was, she waited until he lifted his head, and then she kicked him as hard as she could. He laughed and held her away from him. "Little wildcat! That's all right, my popsy, do your worst. I like 'em wild."

Suddenly he pulled her to him again and began to caress her breasts, now heaving under her neat apron and dark gown with her efforts to escape. With one hand he began to undo the buttons at her throat, and Emily knew it was only a matter of time before he would have her naked, right there in the salon. All at once he put his hand inside her bodice and yanked, too impatient to bother with the buttons, and the whole top of her dress fell away, leaving her breasts exposed under a thin camisole. As he moved his hand, she ducked her head and bit it, drawing blood. He let her go immediately, but only to raise his other hand and slap her viciously. She staggered away and fell into a chair.

"Don't ever do that again!" he growled, stepping back and licking his wound, while Emily, her head reeling, tried to pull the torn fabric of her gown up over her breasts as she struggled to sit upright again. He had hit her with an open palm, but she could still feel the hot sting of his hand.

"Such ingratitude," he suddenly bellowed. "Here I have every intention of setting you up in such luxury you may meet your mistress walking and nod to her from your own carriage, dressed as fine as ninepence in satin and laces and jewels. Have a care, wench. I will not hesitate to punish you much more severely than *that* little love tap!"

As he came toward her again, Emily spoke in desperation. "Stop! I—I have something to say to you, and you must, you *will* listen!"

The colonel paused, admiring the picture she made, her blond hair tumbled around her face, reddened from his slap, and her green eyes sparkling with the tears she was trying valiantly not to shed. Her creamy shoulders and half-concealed bosom aroused his lust again, but he was perfectly content to let her speak while he admired such gorgeous plunder as she displayed.

"Very well," he said, sitting down and taking up his wineglass once again. Fifty had learned what twenty did not know: that anticipation could be as pleasureable as the act itself, and there was, after all, no need to rush. Lord Uxbridge's receptions always lasted such a very long time.

Emily drew a deep breath and, holding her gown more closely to her, began to speak in what she hoped was a confident, convincing voice. "You asked me earlier, Colonel, if I was aware that you had asked my mother for me, many years ago. As it happens, I did know. Not because she told me, of course, for I was not aware of her activities until after her death, but because I found your letters."

She had held his eyes with hers as she spoke, and now she saw him start up in amazement. It gave her the courage to continue. "You were most unwise to put that in writing, sir. As it happens, I still have that particular letter." She paused and waited for him to comment.

"Well, and so what if you do, girl? What is that to say to anything?"

Even to her ears, Emily felt he was bluffing. "You must be aware, Colonel, that if such a letter should come to the attention of your commanding officer, it would have the most dire results. An officer of the Coldstream Guards, soliciting a mother for her thirteen-year-old child!"

Her voice was scornful, and he flushed and said quickly, "But you would be most unwilling to air such scandal about your mother and yourself, would you not, Miss Wyndham?" The thought seemed to give him confidence, for he leaned back and finished his wine. "No, I hardly think it possible that you would so demean yourself, for then all the world would know who you are, and more important, what kind of background you have."

Before he could rise, Emily held out her hands. Her voice was low and bitter, and it stopped him as effectively as a bullet would have done.

"But what possible shame can come to me that would be worse than your attention, sir? And since I have changed my name and become what you describe as a common maid, why would having my name bruited about disturb me? My mother is dead: you cannot hurt her anymore. I tell you this: I would do anything in the world to escape you. I will even go as high as the duke himself, if necessary, and I imagine your career would be short-lived if the contents of that letter became common knowledge.''

The colonel stood up, and for a moment she felt she had failed, but then he turned away from her and stared into the fire. What she said was true; he knew how he would be scorned, he might even be asked to tender his resignation, and he knew also that if he lost his commission, he did not want to live. He was a soldier—it was all he knew or wanted to know. What was one female beside *that*?

"Touché!" he said finally. "It appears you have won the engagement, Miss Wyndham. My compliments!" He bowed ironically and turned to go. "By the way, you are making a mistake, you know. No one as desirable as you are was meant for anything but love. I count it a definite loss that I am not to be the man to initiate you in its pleasures." He bowed again at the door and left the room.

Emily did not move or even breathe until she heard the street door slam, and then she put her face in her hands and burst into tears. How long she sat there crying, she had no idea, but at last she rose and went up to change her clothes and redo her hair. The gown was ruined, and she was glad it was beyond repair, for she could never have worn it again. She shivered as she took it off, and then, remembering his last words, she stopped and stared at herself in Lady Quentin's mirror. Her cheek was still red from his blow, but she was not looking at that, but rather deep into her own eyes. He had said that she was desirable, that she was made for love, and she remembered that for one shameful moment while he was caressing her, she had felt an answering surge, even in all her fright. Could it be true, that she was just like her mother, and not a decent woman at all? And then she remembered Lady Quentin and her obvious enjoyment in making love, and she felt much better. It had nothing to do with morals, or whether you were good or bad. It was just a normal part of being a woman.

Lady Quentin spent an extraordinary amount of time choosing her gown and jewels for the Duchess of Richmond's ball, for she wanted to look her best for Tony. He had promised her that nothing would interfere with his escorting her to what promised to be a most festive evening.

"Perhaps I will even dance with the duke, Nelly," she said. "He always likes a pretty woman, you know, and he smiled at me so warmly the other evening at Lord Uxbridge's that I am sure I have piqued his interest, even if he is, as they say at the moment, intrigued with Lady Frances Webster. What fun if Tony should be jealous!"

She giggled with laughter at the thought, and Emily smiled with her. She had not seen or heard from Colonel Rogers again, and every day that passed reassured her that he had accepted his defeat.

"I do wonder, though, Nelly," Lady Quentin was saying, "if Tony was right, and the allies are about to go into battle. He says so little of it, but there is a look in his eyes lately." She shivered and went to sit down in the chair by the window that she often used while she watched the street and waited for her husband.

Emily saw that she had forgotten her maid, and left the room quietly.

It would be hard for anyone in Brussels not to know that there was something going on. Units appeared and disappeared; the streets rang with the sounds of booted feet and harsh commands, and at the next moment, they were gone. Supply wagons rumbled in long lines down the street, the horses hooves clattering on the cobblestones in response to the cracking of whips. Emily felt as if the population of Brussels was holding its breath, and a part of her wished the war would begin. Since it appeared to be inevitable, the suspense of waiting for it, day after day, was terrible.

But by June 14 they were still waiting. Emily helped Lady Quentin dress for the Richmond ball in a gown she had been saving for this special occasion. It was a pale-green silk with the fashionable round neckline that only half-concealed her breasts. The sash and the trimming on the tiny puffed sleeves were of grass-green satin, and her sandals matched exactly. With this gown she wore a rope of pearls, and Emily dressed her hair regally high, the curls caught up with pearl combs. She looked stunning, and when she came down the stairs, Captain Quentin bowed very low, his handsome face beaming with his love and admiration.

Emily curtsied to them both as they left, and after carefully locking the front door and instructing the maid that on no account was she to admit the officer who had called the other evening, she went upstairs.

The Duchess of Richmond had rented a house on the rue de la Blanchisserie, and it was here that the civilians and the military gathered that evening—everyone who was anyone, that is, for admission was by ticket only. Lady Quentin told Emily later that even so it was a perfect crush, why, even H.R.H. the Prince of Orange had come especially to Brussels to attend!

The ballroom was situated on the first floor of the house, and the duchess had had it transformed by using the royal colors of crimson, gold, and black. There were brilliant draperies and hangings and many blazing chandeliers, and even the pillars were entwined in flowers and ribbons. The Duke of Wellington arrived rather late, and a young lady whose family was well acquainted with him had the daring to break away from the dance and go to him immediately to ask him if the rumors that were circulating were true. The duke answered her solemnly. Yes, all too true, and they would all be off tomorrow. Instantly a great buzz arose as the news went around. Lady Quentin confided that for a moment she felt quite faint, and it was only by hanging tightly to Tony's arm while he tried to protect her from the crowd milling around that she was able to contain herself, "and seeing a very fat elderly lady having hysterics," she added. Tony left her in Lady Caroline Capel's charge while he sought out his commanding officer. When he came back, there was a grim line to his mouth.

When the Quentins arrived home so early, with Lady Quentin weeping softly as she came up to her room, Emily knew at once what had happened. The captain came in just then, but when Emily would have left them, he asked her to remain.

"We do not have much time, and what I have to say I wish Nelly to hear, too, for she will be involved," he explained.

Emily went to stand behind her mistress and waited while the captain paced up and down, running a hand through his black hair.

"I want you both to make for Antwerp as soon as possible in the morning," he said firmly. "No, Alicia, there will be no pleading. I insist on your promise that you will obey me.

Napoleon is almost to Quatre Bras, and that is only about twenty miles from Brussels.''

Emily gasped, and Lady Quentin turned pale and clenched her hands tightly together.

''In the unlikely event that we should not be victorious, the French could be in the city as soon as tomorrow evening. I shall not be easy unless I am sure you will not still be here. Do you understand, both of you?''

''Of course, Tony, I will do what you say, I promise,'' Lady Quentin said at once.

Emily nodded when he swung his glance to her.

''Take good care of your mistress, Nelly, and do not let her return until it is safe, no matter what news is brought.''

He looked very grim, and Emily realized that he was referring to his possible death or wounding, and she swallowed as she nodded again.

''You are to dismiss the servants and take only what you need when you go. Do not waste time packing finery,'' he continued. ''You had better go by barge; who knows what state the roads will be in? Unfortunately, Boothby and I will be gone too early to see to it. Nelly, you must get a place for your mistress and yourself and obtain passports as well.''

''Yes, sir,'' Emily answered. She was impressed with the captain's quiet orders and the way Lady Quentin was controlling herself, and vowed she would do no less, although she had to admit she was very frightened. Perhaps they all were, but she saw that the only thing to do was not to show it.

''Leave the carriage and team here; better still, I will take it to headquarters. We may have need of it,'' he added, his voice grim, but he did not elaborate. Fortunately, neither girl thought to ask him what he meant.

''I think that is all. Be sure you have enough money with you, Alicia, and do not return to Brussels until I send you word. If the news is bad—if this time we do not win—sail for England immediately. Promise me you will do as I say.''

For the first time he looked so upset that Lady Quentin rose and went to him, holding out her hands. ''My dearest, do not worry. I am just as much under your orders as any of your soldiers.'' She gave him a shaky salute, and the captain's grim expression changed to a smile.

''Best of my troops, Alicia! I am proud of you.''

Emily stole away as he took his wife into his arms, and then, when she heard them murmuring, she went down to the kitchen. There was so little time left. She had to let them have this last night alone.

5

Emily spent what was left of the night curled up in an old chair, but she was up and heating water as soon as she heard the Quentins stirring. Sergeant Boothby had slipped in the back door, and with a jaunty wink he took the jug up so the captain might shave. Emily busied herself making the tea for them both, which they drank hastily in the kitchen. The captain had a grim, faraway expression on his face this morning, and even the sergeant was unusually quiet.

Just before they left, Captain Quentin made her promise again that she would follow all his instructions, and as Emily curtsied, she could not help saying, "Do not worry about your wife, sir. She is not the young girl we both knew a few months ago, she has grown up."

The captain nodded, his expression brightening as he realized she was right. "Go to her now, Nelly," he said, "for I am sure she needs you"

With that, they were gone, Emily wishing the sergeant good luck as he followed the captain out the door.

"Never you worries your pretty little 'ead about *me*, Miss Nelson," he said in his old, irrepressible way. "Oim always fine! Lands on me feet, I does, no matter wot!"

When Emily went to Lady Quentin's room, she found her once again waving good-bye and holding her candle high in the window so her husband might see her. There was only the barest lightening of the sky, although it appeared it was going to be a fine day. At least it is not raining as it has been the past few days, Emily thought, and then had to shake herself for her silliness. What difference did it make whether you fought in in rain or brilliant sunshine? It was horrible either way.

She persuaded Lady Quentin to get back in bed and have a cup of tea, prepared for her to break down, now they were alone. But her mistress did no such thing. While she sipped the hot brew, she instructed Emily to fetch a paper and quill and ink, and take down a list of things they would need to take with them to Antwerp. "We might as well use our time well, Nelly," she said, and even though her eyes were suspiciously bright, she did not weep. She decided a pair of portmanteaus would suffice for the few belongings they would need.

"And my jewels, of course. As soon as it is time, I will go with you to the bank and then to the military commander for our passports. There is no use trying to get a place on the barge without them. Oh, and Nelly, send the housekeeper up to me when she arrives, if you please, so I can give her her wages and dismiss her."

But this Emily was unable to do, for she never appeared, and when Emily went up to the attic, she discovered the scullery maid had gone as well, with all her bits and pieces. It seemed the Belgians were convinced that Napoleon would be victorious, and they had no desire to be caught serving the English. Lady Quentin shrugged when she learned of their defection. "It is only to be expected," she said. "I am sure the populace are already planning a great fete to welcome the French."

Emily helped her to dress, and then the two of them made their way to the bank through the ominously empty streets. Empty, that is, of the reassuring presence of the military, although there were many other civilians hurrying here and there. After Lady Quentin had withdrawn a sufficient amount of money, they had a long wait before they were finally admitted to the military commander's office. He looked harassed, and was impatient to the point of rudeness. When she asked for passports for herself and her maid, he rose and shook a stern finger at her.

"You are not the first one here with the same request this morning, Lady Quentin. I cannot believe it! Why, it is not for us to panic and run, for that will only spread alarm. Remember, you are an Englishwoman! Besides, there is no need for such lily-heartedness; our troops shall beat Napoleon in short order as they did before, and then you will feel vastly silly, will you not, so far from the scene of our triumph?''

"But, sir," Lady Quentin said earnestly, "I promised my husband that I would go, on my sacred honor.''

"No, no! I refuse to issue the passports. You must be brave, madam, and by your behavior show these—these foreigners what the English are made of. What we want now is *blood*, not retreat! And now, you must excuse me, for I have much to do.''

He held the door of his office open, and Lady Quentin and Emily were forced to leave. Outside, in the street, Lady Quentin said, "What a terrible man! As if it made any difference whether we go or stay.'' She did not sound at all upset, and Emily looked at her intently.

Lady Quentin looked a little conscious as she shook her head. "I know, Nelly, that it will mean breaking my promise, but what can we do without passports? Besides, Tony *thinks* we have gone and so he will not worry, and that is the most important thing. And you know," she added as she began to walk in the direction of their rented house, "I cannot help but feel the commander is right. I am sure we will vanquish the French.''

Emily shook her head in despair of ever keeping her promises to the captain as she trailed Lady Quentin. They had not gone very far when they were hailed from a passing carriage.

"Alicia! Are you still here too?'' She looked up to discover Lady Caroline Capel motioning her coachman to pull up. "Come, let me give you a lift home. The streets are so crowded, it is not safe.'' She laughed lightly as Lady Quentin and Emily were handed into the carriage. "I have been to the wharf, and what a crush! All the world is trying to escape Brussels, but it is no use. Wellington has commanded all the barges, and there are none left for us poor civilians.''

Lady Quentin asked the reason, and in a more sober tone Lady Caroline said that they were reserved to carry the wounded. Both ladies were silent for a long moment, and then Lady Caroline patted her friend's hand. "Come, Alicia, you must be as brave as your husband. Do you stay in town? Mr. Capel and I are going to a rustic retreat outside the city. Come with us, I beg you!''

Lady Quentin thanked her, but said that since she was unable to get to Antwerp, she rather thought she would remain where her husband would be sure to find her when he returned from the front. In everyone's mind lingered the thought that he might never return, but no one spoke of it.

Lady Caroline set them down at their door and bid them good fortune. "If I were not so near my time, dear Alicia, I would stay with you, I vow, but Mr. Capel is so worried about the baby, he insists on our departure. Take care, my dear. I shall be praying for you and your gallant captain."

With a last wave she was gone, and Lady Quentin and her maid went into the house.

"I think we should put up the shutters, Nelly," she said as she removed her bonnet. "I know they are no real protecion, but we will feel safer, I think."

She never thought to help, and so it was some time later that Emily had the downstairs windows shuttered and barred, with the front door securely bolted. When she was done, both women felt better.

All through that long, sultry day they waited. Emily prepared some simple meals, which was all she knew how to cook, and Lady Quentin made herself eat. She found herself pacing up and down most of the day, praying silently for her husband's safety, and Emily added her prayers as well. Toward evening, they could hear the guns clearly, and Lady Quentin, quite pale now, asked Emily to go and see if she could find out any news. Emily did not want to leave her alone in the house with dusk coming on, but her mistress insisted. "I shall be worse if I do not know what is happening, Nelly. Hurry back as fast as you can."

Emily slipped outside and made her way to the ramparts, where a vast crowd had assembled to listen to the echoes of the artillery and make speculations about the course of the battle. Emily thought she would remember the booming sounds of the guns as long as she lived, and she could not help feeling very frightened. She was standing a little apart, straining her eyes toward the horizon as if she might see what was happening, when an acquaintance of the Quentins came up and spoke to her.

"Isn't it just terrible, Miss Nelson?" this lady said, wringing her hands in an agitated way. "They are saying we have lost the Battle Round the Crossroads, and Napoleon will be upon us before much longer. I have heard such tales, you would not believe it."

Here, Mrs. Ward rummaged through her reticule for a handkerchief as the tears poured down her cheeks. "Tell Lady Quentin to come to the Greville's house tomorrow if she wishes news," she said when she had composed herself a little. "Lady Charlotte seems to know what is going on for a great deal of information finds its way to her from Wellington and others. I shall be there as well. Give your mistress my love and tell her that I will see her tomorrow."

She paused, and Emily, who had always thought her a silly, overdressed woman concerned only with her own comforts, was disconcerted to hear her add, "Do not tell Alicia this, my girl, but the news is very bad. We have lost almost five thousand of our men. Pray God our troops will hold! Tell Alicia that as far as you were able to discover, the Guards were not engaged, for the Scottish regiments bore the brunt of the fighting."

Emily nodded and curtsied as Mrs. Ward hurried away, and then she turned to peer again through the gathering dusk. Was she imagining it, or were the sounds of the guns closer? She did not know how people could continue to stand there listening to those ominous echoes of the fighting. For herself, she wished there was some place she could go where she would not have to hear them.

"Miss Nelson?" she heard a deep voice ask from close behind her, and she whirled, her hand going to her throat in surprise. The Duke of Wrotherham stood there, and when he saw the panic in her eyes, he said, "Pardon me, I did not mean to startle you. I see your mistress also left her departure too late, like the rest of these improvident people."

He sounded so angry and disapproving that Emily said, "We did try to leave, your Grace, but we could not obtain passports, and all the barges have been commandeered by the military."

Just then there was another salvo, and she swung around to stare toward the sound, clutching her reticule with fingers that had turned white with her grip.

"Come away at once," the duke commanded, holding out his arm. "There is nothing to do here but listen to the echo of the guns, and I see you are frightened. I will take you home, such as you should not be out in the streets alone, with dark coming on. People—men—do strange things in wartime."

Emily hesitated for a moment, and then she put her hand in

his arm, grateful for his escort. As they walked away, she said, "You told me that once before, your Grace, but maids are not allowed the luxury of such social niceties."

He made an impatient movement with his other hand. "I still say that in your case, Miss Nelson, it would be wiser to be more prudent. I wish there was more time to talk; I would like to know in what circumstances you began your service, among other things. But come, tell me your direction."

Emily gave him the address of Lady Quentin's house, and since she had no intention of telling him her origins, she was glad it was not very far away. She felt strange being so close to him, close enough to feel the hard muscles of his arm under her hand, and yet it was somehow comforting to be in his care. Since her head came only to his shoulder, he made her feel protected, and small and feminine. They walked through the streets in a silence that seemed to be casting a spell over her, and Emily wished the duke would say something, but when she peeked up at his dark face, it was to see him lost in thought, his dark brows drawn together in a ferocious frown.

They reached the Quentin house at last. Emily withdrew her hand and curtsied, saying, "Thank you for your escort, your Grace. I hope it did not take you too far out of your way."

He stared down at her for a moment and then said absently, "That does not signify in the slightest. Have a care for yourself. A girl like you should not have to endure all this." He waved his arm and then he turned and strode away.

Emily stared after him for a moment, wondering whether he meant her being a servant in such a mean little house, or being caught in a country at war. She watched him until he disappeared around a corner, and then she ran inside to give Lady Quentin the news she had learned.

The next two days were even harder for the civilians trapped in Brussels. Rumors flew—some true, some false, and no one had any way of knowing which was which. Some people shook their heads and insisted that the French were even then marching on the capital; others claimed a great victory for the British. To Lady Quentin and Emily it was all a nightmare.

Lady Quentin had gone to Lady Charlotte Greville's the morning after she had sent Emily to the ramparts. This lady had reassured her that the Guards had not been engaged as yet, but while this news sent her heart soaring, it was not much longer before a gentleman arrived and claimed that indeed they had been in the fight, and sustained heavy losses as well. Lady Charlotte frowned at this Mr. Barton, and when he saw Lady Quentin's pale, strained face, he desisted, adding only, "Perhaps it is not so. Who can tell what is happening? And remember, ladies, the French are not here yet. We must remember Torres Vedras!"

It was a very long day, and an even longer night. By the next morning, Emily felt sure that Lady Quentin would break her iron control if she did not have some definite word soon. Captain Quentin had not sent word, of course, for he believed that his wife was safe in Antwerp, so she did not even have the consolation that some of the other wives did, whose husbands wrote to them to tell them of their safety.

They returned to Lady Charlotte's house to wait. Toward afternoon, Lady Frances Webster came in, her face showing her worry and strain, and told those assembled that she had had a letter from Wellington written very early that same morning in the village of Waterloo, some eight miles from Brussels. She read out part of it to the shocked, silent gathering, and now they knew the worst. A desperate battle had been fought on Friday at Quatre Bras, which Wellington claimed to have won. But he cautioned her that the troops had had to retreat and that in the course of further fighting, he might have to withdraw even more—to Brussels, in fact. He advised her to get her family ready to evacuate to Antwerp in a moment's notice. There was an excited, frightened buzz of conversation as Lady Frances read this section, and Emily, from where she was standing behind Lady Quentin's chair, could see her mistress clenching her hands together so tightly that the knuckles were white.

When Lady Frances was able to be heard again, she said loudly, "But have faith, my dears. The duke concludes by saying that he knows of no danger to us at present, and he promises to send word immediately if it should so come to pass."

Lady Quentin sat quietly for a moment, her head bowed. In spite of her fright, Emily wished she might help her, but there was nothing she could do, nothing anybody could do who had to sit and wait for news.

"It is all right, Nelly," Lady Quentin said with a faint smile when she glanced up to see her maid's white, concerned face. "I thank you for your kindness, but Tony is all right. I would know if he were not, I am sure."

No further news came that day, and although Lady Charlotte tried to convince Lady Quentin to remain with her that night, she insisted on returning home with her maid. Two gentlemen went with them to ensure their safety. Emily had never seen the streets so quiet and empty, and she was glad to reach the little house and bolt the door behind them. It was raining again, which added to the general gloom.

Lady Quentin sank down before the fire that Emily lit in the salon before she went to the kitchen to get her something to eat. There were a few eggs left, and some bread, and she shook her head over the state of their provisions while she made the tea.

Lady Quentin insisted she sit down and join her when she carried the tray to the salon, but after making a little inconsequential conversation for a moment and sipping her tea, she rose and began to pace up and down the salon while Emily watched her anxiously.

"Something has happened, I know. I am afraid, suddenly so afraid," she exclaimed. "I have a feeling—I wish I could describe it, Nelly, a feeling that Tony needs me. Dear God, keep him safe!" She ended with a sob, and Emily sprang up and went to put her arms around her. For a few moments there was no mistress, no maid, only two frightened girls. After a moment Lady Quentin pulled away, wiped her eyes, and announced that she thought they should both retire.

"I will need my strength tomorrow, Nelly."

After she had been undressed and helped into bed, she said, "Call me at seven, Nelly. We have a vast amount to do; I really do not feel I can delay any longer."

The next morning, Lady Quentin sent her to Lady Charlotte's to learn the latest news, and she almost ran home through the streets when she heard, Napoleon was vanquished, the French were in full retreat, and Wellington and the allies were victorious! Lady Quentin exclaimed, but she did not stop what she was doing. Emily saw she had packed a portmanteau with a change of clothes, and laid out her waterproof cape and a severe bonnet. The medicine case lay open, and to it she had added several clean sheets. Emily was

startled to see the captain's dueling pistol as well. Lady
Quentin sent her maid to the kitchen to pack a basket of food,
and told her to be sure to include two bottles of brandy.

"I am going to Tony, Nelly," she said, never stopping
from her packing. "Make haste, now, for you will have to go
to headquarters to fetch the carriage."

Emily would have spoken and tried to make the lady
remain in Brussels, but before she could reason with her,
Lady Quentin snapped, "That is an order, Nelly! You could
never convince me anyway that I should wait here quietly for
Tony's return. We must find him, and quickly! Do not ask
me how I know this is so, I just do."

She was so stern and determined that Emily had no choice
but to do her bidding. When she delivered Lady Quentin's
hastily written note to headquarters, one of the soldiers remaining there, an older man who told her his name was
Corporal Deems, shook his head, but he not only harnessed
the team, he also offered to drive them himself.

"Know the captain," he told Emily when she thanked
him. She had been worried about two women setting out for
the battlefield alone. "Agree with the lady. Must see for
herself that her husband came through the fighting safely."
He seemed about to say more, but thought better of it and
helped Emily to the carriage perch without another word.

When they reached the Quentin's house, her mistress was
ready to leave. She thanked the corporal so warmly that he
blushed as he assured her he was delighted to be of service,
and in a short time they were on the road to Waterloo.

The road through the Forest of Soignes was crowded,
although there were many more conveyances coming from
the front than going toward it. After a few moments, Emily
tried not to look at the carts and wagons, so full of wounded
men, some moaning, some ominously still. Lady Quentin
would have stopped to search every one, until the corporal
told her the wounded officers were cared for nearer the front
and then transported in carriages, not dirty farm carts. Emily
was relieved to be spared such a gruesome search.

It was early afternoon before they reached the outskirts of
Waterloo. The corporal insisted on turning the carriage off
the main road into a farm track, before he went off on foot to
see if he could discover any news of the captain. Lady
Quentin would have insisted on going with him, except he

said, "If we find the captain wounded, your ladyship, he may need transportation at once, and if we drive right into the village, your carriage may be taken for others before we even find him."

At this, Lady Quentin sank back on the seat to wait as patiently as she could. Emily brought out the basket of food and pressed some bread and cheese and wine on her mistress. It was quiet and peaceful in the lane, shaded as they were by large trees; the whole scene was so bucolic that it was impossible to imagine that not many yards away from where they sat and munched their repast, a great battle had taken place. There was still a smell of cordite in the air and some lingering smoke, but the birds were singing again, chirping happily in the boughs over their heads. Emily took a deep breath, but Lady Quentin shivered.

"Hurry, Corporal," she said more to herself than to her maid. "I know Tony is wounded and we must find him quickly."

The corporal did not return for an hour, an hour that seemed interminable to Lady Quentin. There was no news of the captian, and he was not being attended to in any of the makeshift hospitals that had been set up. He seemed encouraged by this news, but Lady Quentin's eyes remained dark and worried. "Did you find out where the Guards fought, Corporal? Has no one seen him?"

Corporal Deems admitted that no one at headquarters knew where he was. "Then we must go on," Lady Quentin said, taking up the reins herself.

"Here, your ladyship," the soldier said as he climbed back into the carriage and took the reins from her hands. "'Tis not fitting! No sight for ladies!"

Lady Quentin shook her head. "I must find my husband no matter how horrible it is, Corporal. I must search until I find him."

The soldier hung his head in resignation as he set the horses in motion to turn the carriage. "Has anyone seen Sergeant Boothby?" she asked next. "I know he would not leave Tony. Why, he has saved his life once before."

But the sergeant was also missing, and it was a silent trio who began their search. Once out of the village proper, the flattened and sometimes bloody cornstalks of the fields told their own story, even without the numerous bodies of men and horses that lay where they had fallen. Here and there were clumps of men resting together, and whenever possible, the corporal approached them to ask for news of the captain. They continued down the road to the still-burning Château Hougoumont. The corporal told them the Coldstream Guards had defended it successfully, and as Emily stared at the few blackened walls that remained, she wondered briefly if Colonel Rogers had survived. It did not seem as if anyone could have lived through such fire and destruction.

Finally the corporal halted the team and turned to Lady Quentin. "We have came as far as the Guards were engaged, m'lady," he said with respect. "What would you like me to do now?"

There was a note of quiet admiration in his voice, for not once had Lady Quentin cried out or put her handkerchief to her mouth, no matter how grim the scene before her. The only time she had made any sound at all was when she saw a looter bending over a body to search the pockets of the dead man, but a shout from the corporal and the angry wave of his pistol made the man scurry away.

Emily had been moved to tears more than once. To see a young drummer boy lying dead by the road, his white trousers as red with blood as his jacket, had sent tears coursing down her cheeks. He could not have been above thirteen, she thought, but she took her cue from her mistress and made not a sound.

Now this lady thought for a moment, and then she asked the corporal to turn around and head back to Waterloo. "I know Tony is somewhere between us and the village. We must look more carefully."

The weary horses moved off, and it was just as well they were tired, for they were plodding along so slowly that Lady Quentin was able to spot a red sleeve with the insignia of the Guards in a clump of bushes near the road.

"Stop!" she commanded, and before the corporal could help her, she got down from the carriage. Quickly she parted the bushes and stared down in horror at the body of Sergeant Boothby. Both legs were missing below the knee, and he had been cut with sabers many times.

Emily, who had joined her mistress, cried out at the sight. Sergeant Boothby would not be "fine" this time, and he would never land on his feet again, she thought, the hot tears beginning to fall as she stared at the body of the cocky little man who looked so much smaller in death than he had in life.

Suddenly she heard Lady Quentin give a cry, and realizing she had gone ahead, she pushed her way through the bushes until she reached her side. The lady was kneeling beside the captain, lifting his head in her arms and calling his name. The corporal, who was close behind Emily, shook his head in sadness, for Captain Quentin looked as dead as his sergeant. His arm was cut in a long, deep saber wound, his uniform jacket was ripped in several places, and his handsome face was ashen pale and still.

Emily went to her mistress to comfort her in her sorrow. "Come away, m'lady," she whispered. "You cannot help him now."

Lady Quentin ignored her as she bent to put her ear to his chest. The tears were running down her face unheeded, but then she sat up and smiled at her companions. "He is not dead! Nelly, get the medicine case out of the carriage at once. Corporal, I shall need your help."

Emily hurried back to the road to fetch the heavy case, trying not to look at Sergeant Boothby as she passed him. When she reached her mistress again, the corporal was easing Captain Quentin's jacket off. His wife opened the case in haste and began to tear one of the sheets into strips for bandages. She gasped when her husband's chest was laid bare, for there was a bullet hole just below his right shoulder. It was bleeding in a slow, sluggish stream, and the corporal put a thick pad over it. When he lifted the captain to secure the bandage over the wound, he nodded in relief.

"See here, your ladyship. The bullet passed through and out his back. That is good news."

"We must get him back to the hospital as soon as we can, corporal." Lady Quentin nodded. "He has lost a lot of blood. Then, too, I do not like the look of that arm, and it is the same one he wounded before."

At last they had the captain bandaged as well as they could manage it on the rough ground. Lady Quentin wanted to help carry her husband, but neither Emily nor Corporal Deems would allow her to assist them. The soldier took the captain's shoulders and Emily picked up his feet, and between them they managed, although Emily was panting when they reached the road, for the captain was a large and heavy man. Somehow the two of them got the unconscious man into the back of the carriage, where Lady Quentin was waiting to support him in her arms on the drive.

"Hurry the horses, if you can, Corporal," she called as he clucked to the team. Emily sat beside him, clutching the medicine case and trying not to shiver. When she looked down at her gown, she saw it was liberally spotted with her master's blood, and she put a shaking hand to her mouth. Behind her she could hear Lady Quentin murmuring and encouraging her husband, but she herself had nothing to do but relive the horror she had just witnessed.

The corporal looked sideways at her white, frightened face and said kindly, "Nothing to be afraid of now, missy. I've seen men worse than that who have recovered, but 'tis a good thing her ladyship found him when she did."

Emily nodded, but she could not speak, and all the way back to Waterloo she found herself praying over and over that the captain would survive.

At the hospital there were many willing hands to lift him down and carry him in to the surgeons, but when Lady Quentin tried to follow, she was firmly denied. A harassed-looking doctor told her she must wait outside. "I shall come and tell you of your husband's condition as soon as I can, m'lady, but at the present, you would only hinder us."

With this, Lady Quentin had to be content and she slumped back in her seat, all her courage gone now that there was no more need for it.

The corporal asked Emily if they had any spirits with them, and remembered the brandy, Emily searched the case until she found a bottle. "Aye, that's what she needs—what you need too, missy," he said with a smile as he poured them both a liberal tot. Emily felt the strong liquid burning her throat, but she felt better after she swallowed it.

As they sat there in the carriage with the tired horses' heads drooping almost to the ground, Emily saw some men come out of one of the still-intact buildings of the village. Then she heard a muffled exclamation and one of them broke away from his companions to hurry toward them. As if through a haze, she recognized the Duke of Wrotherham. He always seems to be there when I need him, she thought. Now why is that?

"Lady Quentin!" the duke called out. "Why are you here?"

Without waiting for her reply, he climbed into the carriage and took her hands in his. His black eyes went over both women, their air of exhaustion and their dishevelment and dirty, bloodstained gowns, and he frowned.

"I came to find my husband, your Grace," Alicia said. "He is with the surgeons now, but they would not let me stay with him."

"Certainly not," the duke agreed. "But forgive me, Lady Quentin, you should return to Brussels now, although how you will get these beasts to carry you that far I do not know."

"I intend to wait so I can take Tony back and nurse him," Lady Quentin said in a firm voice that brooked no argument. "I cannot believe that my care, and Nelly's, cannot help but be superior to anything Tony might experience in that crowded hospital."

"But he may not be able to be moved," the duke reasoned.

"Then we will nurse him here. There must be some place that will take us in, some château, even a farmhouse."

The duke seemed to come to a decision, for he climbed down from the carriage after one more searching look at Lady Quentin and her maid. "Wait here," he commanded as he hurried into the hospital. It was several minutes before he came back and called to a liveried servant nearby, "The horses, at once!"

Emily felt a pang of bitter disappointment that he was leaving them. She had felt so much better after she saw him, sure that he would take care of everything and she would not have to be frightened anymore.

He came up to the carriage again. "Lady Quentin, I have seen the doctors, and although your husband is very weak, there is every chance of his recovery with careful nursing, but they say that he must not be moved any great distance for some time, for he has lost much blood. I will go ahead and make sure that a farmhouse that I know of is ready to take you in. You there," he called to Corporal Deems, "follow the road back toward Brussels as soon as the captain is released to his wife. Travel slowly so as not to jar him, and I will have my man waiting for you at a crossroads some two miles from Waterloo to show you the way."

The corporal nodded and Lady Quentin smiled at the duke.

"You are too kind, your Grace!" she exclaimed. "How can we ever thank you?"

The duke waved an impatient hand of dismissal as his groom brought his horse. "Such bravery as you ladies have shown today must be rewarded, m'lady. All will be well, you'll see."

When he was mounted, his eyes went to Emily's face and he added, as if for her alone, "We shall meet again, presently."

He waited for a moment until the girl nodded, and then he cantered away.

6

As the duke rode away, followed by his groom, he called himself every kind of idiot, for to have embroiled himself in the Quentins' problems could mean nothing but trouble for him. The doctors had told him that there was little chance that the captain would be able to keep the badly wounded arm. They had not removed it because he was so weak from loss of blood that they knew he would not survive the further shock of an amputation, but they fully expected he would have to undergo such surgery as soon as he was stronger. The duke shook his head and resolved to keep that information to himself, at least for now. He had been stunned to see the superficial Lady Quentin there in the carnage that was still Waterloo village, but although he admired her courage in seeking out her husband, if he were to be honest with himself he would have to admit it had been her maid who had inspired his chivalrous gesture. One look at those speaking emerald eyes, filled with such fear and dread even as she succeeded in keeping herself under firm control, had caused him to put his own wants and comforts aside and do what he could to help her. As he rode, he shook his head again. Fool, fool! He knew the signs as well as anyone, and it was obvious that he was fast succumbing to her considerable attractions—and at such a time, too.

He had completed his commission for the War Office and had had every intention of taking ship for England as soon as it could be arranged, but now he had committed himself to a sojourn of indeterminate length in an uncomfortable farmhouse, all for the sake of a common maid—and a maid who had never ever shown any reciprocal attraction for him at that. No, he corrected himself, his black eyes lighting up in memory, there was nothing common about Margaret Nelson except her occupation, but he had never dallied with servants or the lower orders, for he was much too fastidious, or so he had always imagined before now.

As he turned his horse onto the rough track that led to the farmhouse one of the senior officers had told him about, he also admitted he was not at all averse to a period of time spent in her company, no matter how primitive the surroundings. She was an unusual challenge, and perhaps he could make her want him as much as he was beginning to want her; Lord knows he had had numerous successes before this in persuading the feminine sex of his desirability.

The question of marriage never crossed his mind. The Saint Allyns had always been a proud family; when the time came, he would propose to some worthy lady of equal birth and fortune, hoping she would not be too boring or demanding or incompatible, not that that was of any consequence whatsoever. He had been brought up to realize that the only thing that was important was that the Dukes of Wrotherham should continue to descend from father to son in a direct line, as they had done since the duchy was established in 1432 by Henry VI, in reward for some deed of valor or service by the first holder of the title. He had been named for his ancestor, and he had often wondered what the first Charles Alistair Saint Allyn had done to deserve such royal recognition.

He pulled up before a hedge to survey the farmhouse a little way ahead. It was larger than he had expected, but it looked lonely and empty, for there was no smoke coming from any of the chimneys. Outside of a large dog lying before the stable door and some chickens scratching in a dusty yard, there was not a soul in sight. The duke cursed under his breath and heard his groom coughing behind him, reminding him of his presence.

"No one home, Thomas, now what?" he asked, urging his horse into a slow walk. "We shall have to persuade that mongrel that we are worthy of being the next tenants. I hope you are good with dogs, my boy."

"I don't think that will be necessary, your Grace," his groom replied with a grin, and the duke followed his pointing crop to see a man coming out of one of the barns. He urged his horse to a quicker pace.

"You there! *Bonjour, mon homme. Ecoutez-moi,*" he called, and the farmer stopped, taking his pipe from his mouth in amazement at the richly dressed foreigner and his servant who were turning into his yard.

Fortunately the man spoke French as well as his native Flemish, and the duke was able to make himself understood. After the farmer identified himself as Monsieur Bordreau, he did not speak again, but stared impassively at his visitor while the situation was explained to him. There was a long moment of silence until the duke reached for his pocketbook and removed a thick packet of bills. At this, Monsieur Bordreau's eyes brightened, and the price to rent the farm was soon agreed on. There was no one to dispossess but himself, for he had sent his wife and daughters to Brussels before the fighting began, and was not at all averse to joining them there, now that it would be so lucrative to do so. He called, and a boy he called Paul came out of one of the sheds, gawking and grinning. It was plain he was a half-wit, and the duke was tempted to refuse his services until Thomas made so bold as to point out that someone was needed to look after the animals and the other routines of the place, determined it was not to be himself.

While the farmer explained the situation to the boy, the duke was busy instructing his groom.

"Ride back to the crossroads, Thomas, and wait there for Lady Quentin's carriage. Do not bother to escort them here; the corporal can find the place with ease. Instead, ride for Brussels at once. We will need food, supplies, and I shall need clothes for at least a week. Go as quickly as you can. When you return, bring my cook and one of the maids as well, but on no account are you to bring Greene."

The groom hid a grin. Greene was the duke's valet, and a loftier, more high-and-mighty individual he had yet to see.

"He is of no use to us at all unless he is prepared to help nurse the captain. Be sure to explain how I am situated, so he will understand I will not be dressing for dinner every evening and there will be no one to remark my poorly polished boots and less-than-exquisite cravats. Off with you, now. I shall expect you no later than noon tomorrow. Until then, I am sure I can manage."

The groom touched his cap in salute and trotted away even as the duke wondered if his last statement had not been overly optimistic. He shrugged as he prepared to inspect the farm-house with Bordreau. There was, after all, the corporal, and between them they would have to make do.

The farmhouse itself was clean, although the rooms were small and dark and cramped. He set the boy to making up the fires while he tried to decide if the captain would be easier to care for on the ground floor. The only room that was at all suitable was the parlor, but since he could not picture himself sitting in the kitchen with his cook and the half-wit even in a situation like this, he decided they would have to cope with the steep, narrow stairs.

In a short time, the farmer bowed himself away and left in an ancient gig, and the duke banished Paul to the stables.

It was some time before he heard the sounds of a team and carriage. He had aired one of the upper bedrooms, turning back the sheets and fetching a basin and some water from the kitchen while he waited, and now he hurried outside to help.

Lady Quentin was seated in the back of the carriage, once again supporting her husband's unconscious body in her arms. The duke noted the man's extreme pallor and many bandages and darted a glance at the corporal, only to see him shake his head in fearful sorrow. Beside him on the perch was Miss Nelson, holding a large medicine case, which reassured the duke somewhat. He tied the tired horses to a fence and called for Paul to care for them before he and the corporal lifted the captain down and carried him into the farmhouse and up the stairs, being as careful as they could not to jar him. Lady Quentin preceded them, her face white and strained. The duke was perspiring when at last they laid the wounded man on the bed, for the captain was tall and muscled, and the stairs were steep.

"If you will retire for a minute, m'lady," he said, coming to take her by the arm, "the corporal and I will undress your husband and put him to bed. Perhaps you might inspect the other bedrooms and choose one you can share with your maid. There are only three that are at all suitable." For a moment his expression darkened and he added, "I am sorry this is the best I could find in the circumstances."

Lady Quentin summoned up a tired smile as she squeezed his arm. "As if it matters, sir! You have been such a help, Tony and I can never thank you. My maid and I will be content anywhere, won't we, Nelly?"

The girl murmured her assent as she put the medicine case down on the rough bureau and prepared to follow her mistress from the room.

"I shall settle in while you are making Tony more comfortable. Nelly, bring in our cases and then see about making us some tea, if you please, and then . . ."

She moved away and the duke shut the door behind her and stared at the old soldier. "How bad is he, man?" he asked in a quiet voice, for he did not want to distress Lady Quentin.

"Bad as I've ever seen, sir," the corporal said, beginning to remove the captain's coat. "I never thought we'd get him this far alive, your Grace, but there's no telling the lady that. She is sure that, now she has him in her care, she will nurse him back to health in no time." He shook his head as he began to ease off the captain's boots, and the duke hurried to hold his leg still. In a few moments, they had him in one of the farmer's clean nightshirts and beneath the covers. The duke felt for a pulse. It was weak and thready, and he frowned.

"Women can sometimes work miracles, Corporal, and in this case, a miracle is what we need. I'll call her now and fetch some tea for us all."

"Aye, sir. I'll wait here to see if anything else is required," the old soldier said.

After Lady Quentin had gone in to her husband, the duke ran down the stairs and made his way to the kitchen again. Miss Nelson, he saw with approval, had found a voluminous apron that no doubt belonged to the farmer's good wife, and she had put the kettle on the fire and set out a teapot and some cups, but now she was wandering around peering into boxes and sacks, looking confused as well as exhausted. He thought she also looked adorable, even in her disheveled state, with the huge apron wrapped around her almost twice, and he wished he might take her in his arms and comfort her. Instead, he leaned against the door jamb and folded his arms.

"There is some problem, Miss Nelson?" he asked, his face somber. "No tea? Sugar?"

Emily stared back at him. "I have found what there is of the tea, but there is no sugar, your Grace," she said, brushing back one of the tendrils that had escaped her severe chignon. "But what are we to eat? Lady Quentin has had nothing today but some bread and cheese, and there is nothing left in the basket to give her, or indeed, any of us.'' She looked distraught as she added, ''There does not seem to be anything here that will serve as our dinner.''

The duke strolled in and leaned against the deal table. ''In that case we can be thankful this is a farm. I will have the boy kill us a chicken and fetch some eggs as well. You continue to search. Perhaps there is something in the larder?''

He moved toward the door and then he heard a choked little cry and turned back, his black brows rising when he saw her flushed face.

''But that won't do a bit of good, your Grace! I . . . I don't know how to cook anything—so whatever would I do with a chicken?''

At that the duke laughed. ''I take it, then, that you yourself were not raised in the country, Miss Nelson?'' At the shake of her head he added, ''By tomorrow we will have my own cook here, for I sent Thomas into Brussels to fetch her, yes, and a maid as well. Until then, we will just have to figure out between us what you do with a dead chicken.'' He saw that Miss Nelson's eyes were lowered and she was trying not to cry. ''Do not be distressed, my dear,'' he added softly, ''I have no idea what you do with 'em either.''

When he came back some time later, he had removed his riding coat and cravat and loosened his shirt, and he held a dead chicken in each well-cared-for hand. Emily thought she had never seen anything so incongruous as the elegant duke thus employed, but she did not smile. Corporal Deems, who had been seated at the kitchen table rose and took the birds from him, saying, ''Missy has been telling me, your Grace, of her problems. Now, I don't claim to be what you might call a chef, but many a scrawny Spanish hen did I prepare during the Peninsular War. We'll manage!''

''Thank heavens,'' the duke replied, wiping his hands on a towel. ''You are a godsend, Corporal! I was about to, er, pop 'em in a pot and then go away and let them stew for a respectable amount of time. Come, Miss Nelson, let us take some tea to Lady Quentin and give the corporal the peace and quiet I am sure he needs for his culinary endeavors.''

As the two of them left the room, the corporal shook his head as he surveyed the two chickens lying on the table. ''Pop 'em in the pot, your Grace?'' he muttered. ''Before they've been drawn and plucked? Aye, 'tis a good thing I'm here, all right.''

The duke noticed that Miss Nelson stumbled a little on the steep stairs, even though he had insisted on carrying the tray for her. Lady Quentin met them at the door of the bedroom and came out into the hall to whisper to them as she drank her tea.

"He seems to be in a more restful sleep now," she said, her eyes glowing with her relief.

"That is good, Lady Quentin, and since I see we cannot dislodge you from his side, may I suggest that Miss Nelson and I get some rest now? It will be necessary to divide the nursing duties through the night, and it will do no good for all of us to remain awake now. Call us in an hour or so, and then we can care for the captain while you lie down.''

"I shall be happy to sit with the captain first, m'lady," Emily said.

"No, the duke is right, Nelly. There is no need for anyone else at this time, and you know I could not sleep just yet. I will call Corporal Deems if I need any help.''

At that welcome news, Emily concealed a sigh of relief and went away to the bedroom Lady Quentin had chosen. In no time at all she was fast asleep on a pallet she arranged on the floor.

In the future, whenever she remembered that first night at the farmhouse near Waterloo, Emily could only recall a kaleidoscope of hurried impressions: the glow of the old-fashioned lamps and tallow candles, the endless trips up and down the narrow stairs, sleeping for what seemed to be only a few minutes and then being shaken by Lady Quentin just before she fell on her bed in exhaustion, and the huge plate of chicken stew she had devoured, to Corpral Deems' delight. And she remembered the duke: how he had sat with her and the corporal at the kitchen table to eat, as easy as if he were in his own dining room attended by his butler and footmen, asking the old soldier for stories of the Peninsular War when he saw she was too tired to talk. And she remembered how he had insisted on carrying the tea tray for her, and other less pleasant objects as well, the way he had looked holding the two chickens, the armloads of wood he brought in, although she was sure he had never carried wood in his life, and most of all she remembered how he had come to join her sometime in the middle of the night as she sat by the captain's bed.

Tony Quentin had still not recovered consciousness, but he was becoming restless, tossing and turning in the bed until she was sure he would loosen the dressings and start bleeding again. She tried to soothe him and hold him still, but he was a strong man and he was reliving the battle, that much was sure from his disjointed words and cries. She was just about exhausted when she heard the door latch, but she did not turn. "There, Captain," she said as calmly as she could, "you must lie still, please, you must."

"Come on, men! Forward! Sergeant Boothby, get to the right flank and tell the colonel . . . but we will win . . . brave lad, brave lad! Forward! Grantman and Cagell . . . both gone? How many men are left? . . . No, not Dane! Say not that it was Dane who was killed! . . . Where's the Austrian command now? Is the château holding? . . . Ah, it hurts, it hurts!"

Emily could not help but weep as she laid him back panting on his pillow and dampened a cloth in cold water, praying her mistress would not wake at his cries.

"He is close to coming to himself," the duke's deep voice remarked behind her, and she turned a little to see him standing there in his open-necked shirt and breeches. The black curly hair on his chest was clearly visible. As she put the cloth on the captain's forehead, the duke reached out and smoothed back her hair where it had fallen against her cheek, and then he squeezed her shoulder.

"I will stay with you, my dear, until he wakes. Perhaps we can get some of this good broth into him; at the least he should have some laudanum for the pain and to help him sleep."

Emily nodded, wishing he had not moved away to check the broth she had placed on the hob to keep warm. She could still feel the pressure of his strong fingers and it comforted her. I do not think I can stand much more of this, she told herself in despair. The Captain so ill, the mean farmhouse, and having to do things she had never done before—it was all too much. But when the duke stood near her and spoke so kindly, she forgot her exhaustion and terror. He would take care of everything, she told herself, including Margaret Nelson, lady's maid. With Saint Allyn she was safe—they all were.

When the captain woke, it was only for a moment, but they

managed to get him to swallow a few sips of broth, and then some opium. "Nelly, you here?" he whispered, rubbing his eyes with his good hand. "I must be dreaming, for you are in Antwerp with Alicia. She promised."

'All is well, Captain," the duke assured him in a voice of command. "Go to sleep now and we will explain everything in the morning."

Captain Quentin sank back on his pillows and Emily sighed.

"He will be calmer now, Miss Nelson," the duke told her as he replaced the pan of broth near the fire. "If you need me, knock on the wall here and I will come at once. Deems will soon be on duty to relieve you—good girl! My father always said there was nothing like an Englishwoman for bravery and endurance in the face of terrible odds. In fact, he said your sex easily surpassed men in that respect, and I perceive he was right. But even my father could not know that at the same time a woman could be as beautiful as you are."

With a last wave of his hand he was gone, and Emily sat down again to ponder his last words while she watched over her master.

Thomas and a large wagon arrived early the next morning, well before noon. The wagon contained all kinds of food and supplies, the duke's wardrobe, a stout older woman and an even stouter maid, and driving the team and seated somewhat apart from them, an elegant gentleman's gentleman.

"Sorry, your Grace," Thomas muttered as he dismounted and heard the duke's startled oath. "He insisted. Said he had no objection to nursing the captain. What he did object to was having you turned out shoddy, which you would be if you dressed yourself. That's what *he* said, your Grace," he added as his master cast a great frown in his direction.

Emily was asleep when they arrived, and with all this new help, Lady Quentin let her sleep on. She herself, relieved that Tony had woken and spoke to the duke, had been able to sleep for four hours and felt much refreshed.

From that time on, life in the Bordreau farmhouse settled down into an almost placid routine, centered around Tony Quentin and his needs. Madame Vergé, although horrified at the primitive kitchen, fell to work with a will, and Nicole, the stout maid, was cheerful as she took the more onerous chores onto her own broad shoulders with competence. Mr. Greene, although he was heard to sniff now and then in disdain, was worth his weight in gold, for he turned out to be the best nurse of them all. When Tony Quentin was restless from pain and the slight fever he had developed and could not be made to lie still, Mr. Greene had only to lift one eyebrow to gain his cooperation. Lady Quentin remarked on this one afternoon while she was taking tea with the duke in the parlor, which Emily had just served.

"I do not understand what there is about your man, Charles, that makes Tony obey him as if he were no more than two and ten. He is not so good, even for me," she said, nodding to Emily to pass the sugar to the duke.

"I know," the duke replied as he stirred his tea. "But then, Alicia, Greene frightens even me, when he feels I need a setdown. Just one of his sniffs, one frozen glance, and I hurry to do his bidding. A formidable servant, to be sure, and I would not tolerate him except he is such a competent valet."

He smiled his thanks to Emily, and she, noting that perfect coat, the sparkling white of his shirt, and his well-brushed hair, had to agree with him. She got on very well with Mr. Greene, although he never relaxed his formal courtesy to her. Paul was stunned by him, and when he came to the kitchen for his meals, he sat in silent awe of the paragon at the opposite end of the table. Mr. Greene, of course, did not acknowledge the stableboy's existence by the flicker of an eyelash.

Now that a table had been set up in the parlor, the duke and Lady Quentin took their meals alone, so there was no repeat of that first intimate meal for Emily. Even Corporal Deems was seen less often, for he had taken to helping Paul with the stock and the garden, and Thomas was busy riding on the duke's errands and fetching the doctor from the village when it was necessary for him to call. Emily found she had very little to do, once she had dressed Lady Quentin for the day. The duke had sent Emily, with Thomas to escort her, to Brussels to bring back the lady's clothes, but she wore only simple morning gowns, not bothering to change for dinner. It seemed silly, she told her maid, to put on a silk gown even to dine with a duke, when she was going to be in the sickroom afterward.

Lady Quentin had taken to strolling up and down the lane in the afternoons when Mr. Greene was watching Tony, taking Emily with her. The duke found himself admiring the lady's courage in insisting on nursing her husband, but his eyes went more often to the slender figure of her maid as he wished there were some way he could be alone with her.

One afternoon, Mr. Greene came to ask Lady Quentin to come and see her husband. "I do not like the look of him at all, m'lady. He should be mending much faster than he is doing. That arm, now . . . I think perhaps the doctor should be called again."

Lady Quentin rose at once, putting down her book as the duke begged her to send Thomas on the errand if she felt the doctor was needed.

"Thank you, Charles, I shall. I will come at once, Mr. Greene. Nelly? Nelly!" she called, and Emily came in for her orders. "I am going upstairs with Mr. Greene, Nelly, so I will have to forgo my walk this afternoon. Do go out yourself, though, and get some air. It is a lovely summer day and the cottage is stuffy."

It was true the day was hot and sunny, and Emily was glad to thank her before she went to fetch her hat. The duke strolled to the door of the parlor as Lady Quentin and his man went up the stairs, deep in conversation. In the hall he heard Nicole ask Miss Nelson a question, and he heard the girl's soft reply as she tied on her bonnet. Then his brows came together in a frown. The maid, of course, had spoken in French; what was surprising was that Miss Nelson had answered in the same language, fluently and with an elegant accent. The duke was determined to find out more about this unusual lady's maid who was much too educated and refined for her menial occupation.

Accordingly, he noted which way she turned when she reached the lane, and then he took his hat and followed her. She was not in sight when he came around the first bend, and he stopped for a puzzled moment. The women knew they were not to go out of sight of the farm, for there were still soldiers about, some stragglers from the French army, intent on looting and plunder. Corporal Deems had frightened two such men away the second day of their stay, and he had spoken to the duke and suggested he carry a weapon whenever he went out.

Now Charles felt the pocket of his coat to be sure his gun was still there, and then he hurried down the lane after Miss

Nelson. He would have passed by the small path that led off into the woods if he had not heard her cry out with fear. Pushing past the bushes, he made his way down the path at a dead run. There, by a wide brook was Miss Nelson in the arms of a French soldier, his uniform ripped and filthy, and with several days' growth of beard on his dirty face.

"Let her go or I shoot," the duke called in French, drawing his pistol and taking aim.

The Frenchman sprang away with an oath and, seeing the pistol, was quick to jump the brook and take to his heels. The duke waited until all sounds of his flight had disappeared, and then he walked down to where the maid was standing, straightening her gown where the soldier had disarranged it. He noticed that her hands were trembling.

"Little fool! You know you are not supposed to go out of sight of the farm. It's a good thing for you that I followed you when I did."

Emily saw his angry eyes and set lips as she curtsied. "Thank you, your Grace. I am sorry to be such a trouble, but the lane was so hot and dusty I wanted to sit here by the brook for a while."

His expression did not lighten and she turned away to pick up her bonnet where it had fallen to the grassy bank. "*Il me semble que je vois sauve toujours, ma chère. Qu'est-ce-que vous auriez fait si je n'avais pas été ici?*" the duke asked.

"*Il est certain que j'aurais regretté cela beaucoup, monsieur,*" Emily replied, and then her hand went to her mouth in dismay.

The duke came and took her arm. "I think you owe me an explanation, Miss Nelson," he said, still in French. "Since I have vanquished the enemy and have my pistol handy, let us sit down as you wished to do in the first place, and then perhaps you will answer some of my questions."

Emily opened her mouth to deny him, and then shut it.

He nodded. "Yes, so much wiser not to claim you have no knowledge of French when I have found you out."

He indicated the stretch of grass by the brook, and Emily sank down on her knees, her mind whirling. She could not refuse to reply; maids were not allowed such arrogance to their betters.

Charles Saint Allyn sat down next to her, stretching out his booted legs and crossing his feet. He removed his hat and lay back on the grass, propped up on one elbow and completely at his ease. For a moment there was silence except for a bird calling deeper in the wood and the chuckle of the brook as it ran over the stones of its bed.

"Who are you?" the duke asked in English, his voice quiet.

Emily swallowed and stared straight ahead of her. "I am Margaret Nelson, spinster and a lady's maid, your Grace."

"You are certainly *employed* as a lady's maid," the duke agreed cordially. "As to the rest of it, I have my doubts. But we will leave that for now. Why *are* you a lady's maid? One so educated, such a lady herself—it is incongruous!"

"I must make my way in the world, sir," Emily replied in not much more than a whisper. How difficult this conversation was!

"Where were you born? Who are your people? And where did you learn to speak French like that?" He sat up suddenly and took one of her hands. "You ask me to believe that this thin, patrician hand came from peasant stock?"

"I . . . I was born in London, sir. Who my parents are I do not know," she invented.

"A foundling?" the duke asked with rich scorn. "I will concede the point. Perhaps you did have wellborn parents and your mother abandoned you—that is entirely possible and would account for your looks and breeding. But come! If you were a foundling and then put out to service, where did you learn to speak in such an educated way in both French and English?"

"I . . . I went to a house where there was a daughter just my age, and although I was only a maid, Miss liked me and I was allowed to join her for her lessons."

Still all the duke was allowed to see was her elegant profile, for Emily knew she could never look into his eyes and continue to lie to him.

"Look at me," he commanded as if he had read her mind. "That is quite a story and it could have happened that way, although it is very farfetched. Perhaps you will trust me enough someday to tell me the truth. I see you do not trust me now."

His voice sounded so regretful that, without thinking, Emily reached out with her free hand. He was quick to capture it and pull both her hands close to his heart.

"One thing I do know to be true, Miss Margaret Nelson, if that is your real name: you are a very beautiful woman," he said, his deep voice intimate as he bent toward her.

Emily stared into those glowing black eyes and felt a warmth creep over her body until she was sure he could see the blush rising from the neck of her muslin gown. His eyes grew more intent as he leaned still closer.

"Lorelei," he said, and then he bent his head and kissed her.

Emily concentrated on staying very still, afraid that if she moved she would tremble. His kiss was warm and gentle, and without meaning to, her lips opened under his and returned his kiss. At that, he grasped her shoulders in both his strong hands and kissed her more deeply. Emily put her hands up to his chest, but it was only a token gesture, for she had no intention of pushing him away. "So," the little voice in her head said, "so, this is what it is all about."

She felt as if she were sinking deeper and deeper into a soft warm mist. Vaguely she was aware that his arms had gone around her and he was holding her close as his hands caressed her back. When he raised his head at last, Emily felt as if she had traveled a very long distance to a country hitherto unknown to her. She saw a vein beating in his forehead, and his face stern and sober, a little frown between his brows. He did not speak, but she knew he was asking her a question as surely as if she could hear his deep voice. For a moment she hesitated, and then she reached up and put her arms around his neck and his expression brightened. He kissed her cheek and her throat before he began to take the pins from her tight chignon. When he had it loosened, he ran his hands through it until it fell down her back in ripples of pure gold, and he caught his breath in awe. Emily had not taken her eyes from his, and even when he began to unbutton her gown, they only widened and glowed with light. The duke thought he would drown in their green depths, and he found he was holding his breath, as if he were afraid to shatter this perfect moment.

With his hand warm on her breast, he kissed her again, and she closed her eyes at last as he lowered her, unresisting, to the sun-warmed grass.

Later, as she lay on her back, held close to him by one strong arm, she stared up at the blue sky and the few puffy clouds floating so far above her. It was strange. She had thought she would feel differently somehow, that she would be ashamed and remorseful and embarrassed, but her mood was nothing like that at all. Instead, she felt a great peace and a sense of rightness about their lovemaking. He had hurt her a little in the beginning and she had not been able to restrain a little cry of pain. At once he stopped and raised his head to stare down into her face and ask in a gentle voice, "Why didn't you tell me you were a virgin, love?" She shook her head, but she did not speak as she pulled him close again, and in a little while the pain was gone and there was only the duke, his body warm and demanding and all-consuming. Now she turned her head to study that aristocratic face with its strong features and chiseled lips. How much younger he looks with his eyes closed, she thought, and all those lines of boredom gone from his dear face, and then she knew how much she loved him. Her mother might have bequeathed to her the sensuality she still felt, but Emily knew that she would feel it for only one man for the rest of her life. There could be no one else for her, not ever, not after today. She sighed a little and he opened his eyes and smiled at her.

"Are you all right, my dearest?" he whispered, pulling her to him again and kissing her.

Emily lay on top of him, her blond hair making a curtain around their faces as if to hide them from sight.

"Oh yes, I am fine . . . No, that is not the right word. I am wonderful," she said, and he laughed out loud. "More than wonderful. There are no words to describe you. I could search the dictionary for hours and not be able to do you justice."

Suddenly she rolled away from him and sat up, pulling her hair to one side as she studied the sky. "We must make haste, your Grace. See the sun. Why, it must be very late and Lady Quentin will be calling me."

"Charles," he said firmly. "Not 'your Grace,' not now or ever again."

"*Dear* Charles," she repeated as she did up her hair.

He lay and watched her and then he said. "What a shame that you must ever put it up, love. It is so beautiful streaming over your shoulders, as free as we have been."

For a moment her hands stayed on the hairpins and her green eyes darkened as if she had gone far away from him. Then she rose and dressed, and as the duke followed her example, he wondered what that momentary check had been for. He could not know that Emily was remembering that his father had said much the same thing to her mother and that for a moment she had felt a chill of apprehension. When they were ready, he took her in his arms again as if he could not bear to let her go, and kissed her gently.

"I will take care of you, my love. I will always take care of you," he said, his voice husky with emotion.

Emily put up her hand in negation, wishing he had not spoken. She did not want to be reminded, not now, of what the duke would expect of her, or how they would meet again. Time enough to think of that later, she thought, even as she knew there was no way she would allow him to take care of her, giving her money and providing her with clothes and jewels and a house where he could visit her. She loved him, and marriage was impossible, but that she would never consent to. She banished these thoughts as she stood on tiptoe to kiss him good-bye, and then she ran up the path to the lane.

Charles stayed where she had left him. He looked down into the brook, but he did not see the clear water, nor hear its cheerful chuckle; he saw only her face, those marvelous eyes and breathtaking hair, and then he remembered her body, so perfectly formed and supple under his hands, and he shook his head. Truly she was a Lorelei, for see how she had bewitched him! How else could he explain this longing he had to possess her again when she had been gone only for a few minutes! It was some time later before he put on his hat and followed her back to the farmhouse, determined to see her alone again as soon as he could manage it.

Emily was sure that Lady Quentin would be angry at her for being gone so long, but when she reached the farmhouse, it was to find it in an uproar. She could hear the captain cursing and his wife weeping as she hurried up the stairs. She met Mr. Greene carrying a basin and asked, "What is it? What is wrong?"

"The doctor has been, Miss Nelson, and he says that the captain must have that arm removed, that until he does he will not recover. It has been a sad blow, yes, a very sad blow to him and to his lady."

He shook his head as he moved to the stairs, and Emily crept into Lady Quentin's room to check her hair in the mirror and to put on her apron and cap. Poor Lady Quentin, she thought. She had been so sure she could nurse her husband back to health, and now to be faced with this. She straightened up the room, putting away a gown her mistress had left on the bed and hanging up her robe. Her hands paused in their work when she heard the duke's voice and his footsteps coming along the hall as he went to join the Quentins. How strange it is to know he is so close and yet now so far away, she thought.

When Lady Quentin came in at last, her face was pale and streaked with tears, and Emily went to comfort her. "Can I get you some tea, m'lady," she asked.

"No, thank you, Nelly. Have you heard? But of course you have heard." Lady Quentin sank down on her bed as if she were exhausted. "The duke has promised to fetch another doctor from Brussels tomorrow so we might have a second opinion, so perhaps it is wrong to despair just yet, but, oh, Nelly, I have this terrible feeling of dread. And Tony is so upset and distraught. I tried to tell him that it would make no difference to me and that I would rather have him alive even with only one arm, but he will not listen to me. The duke is going to sit with him and take his dinner there, too, so perhaps he can convince him that what happens will be for the best. I am so very tired that I know I must lie down and rest. Do not bother to call me for dinner, Nelly. I know I would not be able to swallow anything this evening."

Emily put a soft throw over her mistress, who fell asleep as soon as her head touched the pillow, and then she tiptoed from the room.

Lady Quentin slept right through the night, and when Emily came to bed, she did not even stir. The duke had remained with the captain all evening, and as Emily paused for a moment outside the door, she heard his deep voice, calm and reassuring, and the captain's subdued answer. He seems quieter now, she thought as she blew a kiss through the panels to Charles before she went to her pallet. She had planned to spend some time thinking about him and what she was to do, but instead, worn out from the emotions of the day, she fell asleep immediately.

The duke was gone when she came down the following morning to have her breakfast and prepare a tray for Lady Quentin. She wondered why she felt almost relieved that she did not have to see him and look into his black eyes with other people around. Perhaps it was because she was sure that everyone would see her love for him at once, and she could not bear to have the world know of it as yet. All day she did her chores as if in a dream, and then in the late afternoon she sat down at a window facing the lane to mend some lace on one of Lady Quentin's gowns. She found her eyes straying to the lane as often as she watched her needle, and just before five she was rewarded by the sight of the duke escorting a gig into the yard. An elderly man climbed down and stretched before his servant handed him a black bag, but Emily had eyes only for the duke. He was searching the windows of the farmhouse and she leaned closer to the panes until he saw her and his face lit up in a warm smile that was full of love. At that her heart gave a great leap of joy, and the familiar wave of warmth swept over her even as she heard her mistress calling her to come at once.

The doctor examined Captain Quentin carefully and came to the same conclusion that the other doctor had. The arm must be amputated as soon as possible. Emily, standing behind her mistress, caught her breath, but Lady Quentin was calm as she held her husband's good hand. Even he seemed resigned to his fate now, for there were no outbursts, no oaths. Whatever the duke had told him had done the trick.

The doctor agreed to assist in the operation, and it was arranged that the captain should be transported to the hospital in Waterloo first thing in the morning. By evening, he said, he could return to the farmhouse.

The duke took him away to the parlor, and Lady Quentin dismissed her maid, for she wanted to be alone with her Tony now. Emily felt hot tears stinging her eyelids as she went down the narrow stairs. How sad it was, and how strange that it had been less than two weeks since the battle began. It seemed much longer than that, for look at all the things that had happened in the interim.

There was no chance for her to see Charles, for he was busy entertaining the doctor and planned to go with him and the captain on the morrow. Lady Quentin had been persuaded to wait at the farm until their return.

"There is nothing you can do to help, m'lady," the doctor said firmly. "Besides, your husband will be much calmer knowing you are here and not exposed to all the horrible sights and sounds of the hospital."

Emily was carrying a pitcher of hot water to her mistress as she prepared for bed, and she met the duke for a brief moment in the upper hall. She could hear Greene at the foot of the stairs, so there was no time for anything but a quick kiss and a murmured endearment before she slipped away to Lady Quentin's room.

The next day was long and tiresome for everyone. Lady Quentin tried to keep to her normal routines, but with Tony gone there was nothing for her to do. It was hot and humid and she did not feel like a walk, although she paced up and down the parlor until both Emily and Mr. Greene remonstrated with her. She drank endless cups of tea, but she had no appetite for any of the delicacies that cook prepared, and although she lay down for a nap at Emily's insistence, she did not sleep.

The carriage returned at dusk, the captain supported in the duke's strong arms. He was under sedation, but his color was good and his breathing normal, and Lady Quentin was able to sigh with relief as she bent to kiss him, trying to ignore that empty sleeve.

On the following day, Tony Quentin made a good recovery, and in a week or so he was able to walk a few steps and then come downstairs for his meals. Sometimes, of course, he was in pain and claimed he could still feel his missing arm, and these were the times his temper was short and everyone in the house trembled before his rage. Everyone but Mr. Greene, of course, and he was always the first one summoned when the captain was in one of his moods. Lady Quentin stayed close to his side as well, talking about the future they would share, and so Emily had more free time than she had ever previously enjoyed. She and the duke met often by the brook on sunny afternoons. She disliked the subterfuge, but she knew there was no other way, and so when the duke would announce he was off for a ride, she would fetch her bonnet and go out for her walk. They went off in different directions and never at precisely the same time, and Emily knew that even if she hated the deceit, she would endure it. Nothing would stop her from going to Charles every chance she got, for she did not know how much more time they would have together.

He talked often of the future now, and she neither denied him nor argued about it, not even when he told her she must leave the Quentins' employ as soon as they returned to England,

and go and live in a house he owned in town; nor when he told her of the gowns and jewels he planned to shower on her, and the team and carriage she would have for her own use. There was something that held her tongue, something that seemed to say that it would never come to that, that she would never have to tell him she could not do it nor why it was impossible. Besides, she hesitated to break the spell of this dreamworld they were living in by speaking of a future she knew they could not share.

Now Captain Quentin was able to walk in the yard for short periods of time, and Lady Quentin was making plans to return to Brussels and then home.

"I am sure Tony will be much better when he is on his own land, Nelly, and so we must get him to Burton-Latimer as soon as we can. I have asked the duke to make the arrangements. What a dear, good man he is! I do not know what we would have done without his help."

Emily smiled and agreed, feeling guilty as she hoped the duke would have difficulty arranging their passage too quickly.

She was picking some flowers for the parlor one morning a few days later when a strange horse and rider came up the lane. The duke, who had been leaning out an open window to watch her, saw the young Englishman before she did, and he recognized Lord Andrews. He knew he was a good friend of the Quentins, but he wondered what he was doing here and how he had found them. Then he heard him call in a loud voice, "Emily! Miss Wyndham!"

Puzzled, the duke looked around to see Margaret whirl and drop her flowers and the shears, her hand going to her white face as she swayed for a moment in shock.

"My dear Miss Wyndham! So it *is* you!" Lord Andrews crowed, and then the duke saw Margaret slip to the ground in a faint, and cursing under his breath, he hurried to her aid.

7

The duke was kneeling beside Emily while Lord Andrew was still tying his horse to the gate, and then he picked her up in his arms to carry her into the farmhouse. As he reached the door, the visitor hurried up, his face earnest with his concern.

"I say, your Grace, I had no idea my surprise would cause such a reaction," he said in an uneasy voice. Charles paid no attention to him as he carried his Lorelei into the parlor and laid her down on the sofa. Picking up her hands, he began to chafe them and said without turning around, "There is some wine there on the table. Pour out a glass, m'lord, for she will need it presently."

Her hands felt ice-cold and he wished he could put his arms around her and warm her, cursing the other man under his breath for his presence as he did so. After what seemed an age, her eyelids fluttered and then opened slowly, as if she was reluctant to return to her present situation.

"Charles," she murmured, her hands turning in his so she might hold them tight.

"Here is the wine, your Grace. I say, I'm most awfully sorry, Miss Wyndham! Never thought you'd go off that way, y'know," Lord Andrews said, and Emily closed her eyes for a moment as if to blot him out.

"Drink this, my dear," the duke ordered, helping her to sit up and supporting her with his arm. "Sit down, man, and stay out of the way," he said to the hovering Lord Andrews. "You have done enough harm as it is."

The young peer flushed and did as he was bid, and Emily swallowed a few sips of the wine. Her eyes went to the duke's angry face, and she shook her head a little at him before she sat up straighter as Lady Quentin came in.

"What in the world? . . . Good heavens, Hubert, you here? My word, what is wrong with Nelly?"

The duke could see that Lord Andrews was big with his news and would be delighted to relate it, so before he could speak, Charles said, "Do me the kindness to take Miss Nelson upstairs, Alicia. She fainted in the garden just now, probably from the heat."

Emily stood up and her mistress slid her arm around her. "Poor Nelly! Come away, and I will bathe your forehead until you feel more the thing." Still talking and soothing, she led her maid away and the two men were left facing each other in a pregnant silence. At last the duke's eyebrows rose and he gestured Lord Andrews back to his chair.

"A glass of wine, m'lord?" he asked. "You look as if you could use one before you tell me the reason for this extraordinary intrusion, and what you meant by your words to Miss Nelson."

He poured out two glasses and, after serving the guest, sat down and crossed his legs, the picture of calm and ease. No one could have guessed at the anger that still seethed in his breast, nor his burning desire to hear the whole story.

Lord Andrew sipped his wine and then sat staring at Farmer Bordreau's worn carpet until the duke purred, "Yes? You were about to explain, I believe . . ."

At that, Lord Andrew burst into speech. "It is just that after I saw Alicia's maid in London, your Grace, I could not get her out of my mind, not even after they had gone abroad. You must admit she is a seductive little armful, eh? Such a waste for her to be someone's maid rather than someone's mistress! You *must* agree, for you have seen her yourself."

The duke nodded, although his fingers tightened on the stem of his glass as if he were tempted to throw its contents into Lord Andrews' fatuous face.

"Well, then, m'mother called me home for a reason that has no bearing on our discussion, and while I was there, I happened to take down a book in the library one day that I had never read. It was a book of old poems, and when I opened it, I discovered that someone, most certainly my father, had carved a niche in the pages in order to hide a miniature of a very lovely blonde. I was stunned, for the lady was the image of Alicia's maid—she could almost have been her twin. The same green eyes, the same patrician nose, even the same smile! I vaguely remember hearing that my father had had a most expensive bit o' muslin in his keeping just before his death, and was sure that this had to have been Miss Nelson's mother. Of course, I thought she had probably abandoned the baby; from her portrait she did not seem to be the motherly type—she had posed, you see, er, with only a flimsy scarf.''

Here he chortled, for telling his story had relieved the tension he had felt at the duke's initial reception.

Charles nodded again. "Do go on, m'lord. I find I have a great interest in your story.'

"Well, on the back of the portrait was written the name 'Althea Wyndham.' I kept it by me when I returned to London, and I asked a few of the older gentlemen who might be expected to remember the lady, if they recalled anyone by that name. Do you know, she must have been notorious, for everyone I approached had heard of her career.''

"Her career?'' the duke prompted as Lord Andrews laughed again, another lascivious chuckle.

"Oh, yes, I think you might safely call it that. Mrs. Wyndham was a famous courtesan, and she moved from one member of society to the next almost without pause. I discovered that she was of the *haut ton* herself, the widow of Captain Thomas Wyndham of the Royal Navy, and the sister-in-law of Lord Gregory Wyndham of Berks, an exceptionally well-thought-of family with its good name and impeccable background—before the lady brought such notoriety to it, of course. She and her husband had a child, a little girl they named Emily Margaret, but after her husband died in battle, the lady began her amatory activities. Why, I found out she was even in your father's keeping at one time, your Grace.''

M'lord sipped his wine again and the duke's eyes narrowed as he inclined his head at this information. "My father had a weakness for beautiful women, that is true,'' he murmured. "It would have been most unusual if he and Mrs. Wyndham had not, er, come to an agreement if she was as famous as you say. But do go on, m'lord.''

"There the trail ended. I could not find anyone who knew what happened to either the mother or the daughter. They just disappeared one day and were never seen again. And then I discovered from Tony's sister, Arabella, that the Quentins were staying at a farmhouse near Waterloo, and I knew I could not wait for them to return to England. I *had* to come and claim her. The memory of her was driving me mad, your Grace, and if she is anything like her mother, why is she wasting her time as a maid? The whole thing is incomprehensible. Why did she change her name? Were there no relatives to take her in? And where is her mother now? But let that go. I don't care about her past; I am only concerned with her future." Here he leered before he added, "I am sure I can convince her it would be much more suitable for her to follow in her mother's footsteps, with *me*, of course, as her first protector."

The duke rose and advanced to where Lord Andrews was sitting. As he towered over him, there was that in his manner that caused the other man to lean back in his chair in fear.

"I am desolated to have to deny you the adventure, m'lord. The lady is not available for your purposes," the duke snapped, his black eyes menacing and cold.

"Oh, I see. Like that, is it?" Lord Andrews mourned. "Too bad, too bad. I had no idea you had the prior claim, your Grace."

The duke ignored him. "Furthermore, you are to say nothing to either Tony or Alicia, or indeed to anyone else, about what you have discovered, do you understand? If a single whisper comes to me that you have been indiscreet about Miss Nelson's background or present occupation, it will give me a great deal of pleasure to make sure you never see another dawn. Do I make myself clear?"

The duke leaned over the cowering man and he said quickly, "Of course your Grace! Happy to oblige, 'pon my word! Not a sound from me, word of an Andrews!"

"Very well," the duke said, moving away, to milord's relief. "Now, I think you should pay your respects to the Quentins and perhaps join them for luncheon before you ride back to town. I do not want Miss Nelson to have to see you again."

Lord Andrews was most agreeable, and Greene was summoned to take him up to Tony's room. Charles poured another glass of wine for himself and sat down to consider the story he had just heard. He never doubted the truth of it for a moment, for it all made so much sense. The way she looked and moved, her education, and her manners, all proclaimed a noble background. He did not know why she was here serving as a maid, but he would find out. Now he remembered something that had puzzled him. Whenever he had spoken of her future as his mistress, she had never agreed, not in so many words, nor had she ever alluded to that time herself. It was as if she were content merely to love him in the present time frame, and to have him love her in return the same way. Miss Nelson—or Miss Wyndham, as he believed she was now—obviously did not feel she could consider a future that included being the Duke of Wrotherham's light-o'-love, and now he knew why. He got up to pace the parlor. How silly she was not to have told him her real name.

But then he asked himself why she had let him make love to her. He knew she was not like her mother, for she had been a virgin when he first took her, and even though she showed her delight in their lovemaking and was the most sensuous woman he had ever known, he knew that she was not wanton and that it was not only physical attraction that had brought her into his arms. All those afternoons at the brook had not been spent entirely in passion. They had spoken of many things—books, politics, history—and he had enjoyed following the convolutions of her quick mind as it advanced from one subject to another. It was certainly not what a man usually expected from his mistress, but he had enjoyed every moment of it, even the arguments they had about small points of fact where she would not agree he was right.

Suddenly his eyes brightened and he stood very still. What was there to prevent him from marrying her now? Surely as a Wyndham of Berks she was an acceptable if not outstanding candidate for the role of his duchess, and then he would be able to have her with him always. It would mean happiness he had never imagined he would enjoy as a husband. And someday, he mused, there will be another Emily, my little daughter. I hope she looks just like her mother, he thought, and then he frowned. He had forgotten her mother's reputation. Did the Duke of Wrotherham have enough credit with the *ton* to live it down?

Suddenly he knew it did not matter in the slightest. Now he had the chance to have her always—not as a mistress tucked away in some little love nest awaiting his pleasure, but with him every day they would live. From waking in his arms, sitting across from him at table, entertaining his guests, or entering a ballroom on his arm, to attending a coronation with him, dressed in crimson and ermine, she would be with him, and what a superb Duchess of Wrotherham she would make!

He felt a surge of emotion that almost carried him up the stairs and into Lady Quentin's room, but he controlled himself with an effort. No, he would wait. For Miss Emily Wyndham everything from now on would be done in correct order and with perfect politeness, for only that way could he show her how much he honored her. He would wait until this evening, and then he would ask her to meet him in the tiny garden and he would hear her story from her own lips before he proposed.

Hubert Andrews took his leave shortly after luncheon, much to the captain's disgust. He could not be persuaded to remain overnight, not even when Alicia added her own entreaties, telling him how much good it had done Tony to see one of his old friends. The young peer looked around as if he were nervous when Lady Quentin strolled with him to the gate, but there was no sign of the duke, for he had had his horse saddled and was indulging in a strenuous ride to help pass the time until dark.

In Lady Quentin's bedroom, Emily watched her nemesis depart, standing well back from the window so she would not be seen. She had a very good idea what Lord Andrews had told Charles, although she did not know how the duke had reacted; she had almost expected to be summoned by him to explain. Careful questioning of Greene revealed his absence. For a moment she felt some doubts. Was he angry with her? Was he upset to discover her true identity and her mother's waywardness? She hoped that was not the case. They had had such a little time together, she and Charles, and now perhaps it was over and done with forever. But then she told herself there was no reason why he should not still want her to be his mistress, not now when he knew about her mother's reputation. She knew her own feelings had not changed. She would not let him support her, even though she loved him. There was enough left of Emily Wyndham's character to recoil from such an arrangement, and she had planned to disappear quietly when they returned to London, changing her name again if she had to. She had not been able to resist him that first day at the brook, and now she was glad to have such wonderful memories to store up against the rest of what was sure to be a bleak single life of unremitting toil. But coming to him freely was one thing; allowing him to pay her bills, clothe her and feed her was another. What she gave to him, she gave without asking for return. It was the only way she could have done it at all.

Lady Quentin had told her to rest for the remainder of the day, but Emily could not lie still. For a while she paced the small bedroom, and then she took up a pile of mending to keep her hands busy. It was a very long afternoon.

When she had arranged Lady Quentin's hair and seen her down to the parlor for dinner with her husband, she straightened the room and then prepared to go and have her own supper. As she opened the door, she came face to face with the duke, his hand raised as if he had been about to knock.

"My dear," he said in a quiet voice, "I have only a moment, but I would appreciate it if you would join me in the garden after dinner. Shall we say at about nine? There is a great deal we have to discuss."

Emily stared up into his face. It was serious, but there was a light in his eyes that showed her that he was not angry or upset. She heard Nicole clumping up the stairs to fetch the slops, and nodded her agreement, and the duke went down to join the Quentins.

At nine, she made her way out the back of the farmhouse and around to the garden. The duke was there before her, holding the flowers she had cut that morning, now wilted from the heat and her neglect, but he threw them away at her approach.

Without a word, he took her in his arms and kissed her, and Emily put her arms around him in return, glad that nothing had really changed. They had never dared to meet like this before, but she was not in the least afraid that they would be discovered.

"Sit down beside me on this bench, love," the duke murmured when he raised his lips from hers at last. "I meant to bow to you, like any gentleman greeting a lady, but I could not resist kissing you. And now I think you owe me an explanation, Miss Wyndham. You *are* Miss Wyndham, are you not?"

Emily stared at him, feeling his warm strength, and she

nodded. "Yes, Charles, that is my real name. If you have heard of my family, and especially my mother, you will understand why I had to change it, although Margaret is my middle name, and my mother was a Nelson before her marriage."

"Perhaps I should tell you what Lord Andrews revealed, and then you can fill in the mysterious parts, which are sure to be more interesting to me," the duke said, holding both her hands in his.

Emily sat in silence, her head slightly bowed, as he sketched for her the story he had been told, omitting all references to what Hubert Andrews had in mind for her. When his voice died away, she looked up into his eyes.

"That is all true, Charles. My mother is dead. She died of consumption three years ago. It was only then that I discovered by what means she had supported us all the years I was growing up. I found some letters, you see, the day of her funeral . . ." She paused for a moment and the duke's mouth tightened. How terrible that must have been for her, so young and alone and still in shock. He pressed her hands and she continued, "My mother was almost penniless at her death, and there was nothing left to me but a small cottage. My uncle, Lord Wyndham, had been one of my mother's lovers and his wife knew of it, so there was no help for me there. Indeed, I did not want his help in any case, but I could see there was no way I could survive without some work to do; and since I did not feel I could ever be Emily Wyndham again, the object of gossip and scorn, I decided to change my name and take up my present occupation. I had waited on my mother for several years after she could no longer afford a dresser—it seemed the easiest thing to do."

She paused again, for the duke was frowning now. She did not know he was trying to imagine what that must have been like for a gently raised girl, used to being waited on herself, and although he had no real conception of it, he was sure it must have been difficult for her, and tiring, discouraging, and demeaning as well. And yet she had retained her poise and elegance. He could only guess at the strength it must have taken to remain so lovely and untouched by her ordeal.

"How old were you when your mother died, Mar—Emily?"

"Twenty-two. I was not a child, you see."

He smiled for the first time and raised one of her hands to

his lips to kiss. "Of course not! You were awake on every suit, I am sure."

"Indeed I was not, Charles. I had had a very restricted childhood, with no friends or family, and when I think how naïve and optimistic I was . . . well!" Her green eyes darkened as she remembered the Marquess of Benterfield and the colonel. "If I had known then what I know now, I do not think I could have done it. But now I am used to the work, and Lady Quentin is not a bad mistress—"

"Lady Quentin, kind though she may be, must find another maid," he said, letting go of her hands.

Emily wondered why she felt so much disappointment, when she had expected him to ask her to be his mistress still. If he had any doubts before, now, of course, he must be thinking "like mother, like daughter," she thought drearily, and then she was startled to see him go down on one knee before her.

"Miss Wyndham . . . my bewitching Lorelei . . . I have the honor to ask you to be the next Duchess of Wrotherham, and what is more important, especially to me, my wife. Believe me when I tell you that I will love you and cherish you always."

"Your wife?" she whispered.

"Of course. And that as soon as we can contrive it. Perhaps we should marry here at the embassy in Brussels and return to England as man and wife, unless you have a great fancy for white satin and Westminster Abbey, my love. However, I beg you not to delay, for I do not think I—"

"No, no," she cried, pulling her hands from his and shrinking back on the bench as if she wanted to escape him.

The duke rose to his feet, a bewildered frown on his dark handsome face. "No? What do you mean, *no*? Do you deny you love me?" he asked, his voice demanding.

"Too much to marry you," she said, glad that the pale light from the sliver of new moon made it impossible for him to see the tears in her eyes. "You cannot have thought, Charles. What, the mighty Duke of Wrotherham marry Althea Wyndham's daughter? It is not to be considered. Why, there would be less consternation and gossip if you married Margaret Nelson, lady's maid. I would not bring such shame to you as my only dowry."

The duke had listened to her without interrupting, and now

he took his seat again. His voice was quiet when he spoke, but there was a note of steel in it she had never heard there before.

"Emily Wyndham or Margaret Nelson . . . it does not matter to me which one I wed. I do not care what the world says, nor shall you, for if I cannot have you as my wife, I see there will be no happiness in my future. I admit I thought of you only as my mistress before I learned your true identity, but now that I know your family and your background, there can be no impediment to our marriage, except for foolish pride. Foolish pride, my dear, that I do not intend to indulge in, nor let you do so either."

"Listen to me, Charles! I *will* not marry you. Rather than that, I will even promise to be your mistress, and—"

"So you never intended to fill that role, eh? I thought as much; it was too much out of character. But why did you let me make love to you, then?"

Emily turned away, but the duke reached out and with strong fingers turned her chin so she was forced to stare into his eyes. He saw her tears and steeled his heart against them. "Well?" he asked. "I am waiting for your answer."

"Because I loved you so," she whispered. "I knew I could bear the rest of my life alone only if I could be close to you here. When our idyll ended, I was prepared to try and forget. I knew I could not bring myself to follow in my mother's footsteps, but here at least we were free to love each other without thought of payment or shame."

The duke bent toward her as if to kiss her, and she drew back. "No, Charles! You must believe I mean what I say."

Suddenly he rose to pace the path before her, and she watched him through swimming eyes.

"But you must marry me now, Miss Wyndham," he said suddenly in a harsher, more formal voice. "I do not ruin ladies of your quality. Acquit me, please, of such boorish behavior. No, I was your first lover, and for someone of such exquisite sensibility as you have shown you possess, you must see that our marriage is as good as accomplished. Why, any true gentleman would do the same if he found out he had taken, even unwittingly, a lady of your standing in the world."

"So, it was all right to seduce the maid, but Emily Wyndham is another matter?" she could not help asking.

"Of course. That is the way of the world, my dear,"

he agreed. "Resign yourself to it and to our union as well. You have told me you love me, know that I will always love you. You'll see, it will all work out for the best in the end, after you overcome these foolish scruples of yours. I honor you for them, but I will not let them stand in our way."

Emily bowed her head. "I will promise you only that I will think about it," she said at last, and the duke had to lean forward to catch her soft words.

"Do me the kindness to do so quickly," he said. "For I have promised myself I will not touch you again until we are married. You are not the only one with foolish scruples, my dear. You do understand that you must not cross me in this or try to escape me with some notion of saving me from my folly, do you not? I would never rest until I found you, and there is no place for you to hide that I would not search you out. You *will* be my duchess!"

Emily swallowed as he continued, "How I wish you had consented tonight. I meant to tell the Quentins and perhaps have a small celebration. Instead, I find that you insist on remaining Miss Nelson some little time longer."

"Oh, please do not tell them, promise me, Charles," she begged. "I could not bear it."

"Very well, although it goes against the grain with me to see my future wife engaged in such menial work. I sent Thomas into Brussels today to make all ready, for we will take coach tomorrow afternoon for the capital. Our stay in the country is over. When we are settled in town again, I expect to hear that in this instance you will comply with my wishes."

He waited until she nodded a little, and then he added, "I intend to see about a special license as soon as I reach town. You see, my dear, I cannot wait for you. Dukes are very often imperious and demanding, but you know you have only to command me, save for this, and I will obey you in everything. And now, if I am not to forget myself completely and take you in my arms again to show you how much I love you, I had better take my leave now. So much for vows of celibacy. Sleep well, Lorelei."

He gave her his most elegant bow—as if I were a queen, she thought—and then he went away. Emily remained in the little garden for some time longer. She had not known it was possible to feel great elation and great sorrow, both at the same time. He loves me, she thought, he loves me enough to marry me in spite of whom I am, and her heart leapt even as the little voice in her head replied, "And you love him enough to be sure it will never happen, don't you, dearie?"

When the moon slipped behind a cloud, she went back into the farmhouse, sad but determined on the course she had set for her future.

8

Emily had every intention of confiding in Lady Quentin, for she knew she would need her help, but she found no opportunity of doing so until they were once again in Brussels. First there was the captain's comfort on the journey to see to, and then the packing and the many interruptions of the other servants while they were thus engaged. In the carriage, of course, Captain Quentin sat beside his wife, so she could not speak there.

In Brussels, Emily was glad to have the help of Corporal Deems, who had attached himself to the captain as his new batman, and she was also glad to find that the cook and the maid had returned to the Quentins' rented house as if they had never deserted it at all.

It was late the following morning before she could ask Lady Quentin for a private interview, and by that time her nerves were on edge, for she expected the duke to knock on the door at any moment and demand his answer.

She was bidden to enter the little drawing room with a smile, but it was not much longer before her mistress was frowning in distaste. Emily had not thought she would be so shocked and horrified, even to the point of drawing her skirts away as if Emily were somehow unclean, and she had never felt so ashamed in her life as when she saw Lady Quentin's cold look of disgust for her wanton behavior, even though she had not told her everything about her adventures by any means. It was not like that, her heart cried out silently. It was not dirty and sordid and common! But, of course, she could not say that, and so, only stumbling a little in her tale, she concluded by saying, "You must see, m'lady, I cannot marry him. It would not be at all seemly."

"Oh, no, it is not to be thought of," Lady Quentin agreed, inadvertently stabbing Emily to the quick. "Oh, Nelly, er, I mean, Miss Wyndham, how could you be so . . . so *lewd*? And to think I never guessed that you and the duke . . . Oh, dear!"

"Please continue to call me Nelly, m'lady," Emily said, swallowing hard and trying to keep the tears from falling down her flushed cheeks. "There is no Miss Wyndham anymore. But how can I convince the duke of that? You must see I have to leave here and escape him as soon as possible."

"And I will help you, and so shall Tony. No matter how you have behaved, I cannot bring myself to abandon you when you have been so good to me, and so kind. But even if you did not wish to escape the duke, you do see that it would be impossible for me to keep you in my service. I am sorry that you must leave this way, but your immoral conduct gives me no other choice."

"I understand, thank you, m'lady," Emily murmured, lowering her eyes, her face now ashen. "But what shall I do? The duke has told me he will not take no for an answer."

Lady Quentin knit her brows in thought. "First of all, you will need some money, but that is no problem, for the duke would not let me pay any expenses at Waterloo, so I have a large sum by me. Then you must have a passport and arrangements made for your passage home. We must think of another name for you as well, so I can write you a letter of reference. How else will you be able to get another position? And I am sure you have learned your lesson, Nelly, and you will not be so abandoned again, so I need not fear I am recommending a wanton. You are, after all, an excellent lady's maid. But more of that later. You and I will go out and get the passport, and I hope that horrid man at the War Office will be more accommodating now that our troops were victorious at Waterloo. I will send Corporal Deems to secure you a place on the next barge and arrange your passage to England as well. What a shame you have that distinctive blond hair. It is the first thing the duke will ask about, and even with a different name you are much too lovely to travel unremarked."

"Perhaps I could wear a wig, m'lady?" Emily asked.

"The very thing! Do you fancy being a redhead or a

dashing brunette, Nelly? Oh, this would be just like a novel if it weren't all so sordid and so sad,'' Lady Quentin mourned. ''First I had to lose Daffy, and now you as well. But while you fetch my bonnet, I will just tell Tony we are going out. Make haste! I shall never be able to dissemble if the duke arrives and finds me here alone.''

By evening it was all accomplished, and after a strained farewell, the handsome brunette who was now Mrs. Regina Wiggins was happy to be on her way to Antwerp by barge. Lady Quentin had chosen the name herself, and Emily had not dared protest that she would really rather not go through life as a Mrs. Wiggins, for Lady Quentin, for all her disgust, had been so helpful.

When the Duke of Wrotherham knocked on the Quentins' front door the next morning to beg for a few moments of Miss Nelson's time, he was ushered into the drawing room and left to pace up and down in his impatience.

Everything had taken much longer than he had thought it would. First, he had to move his household back to Brussels and see that the Quentins were settled before he could go about the business of the special license and all that that entailed at the embassy. The ambassador had been skeptical, but since the duke had secured the Duke of Wellington's promise to attend his wedding, his misgivings were soon overcome. Wellington was your true English hero, the idol of the moment, and if he was to attend the service, then surely it must meet with everyone's approval.

Since it had been more than Saint Allyn could bear, to see his love waiting on Lady Quentin and fetching and carrying for her, he had not returned to the Quentins' house until this morning when all was in train and he had every intention of removing her from her menial work at once.

Now he heard a sound at the drawing-room door and turned with a smile only to see Tony Quentin there, his face stern and pale. The duke frowned, aware that his plans had miscarried.

''She is not here?'' he asked. ''Then she told you, after all?''

''Sit down, your Grace,'' Tony said, motioning him to a chair. ''You know I cannot sit in your presence, and I am not well this morning.''

The duke took the seat he indicated, and refused a glass of wine.

"Miss Nelson is not here, that is true. She has left our employ," the captain said at last. "She told Alicia why she must go, and may I say, both my wife and I respect her for her honesty. I do not know why you wanted to force her into this unsuitable marriage; indeed, I am sure the girl must have been imagining your intent, but even if you did mean to marry her, she has certainly chosen the nobler, saner way."

"Nobler! Saner!" the duke raged. "Allow me to know what is best in this instance, if you please, Tony." His tone was icy as he added, "I never thought to see *you* serve me such a turn."

The captain had paled a little. "It went against the grain, believe me, Charles, but I saw what had to be done. The girl was almost frantic in her desire to escape you. What could I do but help? Besides, it is just as well for you that I am so badly wounded, for I would feel honor-bound to call you out for such dastardly behavior as you have shown. Seducing a young maid in my employ, dallying with her with the intention of making her your mistress. At least by offering for her when you discovered her real name, you behaved as a gentleman."

The duke's face was white with rage, for he was seldom treated to a lecture on his behavior, and he found it hard to bear with any degree of equanimity. Then Tony continued, "But the girl does not want you, so there is no more to be said, and you may count yourself lucky to have had such a narrow escape."

The duke had buried his head in his hands, but now he looked up, and Captain Quentin was surprised to see the anguish on his face.

"A narrow escape, was it? I *love* her, you fool! I shall always love her. And she loves me as well. Why else do you think someone so fine as Emily would give herself to me? I did not rape her, you know; she came to me willingly. No, what you have done is just to delay the inevitable, for I shall find Miss Wyndham, and when I do, I shall marry her out of hand. I wish you and Alicia had not meddled, Tony. Emily may have said she did not want to marry me, but she was lying, and I have no intention of letting her ruin both our lives simply because of what society may say."

He got up and stood over the captain, and his voice was quieter as he added, "She will be my duchess, make no mistake about that. I have seen how happy you are in your marriage—mine will be just as happy. I tell you this, if I cannot marry Emily Wyndham, I shall never marry at all." He paused for a moment and then he said, "But I suppose, even with these assurances, you will not tell me where she has gone, or when she left, or even give me a clue as to how I might find her?"

"I cannot, Charles. She has my promise. No, if what you say is true, I am sorry, but not being aware of your real feelings, what should I be apt to think except that you were merely amusing yourself?"

Tony watched the duke stride up and down the room in his agitation and wished the girl had not thought to wring that particular promise from them both. Then he said, trying to help now, "But consider this, your Grace. You might not be able to find her, but she can always find you. Don't you think she might reconsider after she has been away from you a little while?"

A wry smile twisted the duke's mouth. "You do not know the lady very well, Tony. She has shown me how stubborn she can be and how determined on her noble course. No, it is up to me, but I will find her, never fear. I promised her that, if she tried to run away. And now you must excuse me so I can begin my search. May I wish you a speedy recovery from your wounds? Be sure to give my best wishes to Alicia, and ask her to forgive me if she can. I shall not see either of you for a while, but if it would not displease you, someday I shall bring the duchess to visit you in England."

The two men shook hands, a little stiffly on both sides, and parted company, and the duke rode home to the seclusion of his library. A short time later, he called his groom and gave him instructions to search every inn and rooming house for Miss Nelson. Thomas was amazed at his orders, but being well trained, he did not show his surprise as he went out to begin his inquiries at once.

The duke went to the canal himself to ask about the people who had taken passage on the barges within the last two days. When he questioned the shipping agent, the man was stunned, for although the gentleman gave him an excellent description of the lady's age, height, and demeanor, he could not remember the color of her hair, nor, more importantly, her name. Unfortunately for the duke, only one of the three unaccompanied females who had traveled on the barges the past week could be discarded as unsuitable, for she had been carrying a baby and had another child toddling at her skirts. That left a Mrs. Regina Wiggins and a Miss Mary Berkley. The duke nodded, distributed largesse with an easy air for this intelligence, and returned home, pleased with the start he had made.

Thomas did not report until the following afternoon, too late for the duke to travel that day. There was no sign of Miss Nelson anywhere in Brussels, not even under another name or with her hair disguised. The duke sent him running to secure places for them on the morning barge to Antwerp, and then he summoned his valet.

"Pack me only such necessities as I shall need for a few days, Greene, and then you will close the house here, dismiss the foreign servants, and return home with the rest of the staff and my belongings. Thomas goes with me."

"Very good, your Grace," Greene said, completely unperturbed as he accepted the large roll of bills the duke handed him for expenses. "May I ask the nature of the clothes you will require? Shall you be going directly to town or traveling about the countryside?"

The duke shook his head. "I have no idea where I will be. You are to go to Wrotherham House in Park Lane and await me there. My quest may take a week—a month—I have no idea."

Greene bowed as if he received orders of this nature every day of the week and retired. Via Thomas, the duke's involvement with the lovely Miss Nelson had become well known throughout the servants' quarters, and although Greene could sympathize with the duke's infatuation, he could not help but hope that his master would be unsuccessful in his search. He considered the duke's marriage to be long overdue, and dallying with a lady's maid, no matter how beautiful, could only postpone that inevitable event.

The duke did not bother to inquire for Emily at Antwerp, for he was sure she had sailed for home as quickly as she could. Accordingly, he arrived at the coast and took ship without delay. He spent the Channel crossing on deck, his dark eyes intent and impatient as he watched the shores of

England slowly loom ever larger before him. Which lady should he pursue first, Miss Berkley or Mrs. Wiggins? He was inclined to favor the former, merely because she had much the more attractive name. To imagine his Lorelei as Mrs. Wiggins was offensive to him, but he knew that was not rational thinking. Emily was intelligent; might she not have chosen a common, homely name as a means to confuse him? He ended up tossing a coin, and when it landed at his feet, he was pleased nevertheless to see that it had come up "tails, Miss Berkley," and considered it a good omen for his success.

The lady had made no secret of either her presence or her activities. At one of the smaller inns the duke learned that she had remained there only overnight before taking the stage to London. The innkeeper was most accommodating, agreeing that indeed the lady had been young and pretty, with large blue eyes and brown hair. Upon the duke's sudden frown and barked query, he was quick to admit that of course the lady's eyes had been green. What was he thinking of? A very pure and glowing green, your Grace, he assured his impatient questioner. The duke paid him well for his confidences and strode away. While Thomas was hiring them suitable mounts, he also inquired for the other woman, not quite trusting the innkeeper's memory, or the ease with which he was tracking Miss Berkley, but he was disappointed. Mrs. Wiggins had disappeared without a trace. The duke shrugged. He had never favored Mrs. Wiggins anyway, and was sure that, as Miss Berkley, Emily would make for London. Probably she had it in mind to take another position as soon as she could. His lips tightened with anger and concern. To think she might be in need! Did she have enough money? Had the Quentins' kindness extended that far? He was brusque with Thomas when the groom arrived back at The Ship Inn with two horses, and spoke very little as they rode to town.

It was late afternoon and the shadows were already lenghtening in the streets when the duke arrived at Wrotherham House in Park Lane, and so he was forced to delay his search until the morrow. He told himself it was just as well, for then, refreshed by a night's rest, he would be ready to find his lady and deal with her as he had promised.

He was taciturn with his butler and housekeeper, but since Thomas had been quick to put the other servants into the picture, none of these worthies were at all upset by the duke's frowns and absentmindedness, and were not surprised that he did not go out to one of his clubs, but remained in the library after his excellent dinner with only a bottle of port and his thoughts to keep him company.

After he filled his glass for the last time, he raised it in a toast. "To you, Miss Wyndham-Nelson-Berkley! You have changed your name many times; I shall see to it that you change it once more, and for the last time. I drink to her Grace, Emily Margaret Saint Allyn, Duchess of Wrotherham."

He went up to bed in a happier frame of mind than he had enjoyed for some days, but it was not long before his spirits sank again into depression, for only two days later he had the felicity to meet Miss Mary Berkley and discover that not only was she not Emily Wyndham, she did indeed have blue eyes, a common voice, and was not averse to flirting with him in the little house where she was at present residing and which was owned by a peer not unknown to the duke. He took his leave of her abruptly, much to her dismay, for she had been dreaming of exchanging her present protector, who had sent her home ahead of him from Belgium, for a nobler, more wealthy paramour.

The duke forgot her immediately and began to inquire at the various employment agencies. It was the only thing he could think of to do since he knew there was no sense in trying to retrace his steps to Dover and search for Mrs. Wiggins after all this time. Where *was* she? Where had she gone?

Emily had taken ship for England with more than a little trepidation, but the sea that day was not rough, and she was so glad to escape Belgium undetected that she did not succumb to the seasickness that had afflicted her on the outgoing journey. Like the duke, she had remained on deck wrapped in her cloak, but unlike him she gazed astern at the land where she was leaving the man she would love forever.

As she stared at the wake of the ship, bubbling so cheerfully below her, her thoughts were sad and chaotic. Lady Quentin's reaction and revulsion had upset her very much, forcing her to realize that in the eyes of the world, there had been no beautiful idyll, no love so pure and precious that she had been unable to deny it. Lady Quentin made her feel soiled and cheap, no better than her mother. She writhed a little remembering, but then she felt a spurt of anger. It was all so unjust! When she was a lady's maid, she was only good enough to be the duke's mistress and, as such, an object of scorn and derision to the good women of the world. But when she became the niece of Lord Gregory Wyndham and the daughter of the late Captain Thomas Wyndham of the Royal Navy, why, then, as a member of society, her behavior in taking the duke as her lover was even worse! Yet was she not still the same person? How unfair the strictures of society were! And here was the duke, determined now to marry her because his lovemaking had led to her downfall. She recalled how formal he had been when he asked for her hand, his stern control and measured words. Perhaps he felt trapped and betrayed, and although he had made the offer he did not really want to marry her? Well, then, she had done the right thing in running away from him and he would not bother to follow her, now his honor had been appeased.

She knew that dukes were not as free as other men, and that even a mere baronet would hesitate to align himself with her, because of her occupation and her mother's reputation.

It may be the nineteenth century, she thought, her green eyes growing dark with her anger, but single women are as confined as they were in 1700! Only men were allowed the freedom to take any number of mistresses both before and after marriage. She knew too that wives had more license as well. She had heard the gossip about a certain Lady X, who, after presenting her titled husband with his firstborn son, had foisted several other children on him over the years, none of whom he could be sure were his. Even Lady Quentin had giggled over the juicy *on-dit* last year when Lady X, finding herself pregnant once more, made a hurried trip to Vienna, where her husband had been for some months, to observe the proprieties. What hypocrites members of society were! Strict morality, it seemed, applied only to virgins, and what grand ladies could do had no bearing on Miss Wyndham's behavior.

Ideally, she should have been accompanied by a footman or maid at all times, and shielded from unchaperoned contact with any male not directly related to her, until her hand were given in marriage. She was certainly not supposed to fall in love, and if she was so foolish as to do so, she was never to succumb to her emotions and let the gentleman make love to her until she wore his wedding band. She had flaunted all the rules, spoken and unspoken, from the very beginning, and now there was nothing left for her but loneliness and continued exile from the ranks of the *ton*.

She shook her head sadly. She was no Lady Hamilton, able to cuckold an elderly husband and gain at least token acceptance because her lover was a national hero. There was no Lord Admiral Nelson for her, even though she was much better born than Lady Hamilton, who had been nothing but a little demimonde from a working-class background before Lord Hamilton married her and brought her into society's ranks. Together the Hamiltons had lived openly with Nelson both in Naples and here in England, and she had created a scandal when she caused him to abandon his wife and had even borne him a child. Emily had seen some of the coarse cartoons about the lady that the print shops distributed to amuse society at that time. But now Nelson had been dead ten years and the *ton* was paying Lady Hamilton back for her temerity. She was not so much reviled as she was ignored, contrary to all Nelson's dying wishes that England treat her kindly for his sake. Society always extracted payment from those who flaunted its conventions. What heavy penalty would the duke have to pay if he married her? Emily raised her chin, her eyes bleak, as she vowed that day would never come.

By the time she was again installed at Bradley's Hotel, she began to feel a little safer, although she did not dare to remove the heavy, uncomfortable brunette wig Lady Quentin had bought for her. She knew she had to find a position quickly, not because her money was low, but because the longer she continued to be abroad on the streets, the greater the chance the duke would have for finding her. She did not know when he would be in London again, but felt surely she had at least a few days' grace before that time. She had traveled to Canterbury from Dover instead of taking the stage directly to town, hoping to throw Charles off the scent and never dreaming he was pursuing quite another lady and her precautions were unnecessary. She could not return to the Free Registry for the Placement of Faithful Servants, for it was possible that Mrs. Bromson would still be there to remember her, and her letter of reference spoke only of a Mrs. Wiggins, lady's maid. Emily resigned herself to the name. What difference did it make after all what she was called now?

She was not any more successful in her search for employment than she had been the first time she was in London, for it was now July and a hot, humid summer. Most of society had retired to their estates, those who did not rent a house at one of the more fashionable spas, and Emily was beginning to feel a little desperate after several days passed and she had trudged from one agency to another, finding nothing that was suitable.

Finally, at Mrs. Finches' agency, she was told to return the following day when there might be the chance of an interview, and she was climbing the dusty stairs with a glimmer of hope in her heart at last, when the door of the agency opened and a familiar voice spoke harshly above her.

"Thank you! If the lady you have just described returns here, I shall certainly reward you for your trouble if you send me word at once and keep her here until I come. You have my direction."

Emily stood frozen for a moment, her heart pounding, but then she turned and fled down the stairs and out into the street. She saw Thomas holding the duke's team, but fortunately he was deep in conversation with another groom, and so she was able to escape around the corner before the tall, lean figure of the duke appeared. She watched him leap up into his curricle and drive away, and then she leaned against the palings, trying to control her breathing, and oblivious to the stares of the passersby. What a narrow escape! If he had not spoken when he did, she would have walked right into him. She saw a man leering at her and beginning to approach, and she hurried away, taking the back streets and alleys until she reached the safety of her hotel.

She spent the rest of the day in her room, pacing up and down and thinking hard. London was not a safe haven any longer, and although she felt a kind of glad triumph that the duke had not given her up and was still trying to find her, she knew she had to leave immediately. But where could she go? Perhaps it would be best to travel to some factory town where she would never see anyone but cits, but if she did that, how was she to support herself? Her money would not last forever. Emily ran her hands through her hair in distraction. She was only trained as a lady's maid, therefore she had to go somewhere the *haut ton* assembled and trust to luck that she could evade the duke.

As she went down for her supper, she passed a middle-aged couple on the stairs. The lady was complaining that they had to return to the heat and dirt of town when the sea air and breezes of Brighton had been so delightfully refreshing. Taking the conversation as a good omen, Emily made arrangements with the porter to take the first Brighton stage in the morning, and retired to her room as soon as she had eaten, to pack her bags. Brighton, Bath, Worthington, Tunbridge Wells—what did it matter where she went as long as she was out of the duke's immediate vicinity?

She went to bed remembering his deep voice at the employment agency, that voice that never again would roughen with passion as he made love to her, or soften in contentment when she came laughing into his arms, and she shed a few tears before she slept.

When she reached Brighton the following afternoon, she was quick to ask the innkeeper for the address of the best employment agency, and she made her way there early the next morning, not even stopping to stare at the Royal Pavillion.

Mrs. Huddlewick, the owner of the agency, shook her head sadly when Emily explained why she was there.

"I am so sorry, Mrs. Wiggins," she said, and Emily's heart sank. "There's nothing like what you require. Now, if you were a parlormaid or a footman, I could place you in a minute, but there's no call for lady's maids this season. Brought their own with 'em from town, I have no doubt."

Emily thanked her for her time and said she would inquire again, and gave her the name of the inn where she was putting up before she took her leave. If there was nothing in Brighton, she would have to travel farther, she decided, but she would stay here for a few days in case an opening occurred.

As she strolled back to the inn, she took the time to look about her, and wished she might remain here. The salty tang of the air was refreshing and it was nowhere near as hot as London had been. She paused to admire a white straw bonnet covered with tiny pink rosebuds and moss-green netting in the window of a milliner's shop and became aware of a commotion behind her. As she turned to see what the matter was, she heard people shouting, and then she saw them running to escape. For herself, she seemed unable to move when she saw a large horse bearing down on her. There was an elderly lady on the perch of the old-fashioned carriage the horse was pulling, and her bonnet was askew with her efforts to bring him under control. Too late, Emily made a dive to one side, but she was not quick enough and one of the horse's hooves struck her a glancing blow on the head, and she slipped unconscious to the cobblestones and knew no more.

"Oh, dearie me!" the elderly lady exclaimed as a groom ran up and grabbed the bridle of her horse, turning it aside before it could kick Emily again or smash the milliner's window. He backed it into the street, and the lady driver was quick to get down and go to the small, huddled figure of Emily, lying there so still. A crowd was beginning to gather, and the lady pushed her way through, using the point of a large black umbrella to gain her passage.

"Stand back! You there, oh, my, do not crowd the poor dear, she needs air."

At her refined though nervous accents, two gentlemen, the milliner's assistant, and a small urchin obeyed her without question. The lady, who appeared spry for her age, knelt beside Emily and began to chafe her hands.

"Hortense! What is the meaning of this? What *are* you doing?" a querulous voice demanded, and the old lady looked up in relief.

"I am trying to restore this lady to consciousness, Horatia, as you can see. Oh, dear, the accident was quite all my fault, but when Pegasus bolted, I could not hold him . . ."

"Pegasus? *Bolted?*" the other lady asked, turning to stare at the horse in some surprise. The others followed her gaze to where the horse was now tied to a post. He was a very elderly, placid animal. "A likely story! Hmmph! Pegasus has never bolted in his life. I knew I shouldn't have let you take charge of him, for a sillier widgeon I have never seen. Get away from there and let *me* see to the woman."

"Oh, Horatia, I am so afraid she is dead," Hortense moaned, obediently moving so her sister could kneel beside her.

"Nonsense! She has lost consciousness, that is all. But we must get help. You there," she snapped to the urchin, not even looking in his direction, "run ahead to Doctor Spears and tell him what happened. Now, you two . . . lift her carefully into the carriage. And as for you, gel," she said in an acid tone to the milliner's assistant, who was exclaiming and sobbing and wringing her hands, "I don't know what you're carrying on so for. The horse didn't touch *you*. Be off with you, this isn't a raree show!"

"Coo-er," the girl said, her mouth open in amazement, but she was quick to withdraw into the shop again.

The gentlemen deposited Emily in the back of the carriage, and the first lady got in to support her as best she could in her arms, while her domineering sister collected her umbrella, Emily's reticule, and her own packages before she climbed into the driver's seat and took up the reins, nodding to the groom to untie the horse. He did not hesitate, for Pegasus was quiet now to the point of somnolence, and indeed it took Miss Horatia several minutes of determined cluckings and rein slappings across his broad back to stir him into his customary slow shuffle.

"I shall never understand what made him bolt," she muttered over her shoulder. "He never moves above a walk and hasn't for years. Hmmph!"

"I think it was one of those naughty, er, children, Sister," Hortense ventured from the backseat, the bouncing of the carriage tipping her bonnet farther over one eye. "I saw them whispering after you refused to give them a penny to hold the horse when you went into the draper's shop."

"Hmmph. Very likely, nasty little monsters," her sister replied, pulling a willing Pegasus to a halt at the door of the doctor's office. "I knew we should have sent Agnes to do the errands instead of coming into town ourselves. Just see what has happened because we put ourselves in close proximity to *them*."

The two sisters waited together while Doctor Spears examined the young woman. Hortense sat very still, her hands clasped and her eyes closed in prayer, but Miss Horatia used the time to examine Emily's purse. "She is a Mrs. Wiggins, a Mrs. Regina Wiggins, Sister," she announced in her curt voice after she had read Emily's letter of reference. "A lady's maid, I gather. Funny, she does not look like her name is Wiggins, or as if she is in service. I would have taken her for a lady herself."

"A-men," her sister whispered, opening her faded-blue eyes very wide. "Oh, dear, do you think you should go through her reticule? So . . . so unethical!"

"How else can we find out who she is, or her direction?"

Horatia demanded, fixing an equally faded but sharper eye on her sister.

The two were very much alike, although Miss Hortense favored a hairdo of graying sausage curls, a style that had been popular thirty years before. Her sister, although as tall and thin and with the same gray hair, wore it pulled back in a ruthless, tight bun. On her spare, black-clad bosom hung a pince-nez, which she had used to read Emily's letter, and now she raised it again as she investigated the rest of the contents of the reticule, ignoring her sister's distressed murmurs of protest.

"Hmmmph! How very singular," Horatia said at last. "Now if she is indeed Mrs. Wiggins, Hortense, why does she also carry three letters concerning a Miss Margaret Nelson, tell me that?" She bent her sharp eyes on her sister's face as if she fully expected the lady to come up with a plausible explanation, although it was plainly not in her power to do so.

Just then the doctor entered the waiting room, and Miss Horatia turned her back on him, leaving a flustered Miss Hortense to question him about the patient. Doctor Spears had known the Rutherford sisters for a good many years, and so he was not in the least offended by Miss Horatia's rudeness or the sight of her rigid back.

"She is still unconscious, but I do not think there has been any permanent damage. Fortunately she was wearing a heavy wig that cushioned the blow somewhat," he said, patting Miss Hortense's hands and smiling kindly at her.

"Thank heaven for that," Miss Hortense cried, feeling her prayers had been answered.

"Ask him what treatment he prescribes," Horatia ordered her. The doctor waited courteously until Miss Hortense had relayed the message he had just heard so plainly before he recommended complete quiet and bed rest in a darkened room. "She is apt to have the headache when she comes to herself," he added. "I should like to see her again to be sure there is no danger of concussion. Head injuries are not to be taken lightly. Can you give me her direction? I take it she is a friend of yours."

"Oh, dear me, no," Miss Hortense explained. "We have never seen her before in our lives, Doctor, but it was our horse who kicked her in the head in the first place. What should we do? We do not know where she lives, or . . . or anything about her, but—"

"Nonsense, Hortense," Horatia interrupted. "At least we know she is not what she seems to be, at all accounts. However, since it was your fault and Pegasus' that she was injured, and since I can find no address for her in Brighton in her reticule, I suppose as Christians we must take her home to the hall to recover."

"Oh, thank you, Horatia," Miss Hortense whispered. "I did not like to suggest it, but I do feel it would be the kindest thing, and—"

"I hope I know my duty, Sister, as well as you do. Ask the doctor to carry the girl to the carriage. I will wait outside."

She moved abruptly to the door and slammed it behind her, and the doctor twinkled at the look of confused distress on Miss Hortense Rutherford's face.

"No need to explain, dear lady," he said. "I quite understand. I shall come out tomorrow to see the patient. Shall we say about ten?"

Miss Hortense agreed to the visit and once again climbed into the back of the carriage to hold Emily safe for the journey home.

Rutherford Hall was some six miles from Brighton, and since Pegasus did not feel the slightest urge to hurry, it was some time later before the carriage turned into the gates and made its way slowly up the weed-choked drive. The two sisters had spent the trip speculating about Emily, and now Miss Horatia said as she climbed down from the perch, "We will have to wait until she wakes before we find out any more, Sister. Now we must get her to bed." She turned and called in a loud voice, "Agnes! Bessie! Gertrude, come at once!"

The door to the hall opened and three elderly maids came down the steps, exclaiming at the unexpected guest and asking a dozen questions all at once.

"Yes, yes, later we will explain everything," Miss Horatia Rutherford said. "Agnes and Bessie, you will help me carry her into the house. We will put her in the blue bedroom. Gertrude, you and Hortense run ahead and put clean sheets on the bed immediately."

Still Emily had not moved or opened her eyes, and perhaps that was just as well, for with Agnes and Bessie each supporting her under an arm, and Miss Rutherford taking her feet, she had an awkward journey. The women were not able to avoid bumping her arm on the door jamb or knocking her foot against the newel post as they started slowly up the stairs.

Miss Hortense spared a glance back over the railings as she hurried to the blue bedroom, and not for the first time wished for the assistance of a pair of tall, strong footmen, but she was careful to keep this thought to herself.

9

Four days later, Emily had still not regained consciousness, and Doctor Spears, who drove out every day, was beginning to become alarmed, although he hid this from the dithery Miss Hortense as best he could. He would like to have discussed the case with her more sensible older sister, but Miss Horatia was never present for his visits, and he knew he had not the least expectation of seeing her. Now, as he gazed down at the still, white face of his patient, he frowned, and Miss Hortense shook her head sadly, her gray sausage curls bobbing in her distress.

"Dear Doctor Spears," she whispered, as if a normal voice would disturb the sleeping girl, "what are we to do? I am so afraid that Pegasus has killed her, after all." She sobbed and raised her handkerchief to her face, and the doctor took her hand in his to comfort her.

"I must admit I expected her to rouse long before this, but even so, there is no immediate danger that I can see. There is so little we know about head injuries; perhaps this long spell of unconsciousness is nature's way of healing. Let us hope so. You will continue to administer the drops and give her as much water as you can get her to swallow. I know it takes a long time, but it is most important."

"That does not matter, Doctor, indeed it does not," Miss Hortense said as he picked up his bag and started for the door. "My sister and I will naturally do all we can for the poor girl. Oh, I almost forgot," she added as she escorted the doctor down the stairs. "Have there been any inquiries for her in Brighton? We would be so much more comfortable if we knew who her family is. That is almost the worst thing of all, knowing that somewhere someone is worrying about her, in an agony for not knowing what has become of her. Oh, dear!"

The doctor shook his head. "No, no one has inquired. It is very strange. Surely there must be some kin, a servant even . . . most strange!" He shook his head again and then remarked as he took his hat and cane from one of the maids, "Be sure to send for me immediately she wakens, Miss Hortense. I will come at once."

Hortense saw him out and then went back to the sickroom to find her sister sitting beside the bed. She did not explain what the doctor had said, for she knew Horatia had been hiding in the adjoining dressing room during his visit, listening carefully. Now she rose, and Miss Hortense took her place beside Emily.

"I shall be back at noon, Sister," Horatia said in her curt voice. "I do hope it will not be much longer before the girl comes to herself, for then we can dispense with all these visits. It is not at all what I like. Hmmmph!"

She whisked herself from the room, and her sister picked up one of Emily's limp hands and patted it gently. Even if she is unconscious, the old lady thought to herself, perhaps she will know that she is not alone, that someone cares about her and waits with her.

It was late that same afternoon when Emily slowly opened her eyes. There was a dull throbbing at her temple, and she raised her hand to her head, staring about her in wonder at the quiet, dim room. It hurt to move her head, so she lay still, wondering a little where she was.

"Oh, my dear, at last," she heard a breathless voice exclaim. "What lovely eyes you have, so unusual. But don't move, I must tell Horatia at once and send one of the maids for the doctor. Mind now, you must not move."

Emily watched the tall old lady bustle to the door and smiled. She felt so weak she did not think she could flex a single muscle, and yet the lady seemed to feel she was about to leap from the bed and disappear before she could return. She closed her eyes again and stayed very still until she heard footsteps coming back into the room. "You are silly, Sister," a harsh voice exclaimed. "You say she woke? She looks remarkably unconscious to me. Are you sure you are not just making it up?"

"Of course not, Horatia, she was awake. I saw her eyes, a lovely shade of green. Oh, my dear, have you left us again?"

Emily opened her eyes then and tried to smile. "The Lord be praised," Miss Hortense said, bending over her. "Now, you must not worry, my dear. The doctor will be here soon."

"But . . . but what happened? Why does my head hurt?" Emily whispered. "I do not understand . . ." Her voice, coming from a dry throat, seemed stiff and rusty to her ears.

"You were in an accident, young lady," Miss Horatia told her as she poured out a glass of water.

"We have been so worried about you," the other lady added. "But we will tell you everything that happened, I promise."

"No more talking now, it will tire you," Miss Horatia said, helping her to sit up a little so she could drink the cool water. As grateful as she was, Emily was glad to lie down again, for her head was swimming. "Now you must rest until the doctor comes," Miss Hortense added.

Emily closed her eyes obediently, for she felt very weak and shaky and so she did not see the two old ladies tiptoe to the door. As they went out, Emily frowned. It was all so confusing. There was no sound in the room but the soft ticking of the clock on the mantel, and comforted a little by the homey, familiar sound, she dropped off to sleep.

She slept until the doctor came an hour later, and she woke feeling stronger when she felt his hand on her pulse.

"Welcome back," he said with a comfortable smile. "You were beginning to worry us, young lady."

Again, Emily's hand went to her head. There was a swelling there, tender to the touch, and she winced as the doctor gently probed the spot. "It was much larger four days ago," he reassured her, and then he asked, "You have the headache, do you not? How else do you feel?"

Haltingly, Emily told him of her weakness, but assured him that she did not hurt anywhere except for the bump on her head.

The doctor nodded and patted her hand. "That is to be expected. You must remain in bed until you are stronger, but I expect some nourishing food will soon take care of that. When you do get up, I do not want you to rush into too much activity at once. I will leave you some powders to ease the pain and help you to sleep."

He moved away to his bag that was set on a table near the bed, and Emily stared at her nurse. "But where am I?" she asked.

"You are at Rutherford Hall, my dear, and I am Miss Hortense Rutherford," the lady replied, bobbing her curls and smiling. "I live here with my sister, Miss Horatia. Do you remember seeing her before?"

"Yes," Emily said. "But . . . but where is Rutherford Hall?"

"It is some six miles from Brighton, where the accident happened. I was never more shocked in my life when Pegasus ran you down. Dear, dear! I would never have forgiven myself if you had been hurt seriously, although it was all the fault of those nasty bo—*children*."

Emily closed her eyes again. Rutherford Hall . . . Brighton . . . Pegasus? Nothing made any sense to her.

"Now, dearie," Miss Hortense said, taking her hand and patting it gently, "you must tell us your name so we can notify your family. We have been so concerned, for we know how they must be worrying about you."

Emily opened her mouth to answer, and then shut it as her eyebrows came back together in a frown. "I . . . I don't know who I am. My mind is completely blank."

While Miss Hortense clucked, Doctor Spears came quickly back to the bedside and stared down at her. "I had not foreseen this, but of course with a head injury it is entirely possible. But you are not to worry about your loss of memory, young lady, for it may reappear at any time. Just concentrate on getting well and do not be racking your brains for your identity. It will come back in its own good time. I will return in a few days to see how you are getting along."

Emily swallowed and nodded a little, as Miss Hortense, her blue eyes wide with shock at what she had just heard, went to the door with the doctor.

As soon as they left the room, Miss Horatia came around the screen set at the dressing-room door. Emily was staring straight up at the canopy of the four-poster bed, frowning a little, as if she expected to see her name written in its soft pleats.

"Now, none of that," Miss Horatia commanded, straightening the bedcovers and raising her patient to plump the pillows. "You heard the orders!"

"I know," Emily agreed. "But it is frightening not to know who you are, Miss Rutherford. Oh, what can my name be?"

"From what we can discover, you may have a choice," the elder lady said dryly, but at Emily's bewildered look she took pity on the girl and would say no more. "When you are stronger. Do not worry, there is plenty of time."

Emily drifted off to sleep again and Miss Horatia stalked over to the window to stare with unseeing eyes into the unkempt garden below. "Yes, do not worry, we will keep you safe, my girl," she whispered. "And yet, why do I have the strongest feeling that you are neither Regina Wiggins nor Margaret Nelson?" She closed her eyes for a moment and then shook herself as she added, "I am sure of it! As sure as I am that all your troubles are the doing of one or more of *them.* Hmmph!"

Physically, Emily regained her strength rapidly now that she was able to sit up and eat the good food that the maids brought her so regularly. She had made the acquaintance of them all, but besides wondering why the Rutherfords kept such elderly servants, she did not ask any questions. In a few days, she was able to take a few steps around the room, supported on either side, and she was glad she did not have to call for a bedpan anymore for her needs. She felt she was enough trouble as it was.

The Misses Rutherford were often with her, and although Miss Horatia was kind in her abrupt way, Emily much preferred her dithery sister. No one was allowed to mention her loss of memory, or ask her if it was coming back by orders of Miss Rutherford, but every morning Miss Hortense would bustle into the room in her dressing gown, the papers she put her curls up with still bristling all over her head, and her faded-blue eyes would look eager for a moment, until Emily shook her head with regret.

And so she became "the young lady" or "miss" to the maids, "dearie" to Miss Hortense and "my girl" to her sister.

Miss Horatia had sent Agnes into Brighton to inquire for either a Miss Nelson or a Mrs. Wiggins at all the inns, and the maid returned with Emily's portmanteaus after settling her bill at the hostelry where she had been staying. The Rutherford ladies went through the baggage carefully, but nothing revealing Emily's identity came to light, for all her papers and her mother's letters were at the bottom of her trunk in the box room of Bradley's Hotel awaiting her new direction.

The doctor continued to visit, at carefully specified times when Miss Horatia was sure to be absent, for Emily was still troubled with an occasional severe headache and dizzy spells, but outside of commending her on her returning good health, he had no new suggestions for any way she might regain her memory, merely telling her that nature would take care of that eventually, and all the fretting in the world would not bring back a single remembrance, either good or bad, before it was time.

Some days later, when Miss Horatia felt Emily was strong enough, they told her about the letters they had found in her reticule. They were all three taking tea in Emily's room, and as soon as Bessie had curtsied after bringing in the tray and taken herself off, Miss Horatia laid the four letters before their guest.

Emily read the contents with a frown creasing her forehead. "But this does not make any sense, Miss Horatia," she said. "Why are there two different names? Which one is mine?"

"You were known as Mrs. Wiggins at the Blue Boar, where we found your baggage," the older lady said, frowning at her younger sister as she broke in to say impulsively, "Oh, do not be Mrs. Wiggins, dearie! Such a common, horrid name. Wiggins-Higgins-Piggins! Please *try* to be Miss Nelson."

Emily had to laugh at her. "Of course I shall do my best, ma'am," she twinkled. "I must admit I have no liking for the name 'Wiggins' myself. But where do you suppose, if that is truly my name, is *Mr.* Wiggins?"

Miss Hortense gasped and put her hands to her heart, blushing a bright red, while Miss Horatia turned pale and stiffened. Emily looked from one to the other in confusion.

"Well, my dearie, we cannot be sure there is one. No, I quite refuse to consider that such a lovely girl as you are would be burdened with such a name," Miss Hortense said, speaking quickly and darting little glances at her sister's rigid face.

Emily was rereading the letters and not attending. "It appears I am a lady's maid. How strange. I don't *feel* like one."

Miss Horatia deigned to speak again now that the dangerous subject of the possible Mr. Wiggins had passed. "Your educated words and accent are much at odds with the occupation. Perhaps you have been a lady's maid, but I do not think you were meant to be one. The aura against it is very strong—very strong indeed."

Emily looked confused again, and Miss Hortense patted her hand and said proudly, "Horatia sees auras, you know. She can sense things that are hidden from the rest of us."

"I wish she could see who I am, then," Emily remarked.

"It is impossible to make demands on the spirits," Miss Rutherford said, pouring out a cup of tea while her sister concentrated on selecting another cream puff. "The gift comes and goes; I cannot summon it at will."

"The doctor said it would do you good to go out in the fresh air, dearie," Miss Hortense said next, as soon as she had swallowed the last delicious bit of her pastry. "Perhaps tomorrow you can come outside to a lawn chair if it is a nice day."

"I would like that." Emily smiled. "I feel I must regain my strength so I can leave soon. I have been such a burden to you, and even if I do not know who I am, I cannot trespass on your hospitality much longer. Why, I have been here two weeks now."

Both ladies refused to listen to her plans to go away; in fact, Miss Hortense became quite mournful, and a little tear slid down her fat cheek as she cried, "Oh, do not leave us, my dear! We never have any company anymore and we should enjoy a longer visit."

Emily promised to remain some while longer to cheer her up, but insisted on helping with the work about the hall as soon as she was able. "I cannot sit in idleness like a grand lady forever," she said. "Perhaps if I was a lady's maid, I could take care of you both, do some sewing or laundry, or arrange your hair."

But this, it seemed, was not to be allowed. "You are our guest, and besides, we have more servants than we need already," Miss Horatia said sternly.

"*Many* more than we need," Miss Hortense added. "But Horatia will take them in! Besides Agnes, Bessie, and Gertrude, whom you have met, there is Annie and Gladys and Rose and Millie and Joan and Bertha and Mabel as well."

"Have you forgotten Daisy, Pauline, Jane, and Sally, Hortense?" Miss Horatia asked, passing the plate of cakes to Emily, who was once again looking stunned at the number of maids the sisters employed.

"No, nor Deirdre and Deborah neither," Miss Hortense crowed. "You forgot about them."

"How could I forget when they cook such delicious meals," Miss Horatia replied, rising from the tea table. "Come away now, Sister, and let the young lady rest. Your chatter has tired her, I know."

Emily denied she was tired, but Miss Horatia refused to listen and swept her sister before her to the door. After the two had left, Emily sat on in her chair, her hands tightly clasped in her lap and her unseeing eyes staring at the opposite wall as she tried to still the terror she was beginning to feel rise in her breast whenever she thought about this mysterious lapse of memory she was suffering.

Who *was* she? What was her name? Where did she come from? Was there someone, somewhere, who loved her? Someone who might even now be frantic with fear and concern for her?

And even though she had spoken those brave words to the Rutherfords about leaving the hall, how could she, in this condition? Where would she go? What could she do, not knowing who she was? There had been very little money in her reticule, and even if she had more banked somewhere, how could she claim it?

She felt as if she were lost in a deep, enveloping fog that swirled around her, now parting a little as if to tantalize her, now thickening again into a heavy white curtain that mocked her efforts to fight her way clear of it. Was she always to be lost, never to know who she was and where she belonged? It was almost as if she did not exist—as if she were not really a person at all, but only a nameless shade. She wondered if this was the onset of insanity and shivered in fright. Then she shook her head, determined to put such terrifying thoughts from her mind before she succumbed to panic and hysteria. Wandering over to the tall mullioned windows, she gazed outside. How wonderful it would be to go out tomorrow, she thought. And how kind the Misses Rutherford were to her, a complete stranger. Of course, she admitted to herself as she leaned against the pane, they were a little odd. But then, lots of old ladies have their little eccentricities. At least they do not keep a hundred cats, and if they feel they need so many maids, who am I to say them nay? I do not even know how big the hall is. Perhaps it is a huge old pile, and an army of women is necessary to keep it up.

But the next day when she came slowly down the stairs between the two sisters, followed by Agnes carrying a blanket and some pillows, she saw that Rutherford Hall, although a pleasant manor, was only of ordinary size. It was built of rough gray stone, and all the windows were arched and narrow with tiny panes, so she suspected it was of a great age. The stone hall that they were traversing was decorated with old family portraits, and there was very little furniture to be seen except a few tall chairs and one massive polished table that held a large bouquet of wild flowers.

Emily paused for a moment when they reached the front door, feeling a little dizzy from her exertions, but when that passed, she moved forward between her escorts, both of whom were carefully supporting her. With Miss Hortense clucking encouragement, they went down a shallow set of stone steps to the gravel drive and then made their way over the lawn to a long chair set under a huge old elm that looked at least as ancient as the hall.

When Emily had been settled in the chair, she looked up to see Miss Hortense gasping a little, her rosy face even redder from her efforts, and she said contritely, "I am so sorry, Miss Hortense, for I see my weight was too much for you. You should have called for a groom or one of the footmen . . ."

Agnes, busy arranging pillows at her back, moaned out loud, and Miss Hortense exclaimed, "Oh, no, you must not! Sister, Sister, come back! She did not mean to say it!"

But Miss Horatia was running back to the hall as fast as she could go, her black skirts swinging with the rush of her passage, and she did not turn her head.

"Oh, dearie me," Miss Hortense said, wringing her hands as she sank into another lawn chair. "She will be distressed for hours. Go after her, Agnes, and stay with her until she is calm."

The maid bobbed a curtsy and went away, and Emily asked, "But what did I say? I do not understand."

Miss Hortense sighed. "Of course you do not understand,

dearie, and I should have warned you I know, but you see, we never mention *them* here at the hall.''

''*Them?*'' Emily asked.

Miss Hortense refused to look at her. ''Yes, *them,*'' she whispered. ''*Men!*''

''Why ever not?'' Emily asked in a normal tone of voice.

Miss Hortense looked around, making shushing motions with her little fat hands. ''Sister hates *them,* she always has. I do not really know why, and since she refuses to speak of *them,* I cannot ask. She never used to be quite so bad, but after my father died, she declared he was the last man whose name would ever pass her lips, and the last one she would ever speak to. That is why we have no footmen or grooms or a butler. The maids do it all.''

Emily looked around her in bewilderment. Down at the bottom of the garden near a small stream, two elderly women with sunbonnets and aprons, their skirts looped up out of the way, were busy scything the grass, and she could see three more kneeling in the kitchen garden at the side of the hall. The stone walls and the pointed windows of the hall, as well as all the women servants, suddenly reminded her of a convent.

''But, my dear Miss Hortense, how unfair to you,'' she said after a moment. ''Did *you* never wish to marry? There must have been a man in your life at one time?''

The old lady blushed and simpered. ''Well, yes, there was, but *he* was part of the problem, you see. Horatia said he was not worthy of me and sent him away.'' At Emily's murmur of sympathy Hortense added quickly, ''You must not think I minded too much, dearie. Now that I think of it, he *wasn't* worthy of me. But, of course, there was no chance to go to town for the Season, not with Horatia feeling the way she did, and somehow the years slipped away. You must not be sorry for me, for I declare I have been happy here with my dear sister. Perhaps it is true that there are some women who are happier without *them.*''

''So that is why you have so many maids,'' Emily remarked, trying to hide how appalled she was at the life Miss Hortense had led.

''Not only because of the work,'' Miss Hortense replied. She seemed eager to talk, now the secret was out and her sister had left them. ''Horatia cannot bear to see a woman out of work or in need, for she is sure it is all some of *their* doing when a woman is placed in such a predicament. And, of course, she chooses the older ones because it is so much safer."

"Safer?"

"The younger women want some of *them* around, and when they discover sister's hatred for the sex, they run off to be with *them*. Older maids are not so flighty; they have more sense."

Emily stifled a giggle. "No wonder you were so upset when I mentioned the possibility of a Mr. Wiggins yesterday," she said. "I will be more careful from now on, for I would not distress Miss Rutherford for the world."

Miss Hortense beamed and patted her hand. "I knew I could rely on you to understand. And you will not mention the fact that there are only female portraits in the hall, will you? Horatia even had the suits of armor that used to stand by the stairwell thrown away."

Emily nodded her agreement, determined to enter into the spirit of things. "So that is why Miss Horatia never speaks to the doctor or is present when he comes to see me. It is all clear to me now that you have explained it, Miss Hortense."

"I will be so glad when his visits cease, for Horatia frets so when he is in the house. And then she sulks for hours, after setting the maids to scrub everything he might have touched. But never mind, dearie, as soon as you are able, I will drive you into Brighton to see the doctor, and then Horatia can be comfortable."

She sighed and added shyly, "No doubt this all explains why the dear vicar has not come to call? We never go to church because then Horatia would have to listen to *him* giving the sermon. I do regret it, and I do so worry about my poor sister's fate; it is my primary concern."

Her cheerful face was creased in a frown, and Emily, who thought she had every reason to be concerned about such an unbalanced relative, asked her why it was such a particular worry.

"Well, dearie, what ever is going to happen when she gets to heaven? She has not spoken to a man for thirty years, and how can I be sure I will be by her side to help her?" At Emily's confused expression, she added, "You see, I don't think Saint Peter will like it if she turns her back on him and refuses to speak to him; why, he might even send her to that other place.''

She looked so distressed that Emily swallowed the laughter that was threatening to bubble over and disgrace her. ''Perhaps, being an angel, it will be different?'' she managed to suggest, a little diffidently, and had the pleasure of seeing Miss Hortense's face brighten at the thought. Angels, after all, were not really one of the earthly *them*.

While Emily was recovering in the country, it was not to be supposed that the duke had been idle. When he discovered that Mrs. Wiggins had not returned to the employment agency where he had traced her, and that there was no sign of her at any of the others in London in the days that followed, he turned his efforts in another direction and drove his curricle down to Wantage.

He was received courteously by Lord Wyndham, who, after learning the purpose of his visit, was glad that his wife's absence on afternoon calls prevented her from joining them in the interview. The two men spent an uncomfortable half-hour together, for although the duke was scrupulously polite, Lord Wyndham was left in no doubt as to how he was regarded by the younger man, and in what light the duke considered a family who would not only abandon one of its young female members so callously, but allow her to go into service as well. In vain, Lord Wyndham pointed out that he had had no notion that was her purpose; in vain he expressed his wish to shelter her under his wing again. He was denied in cold, terse words and informed that the protection of Miss Emily Margaret Wyndham would in the future be the sole responsibility of the Duke of Wrotherham, and that this protection would take the form of marrying her as soon as he could locate her once again.

Since Lord Wyndham had no idea where his niece might be, the interview was quickly terminated. As the duke drove away, he was not overly disappointed, for he had never expected Emily to return meekly to her family. He knew her pride. And, he thought as he whipped up his chestnuts and settled them onto the London road, I admit that my journey here was as much for my satisfaction as to discover any hint of her whereabouts. It had done him a world of good to let Lord Wyndham learn of his contempt, and the expression of stunned disbelief and chagrin on the older man's face when he announced his wedding plans had been worth every tiresome mile.

He spent the return journey planning what he would do next. Somehow he did not think that Emily was still in town. He had no real reason for this supposition; it was more a feeling that if she were so close to him, he could not help but be aware of it. He remembered that Captain Quentin's sister lived in London, and on reaching Wrotherham House wrote to ask if he might call on her. He had to wait for a week, for Miss Arabella had gone out of town, and he was disappointed when he was finally admitted to her drawing room to find that she was of little help.

Miss Quentin, trying not to raise her eyebrows at the duke's questions, admitted she had no idea where Miss Nelson might be found, although she did suggest that the duke call on the Quentins' butler and housekeeper at Number Twelve Charles Street, Mayfair.

"Yes, Miss Nelson was very big with the Goodwells, as I recall," she said with a sniff. "Perhaps they might know where she is. You say my brother was making plans to return to England, your Grace? I wonder I have not heard from him."

The duke was about to mention that the Quentins intended to go directly to the captain's home at Burton-Latimer, but something about Miss Arabella Quentin stayed his tongue. She seemed to be laboring under a heavy cloud of pique, as if she had been misused, and he thought Tony would recover faster with only his wife to care for him. No trace of his thoughts was visible as he thanked the lady and took his leave of her sour face and air of cold authority, however.

The Goodwells, although flustered by the attentions of a duke, could not help him either, for Miss Nelson had not called on them since her return to town.

"Such a sweet young maid," Mrs. Goodwell mourned. "I am sorry to learn she has left the Quentins' service, for she did Miss Alicia a world of good."

"You have no idea where she came from prior to her being engaged here?" the duke asked next.

The old butler screwed up his face in thought. "I seem to remember that she said she had been in Yorkshire, your Grace, but she did not mention the name of the family."

Both elderly retainers were agog to know why it was so important for a duke to find a mere lady's maid, but of course they could not inquire, and the duke certainly did not bother to explain.

As he was taking his leave, Mrs. Goodwell came back into the hall from the kitchen, where she had retired when she could be of no further assistance. "Pardon me, your Grace! Perhaps it will not mean anything, but it seems to me that Miss Nelson was staying at Bradley's Hotel in Davies Street before she moved in here."

"Of course!" her husband agreed. "I remember now that the boy who brought her luggage wore their uniform. Does that help, your Grace?"

Charles assured them solemnly that it might be very good news, but he had a hard time returning their smiles. What if she had stayed at Bradley's so many months ago? How did that help him?

Suddenly he stopped dead in the middle of the sidewalk, greatly upsetting an elderly gentleman who stumbled into him before he could stop himself. By the time apologies had been tendered and bows exchanged, the duke was impatient to be off. Perhaps Emily had returned to the same hotel? Perhaps they would know where she had gone?

His spirits rose and he flagged down a hackney cab, all impatience now, for the length of the short journey. So many dead ends, so much wasted time—pray God he would be successful this time!

And successful he was, for the first person he spoke to at Bradley's was the porter, who opened the door of his cab for him and who not only remembered the handsome brunette who was posing as Mrs. Wiggins, but also recalled the vital information that she had gone off to Brighton on the stage only a few weeks ago. The duke clapped him on the shoulder, called him an excellent fellow, and rewarded him with such openhanded largesse that the porter could contemplate treating his particular friends to many a round in their favorite pub for weeks and weeks to come.

If the duke arrived back in Park Lane not exactly walking on air, at the least he wore a brighter expression than had been seen on his face for some time. He discovered a letter awaiting him from his aunt, Lady Staunton, and not even her cold formal words requesting him to call as soon as he could possibly contrive it had the power to dampen his spirits. His butler was astounded to hear him humming as he took the stairs two at a time to change for dinner, and when he informed Greene that he intended to toddle around to Brooks and look up some of his cronies later, and that he rather thought he might take a look-in at Brighton for a few days, Mr. Greene was encouraged to hope that his infatuation with Miss Nelson was at an end and life could return to normal at last.

The following morning, the duke was prompt to present himself in his aunt's drawing room and found his uncle also in attendance. This gentleman looked a little worried, for although the duke was as impeccable as always, he was dressed for riding, a fact he knew would offend his wife. Lady Staunton was a great stickler for the proprieties and would not think it a compliment to be visited by even so exalted a gentleman as the duke unless he wore the proper morning attire. To his surprise, she allowed the duke to kiss her hand and motioned him to a seat without even mentioning the unsatisfactory nature of his dress.

Lady Staunton had no intention of upsetting her nephew this morning. As her butler poured them all a glass of sherry and the duke chatted with her husband, she observed him carefully. She had always considered Charles a handsome man, but this morning there was an air about him of some hidden excitement that caused his black eyes to sparkle, and the look of boredom that was his habitual expression was very much in abeyance. Her heart sank. I suppose he has set up a new mistress, she thought dourly, and just when I have arranged to entertain Lady Beardsley and her daughter. How tiresome men were! She would be hard put to gain his consent to attend her in the country now that he had a new *amour* to intrigue him.

"I suppose you have found yet another suitable, well-bred damsel for my inspection, ma'am? Who is it this time?" the duke began as soon as the butler shut the drawing-room door behind him. His determination to be on his way made him curt, but he did not hear her gasp at his temerity as he added, "This sherry is very tolerable; my compliments, Uncle."

He bowed slightly to the gentleman, who had choked a little at his first remark, and then turned back to his aunt. "Perhaps I should have called on you as soon as I returned

from Brussels, for then I could have spared you the exertion."
He smiled easily at the lady, who sat rigid on the very edge
of a gray satin sofa, her slightly protuberant eyes bulging
with shock.

"I am sure, Charles, that you will be good enough to
explain yourself," she replied in her stiff, colorless voice.
"You know I do not care for careless joking and ill-bred
humor, although I am sure I have always borne my part in
lighthearted conversation."

"I cannot call to mind any occasion that you did so, Aunt,
but no doubt that is a result of my lamentable memory. Come
now, shall we begin again? You asked me to call; behold me,
obedient to your wishes."

His aunt watched him finish his sherry, and as he crossed
his well-polished boots and began to swing one gently, she
knew he was impatient to be off, and she hurried into speech.

"I meant to ask you to come down to Neerings for some
weeks' stay. I am sure you would enjoy it, for your uncle and
I are having a few compatible people to visit. London grows
so tiresome with this heat."

The duke nodded, but said, "Unfortunately I am desolated
to have to refuse the treat, Aunt. I am off to Brighton in an
hour."

Lady Staunton moved forward another half-inch on her
sofa. "Brighton? I do not think we know anyone staying at
Brighton, do we, Jerome?"

In her voice was the suggestion that if none of her acquaintance were there, there *was* no one in Brighton worth knowing.
Her lord shook his head, but he was not required to answer,
for the duke interrupted to say, "Possibly you do not, but I
think I do."

The engaging smile that accompanied this statement did
not endear him to his aunt, who thought that dear Charles was
certainly in an unusual mood this morning. If she had been
anyone else, she would have even called it playful.

"Indeed?" she murmured.

"Indeed. In fact, I am sure that I will find her there."

"Aha! I might have known it was a woman." Lady
Staunton's voice was so full of cold loathing that the duke
remonstrated with her.

"Come, come, Aunt! Such aversion, and to your own sex,

too. But you are mistaken. It is not just *any* woman; it is the future Duchess of Wrotherham.''

"Now I know that you are being frivolous, Charles. I have not heard you were at last contemplating the holy state of matrimony, and I am sure I must have done so if it were true, for the sounds of all England rejoicing that you were about to do your duty at last could hardly have failed to come to my attention.''

The duke noticed his uncle scurrying to pour himself an-other glass of sherry as he replied, "Very well-put indeed, ma'am. That takes the trick and puts me in my place, does it not? But knowing your interest in the matter, I am sure you will be glad to wish me happy. I can assure you, you are the first of the family to know.''

"Who is she?'' Lady Staunton asked baldly, cutting through his rhetoric to the heart of the matter.

"She is a Wyndham of Berks, the niece of Lord Gregory Wyndham, the daughter of Captain Thomas Wyndham, late of the Royal Navy.''

"Wyndham . . . Wyndham,'' his aunt mused.

"It will not be a brilliant match, even though her birth is more than acceptable. However, that is of small concern to me, for I love her and I intend to marry her.''

"Congratulations, my boy, what glorious news,'' his uncle said, coming up to pat him on the shoulder and darting only an occasional glance at his wife, whose one aim in life for the past ten years had been to find the future duchess for her nephew, thereby ensuring his undying gratitude, and more important, that a worthy-enough young woman should fill such a high and exalted post.

"Wyndham . . . Thomas Wyndham . . . the navy . . .'' Lady Staunton murmured again.

"I will spare you any more of these tiring cogitations, ma'am,'' the duke said. "The young lady's mother was Althea Wyndham. Perhaps you knew the lady?''

"*Althea Wyndham?*'' Lady Staunton asked in a voice of doom just before she fainted and fell right off her sofa.

By the time she had been restored to consciousness, the duke was wishing he had gone off to Brighton at dawn, but having opened this Pandora's box, he could hardly go away and leave his uncle to deal with it.

"No, no, say it is not true, Charles,'' his aunt moaned

when she was able to speak again, pushing her husband, who was patting her shoulder, away from her. "Not Althea Wyndham's daughter! You poor, poor deluded boy. Perhaps you were not aware . . . I mean, you cannot have heard that the girl's mother was a . . . In fact, at one time your very own father . . . but maybe you have not offered for her as yet? I beg you to consider the family, your duty to your name. If you marry Althea Wyndham's daughter, I shall have to kill myself, for there will be no other course open to me."

"Uncle, perhaps another glass of sherry for my aunt? Come, ma'am, let us be sensible. It is not Althea Wyndham who is to be my bride; it is her daughter, Emily Margaret. She is nothing at all like her mother, and in this case, the sins of the fathers fall on my head, not hers. Since the unfortunate lady who was her mother is deceased, perhaps we should let her rest in peace? I do not regard her; neither should you."

Lady Staunton moaned. "The scandal . . . the gossip. Charles, tell me you are just funning and you do not mean a word of it and I will promise never to bring another young lady to your attention ever again. Oh, better that you should never marry and the direct line die out than the ignominy of an alliance with the Wyndhams."

The duke stiffened and rose with alacrity.

"Do me the kindness to spare me any more of your lecturing and prosy, puffed-up conceit for the House of Wrotherham, and if you must, ma'am, take comfort in the fact that you are a Staunton and not directly related to the Saint Allyns. Besides, I am almost thirty. What I do is of concern only to me. I can assure you that Emily is much too fine and good for me; I only hope she can be brought to accept my suit. Up to this time, she has been most unwilling to align herself with our family."

He stared at his aunt with considerable hauteur. His mother had died when he was only seven, and her sister, Lady Staunton, had never shown him even an ounce of affection. He could not recall her ever kissing or hugging him; her whole attention was for the title, not the little boy who so desperately needed her love. Remembering this made him add as he strolled to the door, "Oh, by the way, Aunt, Miss Wyndham has been in service as a lady's maid this past year. It is not generally known, and perhaps you would prefer to keep that information to yourself. I *quite* understand, and now I bid you good day.''

There was complete silence in the drawing room as the door closed behind him and the Stauntons heard his booted feet going down the stairs to the front door. Only when they heard it slam behind him did the frozen tableau dissolve and Lady Staunton toss off her entire glass of sherry in one gulp.

''Althea Wyndham . . . a lady's maid . . . unwilling to marry him! I feel much better, Jerome, for it is obvious that Charles, if he is not gone completely mad, which I cannot believe to be the case, is indulging in some childish prank at our expense. I shall not regard it.''

10

Life at Rutherford Hall continued on its former placid way now that Emily had been let in on the secret of Miss Horatia's great distaste for the opposite sex, and she was careful to remove all references to *them* from her conversation. Her normal good health returned quickly, and even the dizzy spells and occasional headaches disappeared, although she came no closer to discovering her real identity. Sometimes, she thought she saw a glimmer of light, and found herself saying, "No, that's not the way I do it"; or she would have a brief vision of a smiling face framed with a cloud of golden hair, or see a pair of dark eyes, intent with passion, but when she tried to force her mind to remember their owners, the hazy curtain would come down again and everything that had ever happened to her before she came to Rutherford Hall would disappear.

She discovered she could play the piano but couldn't cook; that her needlework was exquisite and that she spoke French, but that she could not ride a horse or drive a team, and was worse than useless in the garden. She remembered dates in history and long-ago wars, could recite poetry and discuss philosophy, but she had no knowledge of Napoleon or indeed of any event that had occurred since the turn of the century.

She tried not to brood about it, but even as her strength returned, she began to suffer terrible nightmares. She would sit up suddenly in the dark to find her pillow wet with her tears, but now that she was awake, the dreams that made her so sad eluded her. Why do I cry and sob in my sleep? she wondered. What is there in my past that has caused me such sorrow that it still distresses me now? She began to dread the nighttimes when she had to take her candle from the table in the hall and follow the Misses Rutherford to bed. Miss Horatia, who had the room next to her, had heard her sobbing and had even gone in to her one night to find her fast asleep even as she tossed and moaned in her distress. She watched Emily carefully after that, noting her preoccupation and the frown on her face when she did not think she was being observed. Much concerned, she bade Hortense inquire of the doctor for the cause of this new malady, but that good man could only theorize that the young lady's memory might be coming back at last, and that perhaps there was some painful past event she was trying to avoid remembering.

One night, long after everyone was in bed and asleep, Miss Horatia was roused once again by the girl's pitiful sobs and cries, and she pulled on her dressing gown to investigate.

As she opened the door, she heard her call out, "Charles, I need you. Charles, where are you?" and, steeling her heart, she went up to the bed to take her in her arms. "There, my dear, there," she said in her gruff voice.

Emily woke up startled before she lay her head on Miss Horatia's bosom.

"I am so sorry, Miss Rutherford," she whispered. "Did I wake you again?"

"That is no matter, child. But come, you were calling for someone in your sleep, someone named Charles. Do you know who he might be?"

Emily was astounded to hear a masculine name escape Miss Horatia's thin lips. "I . . . I have no idea. I know no one by that name," she said.

Miss Horatia patted her briskly on the shoulder and rose. "Go back to sleep, then. No doubt it is someone from your past, but you must not let it trouble you."

But the very next morning there was something else to concern the older lady that drove the girl's nightmares right from her mind. Agnes, who had taken their guest to her heart and insisted on serving as her maid, came to Miss Horatia and reported her suspicions. The girl had been with them for over a month now, and none of the cloths that Agnes had provided for her period had been used. Of course, she told her mistress, it might be due to the shock of the accident, but somehow she did not believe it. There was a glow to the girl, a new softness, and although she was sorry to have to mention it to Miss Rutherford, she herself had had four children and could read the signs as well as anyone. Miss Horatia bid her keep her suspicions to herself for the time being and went to seek the counsel of her younger sister, her eyes sharp with her anger and distress.

"I knew all her troubles were directly related to one of *them*, Hortense," she said after she disclosed her fears that the young lady was pregnant. "Hmmph! *They* amuse themselves, but the woman always pays."

"Oh, dearie me," Miss Hortense said, looking nervously at her sister. How would dear Horatia react to their young friend now that there was proof of such a direct relationship with the enemy? Might her dislike extend to her as well?

"So, she is Mrs. Wiggins, after all, how sad," she managed to say at last. "But, Sister, we must find her hus—the baby's, er, I mean . . ."

"I know exactly what you mean," Miss Horatia snapped. "There is no need to pussyfoot about, Hortense. In this instance I shall relax my standards. I am well aware that the young lady did not arrive in her present predicament all by herself. Oh, no, it was all one of *their* doing! I hope she may be Mrs. Wiggins indeed, but I do not count on it. She has probably been abandoned by *him*, unmarried and bereft, and is all alone in the world. That is probably the reason she cries in her sleep."

"Oh, Sister," Miss Hortense exclaimed, clapping her hands in glee, "she is not alone; she has us. How lovely to have a baby in the hall. Do say that we may offer her a home with us, and the child as well."

"That depends, Sister, and we shall have to wait and see," Miss Horatia was quick to remind her. "But that is in the future, and we have more immediate concerns. Since she still cannot remember her real name, this forces us to make inquiries, for even though I do not think it at all probable, knowing what *they* are like, there *may* be a Mr. Wiggins in her past."

"How do we do that, Sister?" Miss Hortense asked, putting aside her dreams of cradles, booties, and little bonnets.

"We shall advertise, of course, in the papers. Then, too, perhaps we should concentrate our efforts in Brighton, since that is where we found her. I shall write up the notices at once, and one of the maids can post them for us this afternoon.

You go and find the girl and tell her what we propose to do. I shall leave it up to you whether or not you tell her that we know of her condition. I am almost positive that she is unaware of it herself as yet.''

Miss Hortense bustled away and found Emily sitting under the giant elm, a pile of mending at her feet.

''Dearie, Horatia has just told me,'' she said as she took a seat and beamed at the girl. ''And soon you will have many more interesting things to sew besides my old petticoats. My, yes, and they will be so much tinier too.''

She giggled and blushed, and Emily put down her sewing in confusion. ''Whatever can you mean, ma'am?'' she asked.

Miss Rutherford not only hemmed and hawed, she started a sentence only to abandon it and bury her face in her handkerchief, peeping around it to wink at Emily before she disappeared behind it once more, and so it was several minutes before Emily learned what the suspicions of the elderly ladies were. At once she felt a great rush of joy, although she did not know why. It seemed strange to be so happy about a child who had no name, whose father was unknown and might not even be her husband, but none of that mattered as she sat clutching Miss Hortense's second-best petticoat to her breast while she smiled a little, her eyes dreamy and far away.

She was recalled to the present when Miss Hortense came and put her arms around her to give her a kiss. ''And you are happy, are you not, my dearie? Yes, yes, I can see that you are. Now listen to me carefully, for what I am about to say is very important. Very important indeed.''

She knelt down in the grass next to Emily's chair and took both her hands in hers. ''We must always, from this moment on, my dearie, *think pink!* Do you understand? The baby *must* be a girl, it must, for I am not entirely sure that Horatia's aversion to men might not even extend to even the newest, wee boy. Now, what do you think of Rachel Rose for a name? Rachel Rose Rutherford—such a nice ring to it, don't you think?''

Emily had to laugh at her eagerness, but even as Miss Hortense had been speaking, the little voice in her head was saying, ''Oh, no, it must be a boy, for his sake!'' For a moment, the dark eyes gleamed in her mind's eye before they faded away. ''Charles,'' she murmured.

''You mean you prefer *Charlotte,* dearie? Well, that is a

pleasant name, too," Miss Hortense said firmly, and Emily shook herself out of her revery as she began to tell her that Horatia was even now writing up some notices that were to be posted around Brighton and preparing a written account for the newspapers.

"But you are not to worry if Mr. Wiggins does not come forward. We are only too happy to have you stay with us, and the baby girl, too," Miss Hortense assured her. "In fact, I shall be very sad if the gentleman does come to claim you, for you have brought such life and spirit to us all."

She got up to shake out her crushed skirts and say as she took her leave, "Remember, dearie, *pink,* only pink, and dear little Rachel Rose."

While Emily dreamed away the rest of the morning under the elm tree, the Duke of Wrotherham was making the acquaintance of Mrs. Huddlewick of Brighton's finest employment agency, who remembered Mrs. Wiggins very well.

"So refined, such a lady herself," she enthused. "Unfortunately I had nothing to offer her, your Grace, and she has never returned, although I am sure she said she would do so."

The duke found himself holding his breath as Mrs. Huddlewick searched her records for the name of the inn where Mrs. Wiggins had said she was staying.

Not quite half an hour later, he strode into The Blue Boar, and began to question the innkeeper. The man remembered Mrs. Wiggins only vaguely, but his buxom young wife was much more forthcoming.

"Yes, the lady was a handsome brunette," she said with an arch smile and a toss of her own black curls. "She 'as been gone over a month now, and 'oo would 'ave thought the likes of 'er would be acquainted with those strange old ladies out at Rutherford 'All?"

"Strange old ladies?" the duke asked, quirking one black eyebrow and trying not to show his sudden excitement.

"Why, yes, your Grace. They sent one of their servants in to fetch the leddy's baggage, so I guess she was going to stay there. Queer do, that was, too. The silly old thing couldn't remember if it was Mrs. Wiggins or some other leddy whose portmanteaus she was to pick up."

"Perhaps the other name was Miss Margaret Nelson?"

"The very one! But when she learned it was Mrs. Regina

Wiggins wot we 'ad 'ere in the inn, she paid 'er shot and took 'er things away to the 'all.''

The duke was quick to learn the direction of Rutherford Hall and, on mentioning that he intended to ride out there immediately to call, was surprised when both the innkeeper and his wife dissolved in helpless laughter.

"I couldn't advise it, your Grace, not if you intends to return to town with a whole skin," Mr. Rathbone said, wiping his eyes. "Apt to shoot you more likely than not, that Miss Rutherford would. No, no, safer to send a message, and be sure to hire a *maid*, not a groom, to deliver it. No male ever gets through the gates."

"Lawks, no," his wife agreed. "Miss Rutherford do 'ave such an 'atred for men. Don't know what she's missing, that she don't,'' she added with another sideways glance at the tall, handsome figure of the duke.

The innkeeper, suddenly aware of his wife's flirting, banished her to the taproom. As he was accepting the money the duke insisted on giving him for the information, he saw an elderly woman nailing up a poster in the street.

"See there, your Grace, there's one o' the wenches from Rutherford 'All now. Best you speak to 'er."

It was unfortunate that Gertrude had been sent into Brighton with the notices, for she was none too bright, and after several years of living with Miss Horatia she had taken her mistress's attitude to males as her own personal aversion, so when the duke spoke to her, she gave a startled scream and ran way, leaving the duke to gather what information he could by reading the notice for himself.

> If anyone is interested in learning the whereabouts of a Mrs. Regina Wiggins or a Miss Margaret Nelson, they should call at Doctor Jos. E. Spears Surgery at 17 Monk Street between the hours of two and four P.M.

There was no signature to the handwritten notice. The duke decided that a call on the doctor was not only handier, but also a good deal safer, and that he would, on the whole, prefer to give these strange old ladies who hated men a wide berth, unless he was forced to storm their citadel to rescue Emily from their grasp.

Accordingly, he was at Number Seventeen Monk Street

shortly after two that afternoon. As he prepared to raise the brass knocker, an old lady opened the door to leave, but when she saw the duke's bow and polite smile, she bustled away with a frown on her round red face.

Doctor Spears was only too happy to welcome the duke and listen to an abbreviated version of his story. "You say the lady is neither Mrs. Wiggins nor Miss Nelson? That her real name is Emily Wyndham?" he asked, moving some papers around on his desk.

"That is correct. Tell me, Doctor Spears, is she indeed at Rutherford Hall?"

"She is there," the doctor said solemnly, and was startled by the duke's sudden, blinding white grin.

"At last! I have searched for her for so long and it is so important that I see her as soon as possible," he said in exultant tones.

"More important than you imagine, your Grace," the doctor remarked dryly. "I have some news of, er, Miss Wyndham for you that perhaps will be upsetting."

"There has been an accident? She is not well?" the duke asked, leaping to his feet and leaning over the desk.

"Sit down, sir, and I will tell you everything. Yes, there was an accident about a month ago. Miss Wyndham was walking on the street here in Brighton and was run down by the Rutherfords' horse. She sustained a blow to the head. No, no, she has completely recovered her health," he added as he caught sight of the duke's strained, anxious face, "but although her body has recovered, her mind has not. I believe she is a victim of what Thomas Sydenham in the middle of the seventeenth century first defined as classical hysteria, for she cannot remember anything about her life before the accident. The Rutherford ladies took her in and nursed her, but there was no way to trace her family. You *are* a relative, are you not, your Grace?"

"Not at the moment," Charles said, his face taut with the shock of what he had just learned. "I intend to marry Miss Wyndham as soon as it can be arranged. I have carried a special license to that effect ever since we became separated."

"I think you are very wise to do so in this instance. The lady who was leaving when you came in was Miss Hortense Rutherford and she came to report a new development in the case. The young lady, er, excuse me, Miss Wyndham is pregnant.''

"Pregnant?" the duke whispered.

"Is there any doubt in your mind, sir, that you are the father of the child?" the doctor asked, bending his pale-gray eyes sternly on the man before him.

The duke got up to pace the office. "None at all, I *know* I am the father."

"And you are prepared to marry the lady, even if she cannot remember you? I must warn you, this hysteria has gone on for so long that there is every possibility she may never regain any knowledge of her former life."

"How much easier it would be if that should be so," the duke muttered, causing Doctor Spears to raise his brows. "I see I shall have to explain it all to you, Doctor. It is not a tale that speaks well for our sex, or of me in particular—perhaps the Misses Rutherford are correct in their misanthropy, for Miss Wyndham has had nothing but trouble in her dealings with men throughout her life."

The story was soon told, for the doctor did not interrupt him. "I understand now," he said when Charles had finished. "I have been reading up on classical hysteria, and although disorders of the brain are in many ways a mystery to the medical profession, Doctor William Cullen of Edinburgh has written a most learned discourse about what he has named neuroses. This condition most often occurs in life situations involving stress, and it is obvious that Miss Wyndham has been struggling under a great load of troubles. Her loss of memory, her nightmares, could all result from such a neurosis rather than from the blow to her head. And since she is pregnant, of course, she probably is even more affected by this hysteria. That word is from the Greek *hystera* meaning uterus, your Grace. You see the connection? Just so. But she is not insane, sir. I have been watching her closely, and she accepts her condition calmly. You can see how valuable this memory loss can be, protecting her mind from any knowledge of her former stressful life."

The doctor seemed to recall himself and shrugged. "But enough of that," he said. "It is an interesting case and all doctors tend to ride their particular hobbyhorses too long for laymen's tastes. The poor young lady! May I say I honor you for your persistent search and for your determination to wed her? And if she does not remember you when she first sees you, I suggest you tell her that you were engaged before she lost her memory. You say she loves you, and in this case her scruples must be disregarded, for her pregnancy makes an immediate ceremony imperative. She cannot be more than six weeks along, if the dates you gave me are correct, and many a first baby is not consistent in his term.''

The duke waved an impatient hand, for he was thinking hard. If Emily was not shocked into remembering him, she would be unaware of her determination not to marry him. She would not know of her mother's reputation or that her tenure as a lady's maid made their union so unequal, and she would come to him without those clouds over her to mar their happiness. He smiled. He would treat her as if her background more than tallied with his, and then she would take her place as his duchess calmly, with no hesitation or remorse. He felt a little ache that he must trick her this way, but his love for her, and the child, made it necessary.

He wanted to ride out to Rutherford Hall immediately, but Doctor Spears convinced him that it would be better if he made preliminary arrangements.

"I do not know if Miss Horatia will even allow you there," he said. "She may insist on bringing Miss Wyndham here. Give me your direction, your Grace, and I will get word to you as soon as I can. We are both dependent on the lady's favor now."

With this the duke had to be content. In spite of an excellent dinner, accompanied by a bottle of good burgundy, his impatience grew. To think that only six miles away his Lorelei was sleeping. To think that possibly as early as tomorrow she would be in his arms again. He spent a restless night, never dreaming that Emily was sobbing and crying his name at the same time.

Early the next morning, the duke received a note from the doctor saying that they were both expected at Rutherford Hall at eleven in the morning. "Not that we will gain admittance to the hall itself," the doctor told him when the duke drove up to his office in a hired carriage shortly thereafter. "No, that would be too much to expect. Miss Rutherford has decreed that we advance no closer than the elm tree on the front lawn, where she promises to have Miss Wyndham awaiting us."

He beguiled the drive by telling the duke everything he knew about the Rutherford ladies.

"I do not care how peculiar they are," the duke declared, his eyes always searching the road ahead. "Their kindness to Miss Wyndham has earned my undying gratitude."

At last the doctor motioned him to turn his team between a pair of rusty gates, and they were forced to proceed much too slowly up the weedy drive for the duke's liking. In the distance he could see the giant elm, and there in a lawn chair was Emily, sitting with the old lady he had seen the day before. There was no sign of the elder Miss Rutherford, but the doctor noticed a large screen behind the pair on the lawn and suspected she had hidden herself there to make sure that the duke was genuine and that no harm would come to her young guest.

It is ridiculous to feel so shy and nervous, the duke told himself as he strode across the grass to his love, followed by Doctor Spears. He noticed she had half-risen from her seat, those beautiful emerald eyes wide and with her hand to her throat. It was obvious that no one had prepared her for their visit. Beside her, the elderly lady had also risen and she looked very agitated.

"May I present Miss Hortense Rutherford, your Grace," the doctor said. From behind the screen came a distinct "Hmmph!"

The duke bowed, dragging his eyes from Emily's beautiful face with reluctance. "Ma'am," he said, "your most obedient servant."

"Oh, dearie me," the old lady exclaimed, much flustered as she waved her hands. "Please to sit down, your Grace, Doctor."

Doctor Spears took the seat she indicated, but Charles moved forward until he was standing before Emily. "Miss Wyndham," he murmured, bowing again, even deeper this time, and taking her hand in his.

Her green eyes stared at him, but there was no sign of recognition there. "Am I indeed Miss Wyndham, sir?" she asked with a little smile. "I am sure I did not know it."

The duke smiled down at her and she felt a wave of warmth flood her body that was somehow familiar. She also seemed to recognize his black eyes, so intent on her face, but she could summon no other memory of him to her mind.

He sat down beside her, still holding her hand. "You are Miss Wyndham for only a short time longer, my dearest," he said, causing Miss Hortense to sob and take out her handkerchief to blow her nose. "The good doctor informs me that you cannot remember anything, but you may believe me when I tell you that you are Emily Margaret Wyndham, and that you are my fiancée and, as such, soon to become Emily Saint Allyn, Duchess of Wrotherham."

Emily's face paled and the little smile she had had for the duke faded as he felt her hand flutter in his.

"Your fiancée?" she asked in wonder.

"My name is Charles Alistair Saint Allyn," the duke told her, causing the screen behind them to tremble from some sudden movement. Neither one of them noticed. "I am sorry you do not remember, but I can assure you that we are in love—very much in love—and that the child that you carry, my darling, is mine."

Emily lowered her eyes after a quick glance at Miss Hortense's blushing face and the doctor's quiet nod.

"See, I have a special license so we can be wed at once." The duke showed her the paper, much creased now from the time it had spent folded in his note case, and Emily saw her name and his written on it.

She took a deep breath. "If what you say is true, sir, and I am truly Miss Wyndham, I am of course grateful to know it. But who were Mrs. Wiggins and Miss Nelson? Why did I carry their names and not my own in my purse? And what was I doing in Brighton?"

"That must remain a mystery that may never be solved, my dear, unless you regain your memory," the duke said firmly, without a moment's hesitation. "You disappeared from London just before our wedding could take place and I have been searching for you ever since. Thank God I found you! Miss Rutherford, I can never thank you and your sister enough for your care of my bride. I shall always be grateful."

"Hmmmph!" said the screen.

It seemed to be indeed the very short time later that the duke had prophesied that arrangements had been made for an immediate ceremony. The vicar was sent for and the maids set to preparing some food while Miss Hortense, wiping a flood of tears from her eyes, took Emily away to pack her bags and change her gown. Miss Horatia came in and kissed her, asking if she were quite sure she wanted this marriage to take place. Emily stared at her reflection in the glass as Agnes, all aflutter at maiding a future duchess, arranged her hair.

"Yes," she said at last. Her face was pale but she was composed and quiet. "I seem to know that I can trust the duke, and I believe everything he has told me."

"Hmmph!" Miss Horatia snorted, trying to hide her feelings, for she was just as upset as her sister that Emily was to leave them, to say nothing of her distaste that she was to marry one of *them*. "If I had not heard you calling his name in your sleep, night after night, I might not have agreed," she said. "But if he is your Charles indeed, then the marriage must take place, if only for the child's sake."

And so, under the old elm, for even for a wedding Miss Rutherford would not relax her standards and admit all of *them* into the hall, Emily Margaret Wyndham became the bride of Charles Alistair Saint Allyn. He was attended by Doctor Spears as his groomsman, and Emily had little Miss Hortense by her side. There was another bridesmaid hidden behind the large screen, but no one mentioned her, not even the large group of elderly maids who came to watch and cry and exclaim.

Charles thought he had never seen anyone so lovely as his bride in her simple pale-green muslin gown. She carried a bouquet of wild flowers in her arms, and her blond hair gleamed in the sunlight under a matching wreath. Nor did he think any wedding ceremony could ever be so meaningful and solemn as the one that now took place on the green lawn of Rutherford Hall, even ungraced as it was by throngs of fashionable wedding guests, large choirs, or pomp and circumstance.

His eyes were worshipful as he said his vows and placed his own heavy signet ring on her finger. Emily could not look at him. Her mouth felt dry and her heart pounded when he took her in his arms at the end and kissed her gently, his lips just brushing hers before he stepped back and placed her arm in his with a proud, proprietary air.

After a short repast of sandwiches and little cakes, and a toast in Miss Horatia's best dandelion wine given by Doctor Spears to the newlyweds, they prepared to leave. The new Duchess of Wrotherham took Miss Hortense in her arms for a final embrace and retired behind the screen for several moments as well.

"Oh, my dearie, you will come back and visit us, won't you?" Miss Hortense begged, looking up at Emily as she sat in the carriage between her new husband and the doctor. "And you will come alone, won't you? Er, that is—I mean, not that I am *wishful* of being unkind, but—"

The duke broke in to assure her that the duchess would come by herself, and Emily added, "I shall bring the baby with me when I come, dear Miss Hortense," and the round old lady beamed with happiness.

As the carriage drove away, the maids throwing rice that the doctor privately thought most unnecessary in this particular case, Miss Hortense called out again.

"But only if it is indeed Rachel Rose, dearie! I quite understand about heirs and direct lines and so forth, but I know you take my meaning."

Emily smiled when the doctor broke into laughter and the duke joined in, and she stole a glance at that handsome, aristocratic face, now so alive with happiness, and knew in her heart that she had done the right thing and that the calmness she was experiencing came from the feeling that she was safe home at last.

But when they left the doctor off in Monk Street, a silence fell between them. Emily chided herself for her shyness, for if she was carrying the duke's child, she must have been very intimate with him at one time, and this terror of being alone with him now must seem both unnecessary and ridiculous.

Charles looked down at her still, white face and turned his team away from the entrance to the inn yard. He drove until they reached a quiet lane that fronted the sea, and then he stopped the team and turned to take her hand.

"Listen, my dearest, it is all right. I know what you are experiencing, for even though I may tell you of our past love, to you, without any memory of it now, I am as much a stranger as if we had just met this morning. I understand and I will not press you."

Emily tried to smile at him through her stiff lips. "I thank you, your Grace."

"Charles, never your Grace, never again," he said, raising her hand to kiss it. "I told you that once before, my love. But come! Are you tired? I thought, if you should not dislike it, to leave Brighton this afternoon. We can be in London by ten this evening, and I have a great wish to take you immediately to Wrotherham House, my love, but only if you feel up to the journey. I would not tire you.''

In his eyes was a concern for her and the child, and Emily smiled. ''I should like that. I have not been unhappy here precisely, but for some reason I should like to leave Brighton and all its memories behind,'' she told him.

The duke drove briskly back to the inn and secured a private parlor for his new wife so she might rest while his clothes were packed, his curricle brought around, and his groom informed of the morning's events.

Thomas' eyes widened for a moment when he learned that the new duchess was Miss Nelson.

''You and Greene are the only ones who know, Thomas, and I know I can rely on you both to keep the duchess's former occupation and identity a secret.'' He went on to explain her memory loss and her rightful name, and Thomas, who had spent so much time searching for the lady, was quick to assure his master that not by a single word would he betray the bride.

They were on the road to London a short time later. The duke's team was swift and his curricle especially built for speed, but still it was almost ten before they arrived in Park Lane. At the last stage, Charles had sent the groom ahead on a hired hack to alert his servants, and especially his valet, of their imminent arrival, and when the duke handed Emily down from the curricle, she found Wrotherham House a blaze of welcoming lights, all the staff assembled in the front hall to welcome their new mistress, and an elegant supper, complete with champagne, prepared for the two of them.

Charles was so proud of her. He knew she must be tired, but she held her head erect and smiled as the butler introduced her to the staff, all of whom, from the tiniest tweeny to the duke's valet himself, were impressed by her quiet, assured manner.

The housekeeper took her up to a suite of rooms adjoining the duke's that had been prepared for her, and after she had bathed and changed, the duke joined her there for supper. It was a lighthearted meal served by Greene himself, and when he had poured the last glass of champagne, and left them, the duke came around the table to take her hands in his, dropping a kiss on her golden hair as he did so.

"You are weary, my love. Go to bed now and I will see you in the morning," he said, looking into her beautiful, troubled green eyes. When she would have spoken, he put his fingers over her mouth. "No, I insist. There is no hurry, my dear, for we have all the rest of our lives together now."

With a final kiss he was gone, promising to send a maid to assist her, and Emily, who was indeed weary, wiped a tear from her eyes. How good he was, how kind, she thought. She was asleep almost as soon as her head touched the pillows, and this evening at least, she was not troubled by nightmares.

The following days were filled with activity. First, the duke insisted on taking her shopping, showering her with gorgeous gowns and ensembles, and furs and jewels. When Emily protested, he hushed her by reminding her that, as the Duchess of Wrotherham, naturally she had an obligation to be beautifully dressed. He insisted on hiring her a lady's maid himself, and he took her all over Wrotherham House so she might see what improvements and new decorations she wished to initiate, and he bought her a large square-cut emerald surrounded by diamonds with a matching wedding band for her hand, and reclaimed his signet ring with a kiss.

The duke had sent an announcement to the newspapers of his marriage, and as soon as some of her gowns had been delivered, he took Emily to concerts, the theater, and the opera, but as if they were really on their honeymoon and wrapped in a cloak of invisibility, he saw none of his friends or relations.

They were in London for only two weeks, and if it never occurred to Emily to wonder why Charles did not introduce her to his family, or mention hers, it was probably because she was so busy, so constantly in her new husband's company that she never thought about it. Besides, he had told her that she was an only child and that both her parents had died some time ago.

At length they set out for Wrotherham Park. Emily was feeling much more at ease with Charles now, although sometimes the light in those black eyes troubled her when he smiled at her, or she was surprised by an eager expression on his handsome face, so quickly controlled, and privately she wondered how long such a virile man as the duke appeared to be would be content with this platonic marriage that they shared.

She herself was not at all averse to having him make love to her now, but she knew no way to let him know she would welcome it, and although she still could not remember being with him before, somehow she was sure it must have been wonderful. Sometimes when he kissed her lightly, she wished she might throw her arms around him and kiss him back until he refused to let her go, and she sighed with frustration. She had no idea how much more frustrating and difficult all this was for the duke, since he had promised himself he would do nothing to upset her until she was ready.

Emily was astounded at the size of Wrotherham Park as they came up the mile-long drive. Made of rosy brick, it had been built many generations ago and added onto as the fortunes of the Saint Allyns grew and prospered, until now it encompassed several stories and wings. She admired the formal gardens, the wide terraces that overlooked the park and ornamental water, and told Charles the peacocks were the crowning touch.

"So . . . so ducal!" She laughed, her emerald eyes mischievous, and Charles had all he could do not to drop the reins and catch her up in his arms then and there. All unaware, Emily continued to tease him, "And I suppose there is another army of servants to be greeted, as well as gardeners, grooms, and gameskeepers? What state, sir! I am not only impressed, I see I shall have to take great care not to grow haughty and proud, and addicted to the use of the royal we."

"You have my permission to be and say anything you wish, child," Charles told her, tooling his curricle briskly around the circular gravel drive and coming to a halt at the bottom of a long flight of stone steps that was lined with footmen in livery and headed by his austere butler.

"I wonder if I should care for it?" Emily mused as the duke came around to lift her down, motioning the footmen away. "Hmm. 'Her Grace is not receiving this afternoon' . . . 'Her Grace would be pleased to dine' . . . 'Her Grace wishes to retire.' "

"May I suggest 'Her Grace would be pleased to love His Grace'?" Charles whispered as he held her close to him for a moment before setting her on her feet.

He felt her stiffen and moved away to greet his butler, cursing himself for his clumsiness. Fool, he told himself. It was too soon, and he had startled her. He was polite and attentive as he shepherded her through the welcoming routine and turned her over to his housekeeper, Mrs. Turner, and so formal that Emily was sure she could not have heard him correctly. She barely saw the beautiful rooms that were to be hers, and was glad when the housekeeper finally shooed the maids out before her and left her alone to rest and think.

She did not see the duke again until evening when they dined in the great dining chamber. Emily was glad that Charles had had her placed beside him instead of what seemed a mile away down the long expanse of mahogany, and she was also glad that he did not refer to the awkwardness that had occurred at their arrival; he seemed to have forgotten it.

She went to bed early, something she had been doing with regularity in these early days of her pregnancy. Charles remained in the library, going over some papers. He came in to her before he went to his own rooms next door, and found her sleeping in the large bed with its satin covers, looking as beautiful as any angel with her blond hair loosened on the pillow. He had to clench his hands and turn away quickly.

But sometime during the night, he awoke to the sound of desperate sobbing, and when he came back into her bedroom, he heard her calling his name. He saw she was still fast asleep, and he sat down on the bed to draw her into his arms and hold her close, as he might have a child who was frightened of the dark.

"Hush now, Emily. It is all right, for I am here," he said, his deep voice husky and unsteady.

Emily opened her eyes, looking perplexed for a moment.

"Why do you cry like that, love?" he asked.

"I don't know. Ever since I lost my memory, I have had nightmares where I seem to be lost and afraid I will be all alone forever," she whispered, trying not to sob.

The duke wiped her eyes. "You will never be lost again, my dear," he reassured her, and then he stayed beside her, rocking her in his arms until her breathing calmed and her eyes closed as she rested her head on his broad chest. But when he made a reluctant move to lay her back down in bed and take his leave, her eyes flew open and she threw her arms around him.

"No, do not leave me! Do not leave me ever again," she cried, and without speaking, the duke got into bed beside her and took her in his arms.

And then it all came right at last.

Throughout his lovemaking, Emily felt the great wave of warmth and joy that she was sure she had known before, and his whispered endearments and strong caressing hands made her reach out in turn to draw him even closer. "Yes," the little voice in her head told her as he kissed her with such familiar ardor, "yes, he is the one, the only one." She was almost fainting with the myriad sensations she felt when his lean body quickened its movements, and she arched her back to draw him deeper inside her, as if somehow she knew this would please him. She felt him catch his breath in a little gasp, and then there was nothing but Charles, in her and around her, permeating every inch of her body with a growing sensation of love and fulfillment. For a long moment, she drifted away from the world, and then she was aware that he had lowered his head to rest it besides hers on the pillow. In the candlelight, Emily saw that his eyes were closed and a little smile curled his chiseled lips. She watched him for a moment, raising herself on one elbow so she might see the expressions that played over his face. Suddenly his eyes opened and he turned toward her, both hands smoothing her hair back from her face so there was no golden curtain between them.

"My dearest," he said, his black eyes glowing, "how beautiful you are. Why, you were made for love!"

For a moment, something dark came into the room, and Emily shook her head to dispel it. A memory from another time, something that had happened to her once—no, she would not remember it! The only thing that is important was that Charles, my dear, dear husband, she amended, has come to me at last. She snuggled down into his arms and sighed as she closed her eyes. She was safe here; he would keep the dark thoughts and memories at bay. She felt his arms tighten around her, and just before she dropped off to sleep, she murmured, "I love you, Charles."

Before the duke could reply, he felt her breathing become deeper, and so he only kissed her gently on the temple and in the little hollow of her throat before he closed his eyes himself.

It was a long time before he slept, however, for he could not help but recall how spoiled and arrogant he had been when he first met her. He remembered how he had only thought to make her his mistress until he discovered her real name, and he was ashamed of himself. How grateful and humble he was now for this precious gift of love she offered him so freely. His wife and his lover, and the child she carried made her even more dear to him. He had not really prayed in years, but now he thanked God for his great good fortune and vowed to be worthy of it before he fell asleep at last, holding her close in his arms.

When he awoke in the morning, he saw that she was still asleep, lying on her side close to him, with one slim arm thrown across his chest and her fingers entwined in the curly black hair on his chest as if she was afraid he might disappear. There had been no further nightmares, for although the duke had slept intermittently, sometimes coming awake to ease an arm aching from the weight of her body, or to make sure she was comfortable, his duchess had slept like one bewitched, her breathing deep and even and her face composed. He had meant to return to his own bed, sure she would rest better alone, but now he made himself comfortable and dozed beside her.

It was sometime later when he was startled to hear a quick knock on the door, which opened immediately to reveal the aproned figure of Reynolds, her maid. The duke had chosen this woman deliberately, for she was so unlike Emily he was sure she would not be reminded of her previous occupation. Now, the tall, gaunt, middle-aged maid flushed and began to back from the room. From the bed beside him, he heard his wife say, almost coldly, "From now on, you must not enter my room until you have been summoned, Reynolds. You may go."

The maid curtsied and shut the door quietly behind her, and Charles turned, afraid from her tone that Emily was upset. He found her grinning up at him, her green eyes alight with mischief.

"Now, didn't I sound very ducal, dearest Charles?" she whispered, and when he put his arms around her and drew her close, she added, "Of course it was very unfair to the poor woman when she has never had to worry about such things before."

"Then her reprimand is long overdue, for I find your bed so much more pleasant than mine that I plan to spend every night here," the duke told her, kissing her on the nose and both eyelids.

"No doubt it is because it is wider, or firmer, or softer," his irrepressible wife agreed cordially. "Perhaps the pillows are more to your liking, or the coverings a more agreeable color than your own?"

"Lorelei," he said, shaking her gently, " 'tis only your gorgeous self that makes the difference, and well you know it! Well, wife, are you pleased to rise?"

Emily put back her head and laughed. "Well, husband, are you?" she asked. Then she put her hands on his shoulders and stared at him with a proud, haughty expression, and in the same voice she had used to address her maid, she added, "Should her Grace be pleased to love his Grace? Hmmm. Her Grace will think about it."

"But his Grace does not have to think," he growled before he began to kiss her over and over again.

It was a long time before Reynolds was called to bring the duchess's breakfast tray, and when she entered the room, there was no sign of the duke, although she could hear him whistling in the adjoining rooms.

"I'm sure I'm very sorry, your Grace," Reynolds whispered in an anguished tone, and Emily looked up to see that her maid was distraught, for she was twisting her hands in her apron and had tears in her eyes. Again there came that little snake of memory, dark and somehow threatening, and Emily said quickly, "It was not your fault, my dear Reynolds. I should have told you my wishes before. Come, forget it! It is such a beautiful day and I would like a bath before I dress. And then I think I will wear the new sprigged muslin and the large straw hat with the matching roses on it. The duke is taking me for a drive this afternoon."

She smiled to show she was not at all displeased, and the maid plumped up her pillows and laid her breakfast tray before her with a grateful look for her kindness, before she went away to get the bath ready. Emily found she was hungry and ate the shirred eggs and a slice of ham as well as a roll. As she sipped her coffee, she smiled to herself. What an appetite her Grace has this morning, she thought, and I don't even have to wonder why!

In the late-summer days that followed, all through September and early October, the Saint Allyns continued to revel in their newfound happiness. Charles promised to teach Emily to ride next spring, after the baby's birth, for both of them found the easy walks and sedate drives that were all they could indulge in, irksome. There was hardly any privacy during the day at Wrotherham Park, not with the army of servants going about their duties, all bowing and tugging their forelocks, or curtsying whenever they saw the duke and duchess. Sometimes Emily would look up and see Charles staring at her, and as she knew very well by this time what that sparkling, intent look implied, she would smile and blow him a kiss as soon as the butler turned his back or the footman bent to attend the fire. She knew that he longed to send them all scurrying so he might bolt the drawing-room door and make love to her then and there, and that he refrained from doing so only with a great deal of effort. It was true that in her early pregnancy, and with her love for the duke glowing on her face, Emily was more beautiful than ever, especially since there was no cloud of regret about "unequal stations" and "unworthy brides" to mar her happiness, and Charles could hardly believe his good fortune and the joy he experienced so continually.

He had summoned London's most famous *accoucheur* to examine his wife, and although Emily laughed at his concern, smoothing her gown over her flat stomach, she acquiesced, for the child—Charles' son—was only a little less dear to her already than his illustrious father.

The duke, over a glass of sherry with Doctor Randall while Emily dressed again, was relieved to hear that his wife was in excellent health and that the Doctor expected nothing to complicate her pregnancy and delivery. The duke questioned him about her loss of memory as well, but the learned doctor had no more insight into that condition than Doctor Spears had had.

"It may be, your Grace," he said as he rose to take his leave, "that the duchess will remember in an instant. Even something as simple as a familiar aroma or sound could trigger her memory. But it is equally possible that she will never recall her past. You said it has been over two months since the accident? That is indeed a long time, but since she is not fretting about it and seems so happy and contented, I cannot see that her condition should be of any concern."

The duke thanked him and, as the butler ushered him out, could not help offering up a silent plea that his wife would never remember her former life. He knew he could not keep her in this ivory tower forever, aloof from the world and its cruel gossip, for he had already received a horrified letter from his aunt, and only a few cold, formal notes of congratulation from other members of the *haut ton* that showed him only too clearly what his duchess would have to face in the future. He refused to think about it now. At least until the baby was born he could protect her here at Wrotherham Park. When they went to London next spring for the Season, he hoped that their love for each other and her attachment to him would be so strong that even when he gave her a carefully edited story of her background, it would make no difference to her, and with him at her side, she would continue to be the gracious and assured Duchess of Wrotherham that she was now.

He put all thoughts of this from his mind as Emily entered the drawing room, radiant in a gown of her favorite green. She came to him immediately with that familiar look of love in her eyes that always caught at his heart, and as she held up her face for his kiss, he vowed he would cherish her always, no matter what the future might bring.

11

By the end of October, Emily began to show her pregnancy a little. Charles admired the new fullness of her breasts, but she and Reynolds did not have to choose her gown with any more care as yet. Emily was glad that the current fashions, with their low round necklines and Empire waists would conceal her condition so well when the time came. She knew her pregnancy was well known among the servants, and a matter of general rejoicing and anticipation, but she was still a little shy about it, and when Mrs. Turner brought her an eggnog and some little cakes the chef had made especially, or Charles' butler, Wilkins, beamed at her and was quick to send a footman to support her elbow when she came downstairs, she was embarrassed.

"I am treated like a china doll," she complained to the duke as they sat one morning in the library. "I do not *want* to be coddled this way. Heavens, I will not break."

Her husband smiled at her over the papers spread on his desk. "I am delighted to hear you say so, Emily, for while you were still sleeping, I went out for an early ride. It is going to be a beautiful day, as warm as summer. Should you like to have a small adventure with me?"

There was an air of almost devilish anticipation in his eyes, and Emily nodded her head.

"Good! Summon your maid, Duchess, and have her bring you your stole and bonnet. I shall say no more, for I intend this to be a surprise."

When they went out, Emily saw two footmen putting a large hamper and some pillows and rugs in one of the landaus.

The top of the carriage had been folded back, and the duke's team of chestnuts stood ready harnessed.

"Where are we going, Charles?" Emily asked after she had been seated in the carriage and the duke took his place beside her and picked up the reins. She noticed there were no attendant grooms, and smiled to herself.

"It is a secret, my dear," he told her as they tooled away down the drive. "But I am kidnapping you and taking you away to a far country where I can have you all to myself, completely alone."

"How nice," Emily said, putting her hand on his thigh and feeling the muscles tense. "And there we can make love whenever we wish, and I will not have to watch you struggle to control yourself until what has become, my dear sir, a disgracefully early bedtime."

The duke laughed out loud. "But the hour I choose to go up is perfectly understandable in a soon-to-be-father. Of course the servants know it is because of my concern for the heir, and not from any designs I might have on your beautiful self."

"Then it is just as well they do not know of the amount of sleep I am really allowed," Emily said demurely. "I hope you may be right, for I have been meaning to ask you to spare my blushes, your Grace. I can almost hear what the footmen are thinking when they bow us up the stairs, and what your so very correct butler makes of it I do not care to know."

"I shall order him to leave our employ as soon as we return," the duke vowed, turning the landau off the main drive into a smaller lane. "But, dearest, are you really concerned? I would not have you upset."

Emily smiled up into his suddenly frowning face. "Of course not. I am teasing you. It is shameless of me perhaps, but I do not care what anyone thinks of us, I love you too much. And after all, surely what the Duke and Duchess of Wrotherham deem proper carries enough credit to overset any of the world's opinions."

She knew she had said the right thing, for Charles' face brightened at once. "Well said, my love! If you would please me, always remember that," he replied.

They traveled on through a section of the woods that Emily had never seen before, and at length the duke pulled up in a small clearing. He gave her the reins to hold while he secured the horses, then he came back to the carriage and took out the hamper and rugs, and bidding her remain where she was until he came back, he disappeared down a narrow path. Emily closed her eyes and raised her face to the warm sunlight. The heat of the day was making her sleepy, and she was content to sit there on the perch, listening to the sounds of the birds and waiting for Charles to return to her.

"Come, love," she heard his deep voice commanding her, and she opened her eyes to see him smiling and holding out his arms. When she stepped down from the carriage, she found herself swooped up in those same strong arms and carried down the path.

"Indeed I think I am kidnapped," she said, one arm around his neck and the other hand holding on to her straw hat. "Horrors! Miles away in the forest, and no one to come if I call!"

"They had better not," the duke said in mock grimness as he reached the end of the path and set her on her feet in a grassy glade bordered by a wide shallow brook and a small waterfall.

"Charles, what a perfect spot," Emily exclaimed, running to admire the falling water.

Her husband spread out the rugs, and after she sat down and untied the streamers of her hat, he took the bottle of wine from the hamper and went to place it in a shaded spot under the waterfall to cool, before he came back to sit beside her. Soon Emily discarded her shawl, and the duke removed his coat and cravat and opened his shirt in the warm stillness.

"Who would take us for the duke and duchess now?" Emily asked idly, one arm shading her eyes as she lay sprawled full-length on the rug and smiled up into the handsome face that was bent over hers, smiling in return. "We look like a couple of servants on their day off."

She wondered why Charles' face darkened for a moment, but then he kissed her sun-warmed lips and she forgot everything but the exciting familiar pressure of his mouth, and the strong yet gentle hands that moved up her bare arms to caress her breasts.

"You are a witch, my love," he said when at last he raised his head. "Come, let us eat our luncheon. To return with a full hamper would only give rise to those speculations you abhor. Why, my desires for early bedtimes would pale in comparison.''

Emily ate the pâté and crusty rolls, nibbled on a chicken leg, and let Charles peel her a peach. They drank their sparkling wine from crystal goblets, but when he offered her a piece of cake, she refused. ''I am full, and besides, it will make me fat.''

Charles lay back on the rug and laughed. ''There is no way you can stop getting much fatter, my dear. And after all, what is one sweet more or less?''

''Shall you mind, Charles?'' she asked, her face earnest. ''I mean, I know I must get heavy and awkward and grotesque in the coming months, but I—''

The duke put one hand over her mouth and the other, protectively, on her abdomen. ''You will be even more dear to me, my love, if that is possible. How can you be grotesque, you, the mother of our child and my dearest love?''

Emily felt a lump in her throat at his words, and she was glad when the duke pulled her down gently beside him and began to make love to her.

For some reason, there in the woods so far from Wrotherham Park and completely alone, their lovemaking was more sensual than it had ever been before. It was the first time since their marriage they had been together outdoors, and Emily gave herself up to it with abandon. The duke, as if sensing her mood, took endless time to arouse her to heights she had never reached before. She cried out in delight when at last they reached that secret peak they had climbed together so many times before, and afterward, she could not restrain her tears of happiness when she lay clasped in his arms against his broad chest before she fell fast asleep.

The duke looked down at her, his own heart full of loving content, and then he wiped all traces of tears from her cheeks and stretched out beside her to sleep as well.

When she woke up, Emily kept her eyes closed for a moment, listening to the cheerful sound of the brook and feeling the warm sun on her naked body. She turned her head idly and saw the duke beside her, his black hair crisp in the sunlight and his aristocratic features relaxed in sleep, before she sighed and stared up at the blue sky and the few puffy clouds that floated above them.

It must be very late, she thought. We must make haste, for Lady Quentin will be angry if I do not return soon.

Suddenly she froze, and then she sat up, her green eyes wide and staring, and one trembling hand crept up to cover her mouth when she heard herself whimpering. Her eyes were dark with horror, and with an involuntary motion, she edged away from the sleeping figure of her husband. Her name was Emily Wyndham. She was the daughter of Althea Wyndham, and she was also Margaret Nelson, lady's maid. A thousand memories flooded her mind. Lord and Lady Wyndham . . . Captain and Lady Quentin . . . Wantage, London, Belgium. Now she knew what she had been doing in Bristol, why she had masqueraded as Mrs. Wiggins. She had been trying to escape the duke again. Miss Rutherford is right to hate men, she thought bitterly.

For now, of course, she was Emily Saint Allyn, Duchess of Wrotherham, the one person she had fought against becoming for such a long time and with such high purpose.

Suddenly she was angry, as angry as she had ever been in her life. Charles had known! He had known how she felt, and he had married her anyway, taking advantage of her when she was unable to stop him in her illness. And he had seduced her with his lovemaking, all the while not telling her anything about her past, so that she might not be reminded of it and perhaps regain her memory. He had been so selfish, so determined to have his own way, that he even hoped she would remain in ignorance of her former life.

She felt a sharp pain deep inside her and leaned over, trying not to retch, and her hands flew to protect the new life there. Dear God, she thought, my baby! In a moment the pain left her, and she straightened, her movements those of an old woman. What was she to do? There was no going back and even if she could bear the squalor of a divorce, she knew Charles would never allow it, for she carried the possible heir to Wrotherham. Suddenly she wished she had never met the arrogant, superior duke, never fallen in love with him, never lain with him and conceived his child. Was her life always to be so horrible and complicated? Was she never to know any peace at all?

She heard the duke stirring beside her, and knowing she could not face him just yet, she lay down again and, turning her head away, closed her eyes. The sun that had seemed so benevolent only moments before could not warm her now, and she hoped Charles would not notice her trembling. She sensed it when he turned and looked at her and then she heard him rise and move away. A moment later, her shawl was laid softly over her, and she could have wept as she felt his hands tuck it gently around her body so as not to disturb her slumber. Charles, Charles, she cried deep inside, why did you do it? Why?

In the little time that it took the duke to dress and repack the hamper, she had composed herself. She knew she was not able to tell him what had happened just yet, for she needed more time to get used to the sudden recovery of her memory and to make plans for how she would handle the future. When he knelt beside her and put his hand on her shoulder, she was ready. She opened her eyes and stared up at him. She had all she could do to summon a faint smile to her stiff lips.

"I shall call you Sleeping Beauty, love," he teased, stooping to kiss her lightly. "I am sorry to disturb your rest, but it grows late and there is a cool breeze come up." He handed her her shift as she sat up obediently, and added, "I will carry these things back to the landau while you dress. Our secret journey is over, but I will never forget it."

"Nor I, your Grace," she murmured as he strode away. "Perhaps it is to be the last really happy day of my life, I cannot tell."

As she fastened the hooks of her gown and pulled on her stockings, Emily mourned the innocence that had been hers in her illness. If only she had not remembered! If only it were possible to go back!

She could not bring herself to talk very much on the return drive, and when the duke questioned her, she was quick to excuse herself by saying she was a little tired.

"I hope it has not been too much for you, my dear," he said, his dark eyes worried as he whipped up the team. "But we will soon be home and then you may rest till dinnertime if you like. I should confer with my agent, in any case. The poor man has been trying to get my attention for some time, but we know, do we not, love, why he has been so unsuccessful?"

He threw back his head and laughed, and Emily tried again to smile. As they drew up to the steps at the front of the house, he added, "And no one will remark on our early bedtime tonight, for you will go up alone to sleep. I will not disturb you, my love.''

He handed her down from the carriage and gave her his best bow, and then, oblivious to the many windows behind him, he kissed her hand. ''My dearest,'' he murmured, ''you have made me so happy, I am sure the gods are jealous. I hope they are not even now preparing their revenge.''

He took her up to her rooms himself and summoned her maid, and just when Emily thought she must scream from the tension of trying to appear normal in front of him, he went away.

She sank into a wing chair before the fire, and when Reynolds came in and curtsied, she could barely summon a normal tone of voice to order tea. How many times had she herself stood just like that, eyes downcast and hands folded meekly before her, awaiting her mistress's pleasure? And since her marriage, how many times had she ordered Reynolds to do this and that with no more concern for the woman than Lady Quentin and her other mistresses had had for her? She remembered the morning when she had spoken so coldly to her maid for coming in while Charles was still in her bed, and how she had laughed about it afterward—laughed, like some grand, cruel lady when in reality she and Reynolds were equals.

Emily was quick to dismiss her when her maid brought the tea, and when she was alone, she got up to pace up and down, her hands clenched and her face pale.

By the time the first dressing bell rang, she was as confused as ever. She had not been able to decide what she should do, for her mind had ranged instead over everything that had happened to her since her mother died. It had been like glancing through a book she had read years before, making the reacquaintance of characters she had once loved but since forgotten.

But always her thoughts came back to Charles and their brief liaison, and once again the anger flooded back as she reviewed every single minute of their time together and realized that he had not introduced her to a single member of his family or ever suggested he wanted her to meet his friends. Oh, no, she thought bitterly, he rushed me down here to the country where no one can see me, and he intends to keep me hidden here as long as he can. In spite of his loving words, he is ashamed of me, for, otherwise, why would he not brazen it out as he had always said he would do? She discounted the opinions of his army of servants; they would take their orders and their cue from him. It was clear to her now that he had married her because he had "ruined" her, a girl from a good family, and because she was pregnant, and for no other reason. Of course he was not averse to making love to her; after all, had he not paid a high price for the privilege?

She did not know how she was to face him, sitting across the table and pretending everything was just the same as it had been before they set out this afternoon, and when Reynolds answered the bell, she asked her to make her excuses to the duke and tell him that her Grace had decided to have a tray in her room and go to bed immediately, and that she did not wish to be disturbed.

She knew that Charles would not go down to his solitary meal without looking in on her, and she pretended to be dozing when he came in. He picked up her hand where it lay on the satin coverlet, and then she felt his soft kiss on her hair. She tried to keep her breathing deep and even until she heard the door close behind him.

When Reynolds came to take her almost untouched tray away, she was about to dismiss her for the night when she had a sudden thought.

"Reynolds," she said, making her voice easy and assured, "I would like to borrow one of your aprons and caps, if you will be so good."

The maid looked surprised, and she added, "It is something the duke and I were discussing this afternoon, and I want to play a little joke on him."

The maid curtsied, still looking confused, but she returned promptly with the required articles before she bid her mistress good night.

Emily got up and dressed in one of her most sober dark gowns, and then she sat down at the dressing table and brushed her curls out before she pulled her hair back into a severe knot. With the apron tied around her waist and the cap in place on her head, she rose to stare at herself in the large pier glass and discovered that the Duchess of Wrotherham had disappeared, and in her place was only another servant.

She sat down by the fire to wait, and when she heard

voices in the duke's rooms, she tiptoed over to the connecting doors.

Charles' deep voice spoke an order, and she heard Greene murmur a response. It seemed to take forever before she heard him say clearly, "Very good, your Grace. I shall call you at eight. Good night."

Charles answered him, and when Emily heard the door close, she straightened up and, taking a deep breath, opened the door.

Charles was sitting before the fire, a glass of wine at his elbow and his chin propped up in one hand as he stared into the flames. At some tiny sound she made, he turned his head, and the smile that was already forming on his well-cut mouth froze for a moment as his dark brows came together in a frown.

"You remembered," he whispered, getting slowly to his feet and staring at the lady's maid who had replaced his duchess. Miss Nelson was back, buttoned into her usual neat dark gown and crisp apron and cap, her beautiful blond hair skinned back in an ugly knot. The only thing that was different was her expression. As a maid, she had never stared at him so directly, and she would never have dared to show such scorn and anger in those emerald eyes of hers that now resembled chips of ice.

"Yes, your Grace, I remembered," she said, dropping him a curtsy before she folded her hands before her in meek submission. "Will there be anything further required this evening, your Grace?"

He came toward her and took her hands in his, and Emily forced them to remain limp and unresponsive.

"Remove those things at once," he ordered, his voice harsh. "You may have remembered your past, Emily, but I beg you also to remember your present. You are the Duchess of Wrotherham!"

"As you wish, sir," she said, bobbing a curtsy before she took off the apron and unpinned her cap. "Of course it must be an object with me to please you, sir. And perhaps you would like me to continue to undress?"

The duke's mouth was bracketed with hard white lines, and his eyes were blazing. "Stop it!" he demanded, putting his hands on her arms and shaking her a little. "What nonsense is this? You are my wife."

"Yes, your Grace, I am, but not through any wish of my own, as you very well know."

"But you will have to admit we have been happy, if you are truthful. Come, Emily, do not deny you love me as much as I love you," he said, trying to draw her closer. Emily twisted away and he released her.

"Yes, I love you, more to my shame," she said bitterly. "And it is obvious that you yourself are ashamed of me. Why else did you hurry me down to the country unless it was to keep me out of sight? Why have you never introduced me to your family, your friends?"

Charles' face paled a little, but he said in a steady voice, "But we were on our honeymoon, love. One does not invite the world at such a time."

"Our honeymoon? A little after the fact, your Grace, wouldn't you say?"

Suddenly the sarcasm left her voice and she said in her normal tone, "How could you, Charles? How could you take advantage of me when I could not remember? You *knew* I was determined not to marry you and bring this shame on you, but you ignored that fact while you gratified your own code. Oh, you knew what a disastrous match you made, but you did not care. Having determined to marry me, you could not bear to be thwarted, could you? Even to the point of taking an unwilling bride, if she had been able to know she was unwilling. But that did not matter to you in the least, as long as you got your own way and satisfied your ridiculous gentleman's code of honor. I shall never forgive you for that, Charles, never!"

"Emily! Come, my dear, you are distraught, not thinking. Of course I had to marry you when I found out you were with child, but you know I was determined to do so long before I learned of that happy event. I told you in Belgium you would be duchess here."

"I think you have been very foolish, your Grace," Emily retorted, her green eyes almost as dark with her feelings as his own. Before she thought, her anger made her add, "For how can you be sure the child is yours, indeed? There were several weeks between the time I ran away and you found me again."

The duke raised his hand and slapped her. It was not a

bruising blow, but it whipped her head back and tears came unbidden to her eyes.

"How dare you, madam?" he asked, his voice taut with rage. "How dare you speak to me that way? I know the child is mine."

"We must certainly hope he has black hair and eyes in that case, your Grace," Emily retorted. "But maids, you know, even the best of them, have uncertain morals. They are not like your exalted self and other members of the *ton*."

Suddenly Charles dropped his hands and walked away from her, going a little blindly to lean against the mantel. Emily stared at his broad back, her breath coming in little gasps as she dashed away the tears with the back of one unsteady hand. For a moment there was a heavy silence before the duke straightened up to turn and face her, his eyes bleak and cold.

Emily took a deep breath and clenched her hands in the folds of her skirt as Charles said, "Your pardon, wife." His voice was so rigid with anger that she cringed. "It was unforgivable of me to strike you, especially in your condition. But may I say I do not believe you? You are not like other women who may cuckold their husbands, although even they would not dare with the *first* child. No, no—not the lady who was Emily Wyndham, with her exquisite sensibilities and stern moral code."

The bow that accompanied this compliment was ironic. Emily never took her eyes from him, for his expression was so forbidding that he looked as if his face had been carved from marble.

"I would remind you again, madam, of something you said only this afternoon. You told me then that you did not care what anyone thinks of us and that what the Duke and Duchess of Wrotherham consider correct matters more than a single one of the world's opinions. I take it you no longer subscribe to that viewpoint?"

Emily wished he would speak to her in his normal tone of voice, instead of with this frozen sneer, and the hurt and anguish she was experiencing made her say, "It is impossible for me to do so. Now that I remember my past, how can I think your behavior proper? Or my own either?"

"I see. In that case I must ask you what your wishes are. Know that I will never permit our marriage to be dissolved, but if my behavior in wedding you without your consent has given you a disgust of me, I shall be happy to relieve you of my attentions. In fact, you have only to tell me and I shall be gone from Wrotherham Park tomorrow.''

"There is no need for that, your Grace," Emily replied, somewhat startled by this turn of events. "This is your home, I would not turn you out of it. Give me leave to go instead."

The duke's mouth twisted wryly. "Unfortunately, that is not possible, for it is also your home now, madam, whether you like it or not. No, I would be very distressed if my son was not born here on his own land. You will remain in residence, but you have my word I will not trouble you again. In other words, Duchess, we will have a marriage of convenience. In public, all will be as before, but in private . . ." He stopped and laughed, an angry bark that had no humor in it. "What am I thinking of? Of course there will be no 'private,' not until you yourself will it."

Emily involuntarily raised her hand, but the duke had turned away again and did not see the little gesture.

"You need not fear that I shall attempt to coerce you or influence you in any way," he said, and then he whirled and pointed one stern finger at her. "Yes, perhaps I *was* wrong to do what I did, but there was no certainty that you would ever remember your past, and there was our love for each other and our child to consider. However, know you will never be bothered by my unwanted attentions. I daresay we shall grow accustomed. But even so, you must pray the child will be a son so you will never be forced to lie with me again. In this, I expect you to do your duty. I *will* have my heir; on that I must insist, madam.''

He glared at her, his brows knit in a ferocious frown, and Emily saw that he meant every word of it, and she wondered how a man so much in love only a short time ago could say such cold, wounding things. She knew her husband was a proud man, and tonight she had struck out at his pride and damaged his image of himself; she saw clearly that he would remain aloof from her forever if she did not relent. She swallowed as he continued, "You have only to ask my steward for anything you need, if I should happen to be absent. Perhaps there is someone you would like to have stay with you and bear you company? Invite whomever you like. I shall arrange for the doctor to make regular visits, and I shall of course instruct my lawyers to put any sum of money you require at your disposal.''

For a moment he paused, his black eyes intent on her face as Emily bowed her head, lowering her eyelids slightly so he could not see the tears that came unbidden to them. Dear God, how was she to live like this? Left alone in this massive house with only the servants, and five long months to go until her confinement? Or what was even worse, sharing it with Charles in a travesty of connubial contentment for the servants' sakes. Why couldn't he let her go? She knew the Misses Rutherford would take her in, and it would be so much easier for her there. But then she realized that this was to be her punishment, if that was the correct word for the situation. She might not have wanted to be duchess here, but now that was an accomplished fact, the duke expected her to grace her position with composure and dignity, no matter how lonely and miserable she felt. She had forced them both to this; she must accept the consequences. Almost, she wished she had never confronted him at all.

''Nothing to say, madam?'' he asked in the lengthening silence. ''How unusual! In that case, and having concluded our business, I give you leave to retire.''

He bowed, and Emily turned away, hurrying to the door of her room, which she could barely see through the tears that now ran unchecked down her cheeks. As she reached the door and grasped the handle, he spoke again in a low voice, husky with emotion.

''Take very good care of yourself, my dear. You and our child will be always in my thoughts. And remember, you have only to send me word to command my instant attendance. I will, of course, be praying that you will forgive me and end this charade soon.''

With her throat thickened with the sobs she was restraining, she could not answer, but she nodded as she passed through into her own room and closed the door behind her.

She had not thought she would be able to sleep, but when she had undressed and climbed into the huge bed, she was so exhausted that she sank into oblivion almost at once, only to toss and turn even as she had done during her worst nightmares.

When she woke to a dark morning, she could hear the rain beating against the panes, and after ringing for her maid, she wandered over to the window to stare down at the gravel drive below her. The beautiful October day they had enjoyed only yesterday was gone as if it had never been, for in one night autumn had disappeared and winter was upon them. She looked at the weeping sky that muted the fall colors as if they were covered by a filmy gray veil. A sudden gust of wind shook the elm trees, and several leaves fell like large tears to the earth. She leaned her forehead against the cold pane, wishing she could weep too. "Charles," she whispered, "Charles."

When Reynolds came in with her tray, she returned to bed. As the maid was arranging her pillows, she noticed her mistress's pallor and silence, and in an effort to cheer her up, said, "Why not stay in bed this gloomy morning, your Grace? Since the duke has gone to London, there is no need to hurry your dressing."

The spoon that Emily was using to stir her tea clattered against the side of the cup. So he had already gone. She could not know he had ridden away at dawn after a sleepless night because he could not bear to remain in such close proximity to her when now, by circumstance, they were so far apart.

Emily felt bereft. Somehow she had imagined she might see him once more, had thought he would be unble to go without coming to bid her good-bye. Then she realized the maid was speaking again, asking for her orders, and she collected herself with an effort.

"No, I shall dress, Reynolds. Be so kind as to tell Mrs. Turner I desire an interview with her in an hour, if that is convenient."

The maid curtsied and went into the dressing room, and Emily forced herself to eat a roll and some fruit. The long solitude was beginning and there was no sense in trying to put it off. With her eyes fixed unseeing on some distant point, she squared her shoulders. Very well. She would be the best duchess Wrotherham had ever known, no matter how she felt.

But in the weeks that followed, there were times when she almost lost her courage, times when she felt so lonely she thought she must die of it. There was no one she could talk to freely. All the servants had begun to love her for the politeness with which she gave her orders and her smiling thanks for a well-performed task, and for her quiet interest in and concern for their well-being; but even though Emily remembered only too well now what it was like to be one of them, the gulf that stretched between the duchess and the staff was as wide as the ocean. She might inquire for the under-butler's sick mother, or arrange for the still-room maid to have a painful tooth extracted, or congratulate Reynolds on her brother's army promotion—she could not confide her own troubles in return.

Charles had remained in town for over two weeks, and when he returned the first time, it was only for a short three days before he was off to visit friends in Scotland. He was scrupulously polite to his wife when they were forced to be in each other's company. At the dinner table, he chatted of the amusements of the Little Season, which was drawing to a close, and told her of the *on-dits* of society and the current plays that could be enjoyed. Emily responded by discussing the estate, the illness of one of his elderly pensioners, and her plans to refurbish the gold salon.

They were so casual and normal, she had all she could do not to scream. If she had thought it horrible to be at Wrotherham Park by herself, she now realized that when the duke was in residence, it was twice as difficult and painful, so it was almost with relief that she bade him good-bye the night before he was to leave for Inverness. Charles stared at her as she curtsied and prepared to leave him to his port. She had announced she was going to bed immediately, rather than waiting for him in the solitude of the drawing room. He almost spoke, for his wife did not look well. Her pregnancy was obvious now, and her face, although still and composed, was pale. His arms ached to hold her close while he begged her to end this farce, as only she could do. Not trusting himself to speak, he nodded, his fingers tightening on the stem of his glass. As Emily moved to the door, which the butler was holding for her, he said, "I shall return by Christmas, my dear. Have a care for yourself."

"I shall, Charles," she answered, smiling a little at Wilkins as he bowed. "Everything will be in order when you return."

"I am sure of it, my admirable Duchess," he murmured, pouring himself another glass of port. He waved to his butler and attendant footmen to leave the room, and then he sat there in a brown study, his eyes frowning in concentration.

Even now he did not trust himself to remain near his wife for any length of time. His anger at her had dimmed quickly, after all, and he loved her so much it was nearly impossible to contain himself when all that he longed to do was sweep her into his arms and force her to admit she loved him the same way. He had hoped that a period of quiet and lonely introspection would bring her to her senses, but he saw no signs that she was relenting, nor even that this stiff, formal marriage of convenience was not at all to her liking. He shook his head and grimaced, wondering what he was to do now.

Emily was awake early the following morning, standing concealed behind the curtains to watch the duke's carriage leave. As he came down the broad steps, followed by Greene, and Thomas opened the door of the coach, he paused for a moment and turned to stare up at her windows. Emily drew in her breath sharply, afraid he could see her there, but his face bore such a tortured look of yearning and unhappiness that, without thinking, she moved forward, determined to sweep the curtains aside and wave to him. Before she could do so, Charles turned away and, bending his dark head, entered his coach, which started down the drive at once at a spanking pace. Her heart sank.

Emily kept busy, making preparations for Christmas. Even though she had no desire for it, the servants would expect the park to be decorated for the season, and there were gifts to be selected for each and every retainer, and special delicacies and wines to be ordered from town. The duke had left his youthful secretary, Mr. Watts, to assist her, and he was very helpful, falling under the duchess's spell as had all the staff.

Emily wished there were guests coming, for spending Christmas alone with the duke was sure to be an uncomfortable experience. But whom could she ask? She knew no one, and the duke had not left any guest list of his own. Her chin went up and her eyes darkened. At least he could have invited some of his family, but of course she knew he had no desire to parade her before them. She quite understood!

One person she did write to, however, and that was her old nurse. She had been inspecting the nursery suite, at Mrs. Turner's request. All the servants knew that something was wrong between their master and his bride, although Mr. Wilkins and Mrs. Turner were careful to keep their speculations to themselves and allowed no one to gossip in their presence. Poor dear, Mrs. Turner thought now, watching Emily rock the ancestral cradle, a little smile coming to her lips as she did so. Why is she so unhappy? I'd like to shake his Grace for whatever is wrong. Seeing that thinking about the baby made her mistress brighten a bit, she began to talk of nursemaids and the refurbishing of the nursery, and Emily remembered her own dear nanny Darty, and wrote to her at once. Mrs. Dartmouth replied she would be delighted to come to Wrotherham Park, and a carriage was dispatched to fetch her. She took charge of the preparations for the baby at once, and more importantly, of Emily herself, cajoling her to eat more and to get her rest as well as some regular exercise, and she would stand for no nonsense in the fulfillment of her instructions. Mrs. Turner was delighted when the duchess seemed happier and more content, although even with Darty, Emily had not gained a real confidante or close friend.

The duke returned shortly before Christmas and the first morning of his stay, he asked Emily to join him in the library. When she entered the room, her heart beating strangely, she found him seated at his desk, frowning over some cards of invitation.

After he had bowed and seated her, he returned to the desk to tap the cards before him.

"We have been asked to a number of festive occasions in honor of the season, madam," he said in a voice that seemed cold and indifferent to Emily's ears. "Would you care to attend? There is no need, of course, to put in an appearance at this time if you should not wish to, for everyone knows of your condition."

Emily felt a surge of anger. "It is a matter of indifference to me, your Grace, but of course I should be happy to accompany you if that is your wish." There, she thought, you cannot know by that statement how mortified I am that you cannot bear to have me meet your friends.

"I do not care," the duke replied carelessly. "I find I am hardly in a festive mood this Christmas."

"In that case, I suggest you refuse them, one and all," Emily snapped, getting to her feet to terminate the interview before she lost her temper. The duke did not notice her mood as he held up one card in his strong hand.

"Perhaps we should at least ask the Earl and Countess of Gant to dine one evening, even if we do not grace their ball.

Nigel is one of my oldest friends, and I am sure you will like Jessica. However, I will not press you. Perhaps in the spring . . .''

"I see no need to put off the inevitable any longer, sir, regardless of my condition, which is, after all, not so noticeable as yet. By all means, extend the invitation. I look forward to it and I shall do my best not to put you to shame."

Her voice shook a little and then she curtsied as the duke rose from his chair and stared at her, his dark eyes intent.

"You could never do that, Duchess," he said softly as she moved away down the long length of the library, her back straight and her skirts swaying with the graceful movement he had always admired. She gave no sign that she heard him.

A few evenings later, resplendent in one of her new silk gowns and the Saint Allyn emeralds, Emily stood beside her husband to welcome Nigel and Jessica Cathcart. She liked the young Countess of Gant immediately. She was a few years older than Emily and not at all a beauty, but her tall, lanky figure and straight sandy hair were more than compensated for by a pair of sparkling blue eyes and a warm smile. Emily thought it was amazing how much she looked like her husband, almost as if they were sister and brother instead of man and wife.

As they all waited in the drawing room for Wilkins to announce dinner, the countess shook her head at the gentlemen, already deep in conversation over by the fireplace.

"You can see how I am ignored, your Grace," she laughed, "but I did not expect the duke to treat his bride in such a cavalier fashion. Charles! Nigel! It is too bad of you to be going on and on about politics and peace treaties, cotton mills, and steam engines when *we* are here. The duchess and I are most offended, are we not, ma'am? But please, if *I* start to discuss people and places you do not know, you must stop me as well, for I do have a tendency to rattle on and on."

Her husband so promptly agreed with her assessment of her character that they all laughed, and Emily begged the countess to call her by her first name. It turned out to be quite the most pleasant evening she had spent at Wrotherham Park since October. She discovered that Jessica was the mother of a seven-year-old daughter and twin boys, age four.

"The monster duo," she remarked in gloomy tones even as her eyes lit up. "I shall pray you do not repeat my mistake, Emily. Harry and Thomas are double trouble, I assure you, and what we are to do when they are a little older, I do not know. Horses and guns and pranks—oh, dear! Marianne was an angel compared to these two. They have quite put me off having any more babies, although Nigel would like a dozen. Do you know what they did yesterday?''

She went on to describe how the twins had stumbled into some of the Christmas decorations and the havoc that had resulted, and Emily laughed out loud. The duke felt a stab in his heart. How long had it been since Emily had laughed with him like that? How long since he had been able to bring such a warm smile to her face?

By the time the Cathcarts left, shortly after the tea tray had been brought in, for their home was six miles away and it was beginning to snow, they were all fast friends. Emily promised to call on the countess soon after the New Year. ''I must see for myself, Jessica,'' she said. ''I cannot believe your twins are as bad as you have painted them.''

''Worse—much, much worse,'' Nigel intoned, his expressive face glum. ''Jessy is too fond a mother to tell you the whole, but if I did not feel it put a blight on your dreams of the heir to Wrotherham, I would tell you the whole horrible tale.''

''Do not listen to him, Emily; he exaggerates even more than I do,'' her new friend advised. ''I will look forward to your visit. Oh, I am so glad we have met at last. And, Charles, you are to be congratulated. Not only is your duchess beautiful, which of course everyone certainly expected, she is *nice* as well. That will come as a surprise to a great many old busybodies, for she is not at all what they have been imagining.''

''Now I know it is time to go home,'' Nigel said firmly, putting his arm around his outspoken wife and marching her to the door. ''You have said quite enough, Jessy, not that I don't agree with you.''

''Have a happy Christmas!''—''Sorry you must miss the ball!''—''Be sure to call.''—''Good night, good night!''

Amid the laughter of the leavetaking and quite without thinking of what he was doing, Charles put his arm around his wife and hugged her. He felt her stiffen and dropped his arm as if he had touched a red-hot brand from the fire.

''I beg your pardon, madam,'' he said softly, so the footmen could not hear, and then he added in his normal tone. "My congratulations on the evening. The dinner was excellent and you were everything anyone could ask for as *châtelaine* here. I was very proud of you."

Emily noticed that his stiff expression was at odds with these warm words as she swept him a curtsy, and her own face grew still and wary. "Thank you, sir. I beg leave to retire now, for the evening has tired me."

The duke said good night, but before he went to his library, he watched her climb the wide stairs, and his eyes were stormy. The pleasant evening had ended, and so abruptly too.

Shortly after Christmas, he announced his plans to leave the park again one evening at dinner. Nodding to the footman who was offering him a platter of veal, he said, "I am off again tomorrow, madam. Viscount Castlereagh, the Foreign Secretary, has asked me to attend him in London. It seems there may be a mission I can undertake for him abroad. I hesitate to refuse Robert, especially now that we are setting up the peace at last, but I will make every effort to return to England before the birth of our baby."

Emily nodded and sipped her wine. Since life at the park had returned to stiff, formal playacting again after their one dinner party, she was not at all reluctant for the duke to take his leave. Knowing that she would not be so lonely, now she could see Jessica Cathcart as soon as the holidays were over, made her able to bid the duke good-bye with a composure she was far from feeling. Indeed, she was sure if Charles remained, she would be more apt to disgrace herself by bursting into tears before him or screaming she could not stand this travesty of a marriage, and she was sure that would disgust him. She was sure he did not want her anymore except as the mother of his son, for, if he did, why did he keep leaving her? Even the gifts he had brought her for Christmas could not change her mind, although the sable cloak was glorious and the pearls the most perfectly matched she had ever seen.

But a week after the duke's departure, Emily received a note from Jessica, canceling their plans. It seemed that her father was very ill and her mother in need of her, and so the Cathcarts had cut short their stay in the country and were even now on the way to London. Jessica begged her to write and tell her about the baby, and to be sure and let her know when she came up to town, before she signed her note in haste.

Emily sighed and took up her solitary existence once again. She had her interviews with the housekeeper, the chef, and Charles' agent; she read and sewed, and she took some gentle walks around the wintry gardens with her maid when the weather was clement. The only time she left the grounds was to attend church, and since she had not met any of society at the Christmas balls and parties, no one came to Wrotherham Park to break the lonely monotony of her days.

She wondered a little at this. Why was she being snubbed when, after all, the Countess of Gant had been so friendly? She did not realize that if a duchess does not show any desire to know you, it would be the height of presumption to try and initiate a relationship. The gentry around Wrotherham Park, one and all, stayed away.

12

By the end of January, Emily could only be glad to be left alone, for her figure was becoming just as heavy and awkward as she had predicted it would.

She was sitting in the newly redecorated gold salon one afternoon, embroidering a small blanket for the baby, when Wilkins came to announce that Lord and Lady Staunton had called. At first she was tempted to deny them, and her expression of distaste for her condition made the butler add in his fatherly way, "It is only the duke's aunt and uncle, your Grace. They are on their way to London and beg to break their journey here overnight."

At that, Emily nodded and folded up her work with suddenly cold and nervous hands. So, she was to meet some of the duke's family at last! A moment later she rose as the middle-aged couple were bowed into the drawing room.

"How do you do?" she asked, coming toward them with a welcoming smile on her lips. "Unfortunately, Charles is not here, but I am delighted to welcome you in his place."

Lady Staunton sniffed and raised her pince-nez to inspect her new niece more closely. "Of *course* you are delighted, my girl!" she exclaimed in an insulting tone of voice.

Emily stiffened. How dare she speak to me like that, she thought, and where was the curtsy that convention insisted the older woman give her in deference to her rank? She could see Lord Staunton all but wringing his hands, his mouth opening and closing at his wife's rudeness, and it gave her the courage to say in a cold, proud voice that Lady Staunton could hardly have bettered, "I fear you have been misinformed, ma'am. I am not 'your girl'—I am Emily Saint Allyn, Duchess of Wrotherham.''

She paused, staring at Charles' unpleasant aunt until the lady was forced to drop her pince-nez and a shallow curtsy as well. "Your Grace," she said grudgingly.

"Won't you be seated?" Emily asked next as if nothing untoward had happened. "I will order some wine for you. Such a raw day, is it not?"

They all spent an uncomfortable half-hour together until Lady Staunton said she would like to go to her room and rest before dinner. Emily escorted them to the hall, where she was delighted to turn them over to Wilkins and the housekeeper.

As she returned to the gold salon, she thought she had seldom met a more impossible woman. Her husband had had very little to say for himself, and when he did respond to one of Emily's direct questions, he kept darting his popping little eyes in his wife's direction. It was obvious that Lady Staunton ruled that roost, that she was less than ecstatic about this newest member of the family, and that she was very proud and formal as well. It was exactly the kind of reaction that Emily had expected from the duke's family, but instead of acknowledging that the lady had a valid point in disliking her and the circumstances, she found herself indignant and angry. Very well, she was Althea Wyndham's daughter, but now she was also the Duchess of Wrotherham, and she expected to be treated as such. In fact, she promised herself as she paced the floor, I demand it. Lady Staunton had better beware.

Dinner, although delicious as always, had seldom seemed to last longer. Thanks to Charles' anecdotes about town, Emily was able to hold her own, and because of the presence of the servants, Lady Staunton's guns were spiked. When, however, the two ladies adjourned to the drawing room, leaving Lord Staunton to his port, she wasted no time in rectifying this error. The fact that Emily was the perfect embodiment of a duchess and filled the role with such grace and dignity she found offensive, and she was especially angry when she saw with what care and respect all the servants treated this shameless chit of a notorious mother, who, according to Charles' own account, had lately been one of them. And yet there was Wilkins smiling as he seated her so carefully at the table, and the footmen hovering behind her, attentive to her every wish. Lady Staunton found the entire situation revolting.

"I see you are with child," she remarked coldly as soon as she was seated. "When do you expect to be confined?"

"Sometime in March, m'lady," Emily replied as she took out her embroidery.

"Or perhaps even February? I am sure no one in society would be at all surprised at a very premature birth," Lady Staunton said bitterly. "Now I know why Charles buried you down here in the country, but how does he expect us to live this down, along with everything else we have had to bear? It is disgraceful!"

Emily threaded her needle calmly. "May I remind you, madam, that that is Charles' and my business? I fail to see that it is any business of yours."

The older lady gasped and Emily looked straight into her eyes and continued, "Since we are now family, no matter how each one of us may regret it, may I suggest at least a semblance of goodwill between us? I am perfectly willing to receive any of the duke's relatives as long as they behave in a correct manner, but as duchess here, I will not tolerate rudeness or insults. Do I make myself clear, Lady Staunton?" She stared until the lady flushed and nodded.

"Of course, I suppose it must be as you say," she agreed reluctantly, and then took another tack. "I am not surprised to find that dear Charles is not here, for I have it from all the tittle-tattles in London that he seldom visits Wrotherham Park these days." In her voice was the conviction that her nephew was regretting his hasty marriage already. "I am told on good authority that he was seen escorting Lady Ackroyd again, only last week. Charles is such a favorite with the ladies."

"I know Charles is the type of man women find hard to ignore," Emily agreed sweetly, as if so secure in her position this did not worry her in the slightest.

"Yes, Helena Ackroyd was quite distraught when she learned of his marriage. However, since she is out of black gloves for her late husband now, she has become quite the gay widow," Lady Staunton persisted, adding yet another barb to Emily's quivering flesh. "How beautiful she is! She was called the Incomparable of Incomparables the year she came out. Perhaps, since you never entered society's ranks yourself, you are not acquainted with the lady? A tall, handsome brunette, the type Charles has always favored. But then, one can hardly expect the duke to allow the act of marriage to reform him. I fear you have married a rake, madam.''

At this point, Lord Staunton slipped into the room and Emily smiled a welcome to him even as she rose. ''I must ask you both to excuse me,'' she said. ''The doctor decrees an early bedtime for me these days. May I ask when you have called for your coach in the morning?''

''We plan to leave at ten, niece,'' Lord Staunton said, coming to take her hand and bid her good night.

''How unfortunate that I will not be able to see you off! I am never belowstairs before eleven. Allow me to wish you a safe journey, and let me assure you, you will always be welcome at Wrotherham Park.''

On this note she bowed and left her guests to fend for themselves. As she went up the stairs on one of the footmen's arm, she berated herself for her cowardice, but she did not feel she could remain in the same room with that horrible woman for another moment without losing both her temper and her dignity.

In the days that followed the Stauntons' visit, Emily found herself in a state of unhappiness that even surpassed her misery at Charles' initial defection. He had never mentioned his aunt and uncle to her, of course, so she had no way of knowing how he regarded them, but could he care for such a woman as Lady Staunton? Surely he would not be influenced by her opinion of his duchess, would he? And this beautiful Lady Ackroyd . . . who was she? Could it be possible that Charles was setting up a mistress already? She clenched her hands as the baby moved within her, and then she looked down at her unshapely form and could not help weeping a little with her frustration. Several times she began a letter to Charles, hoping to hear that none of what she feared was true, but the letter proved impossible to write, and outside of using up a lot of time and wasting several sheets of hot-pressed paper, nothing came of this endeavor, for she found she could not send it.

At last, instead, she wrote only to tell him that the steward had found a large leak in one of the roofs of the west wing. What did Charles wish her to do about it? she inquired. And then she added, as if it was an afterthought, that Lord and

Lady Staunton had stayed this past week and she hoped they had arrived in town safely. After assuring him of her continued good health, she signed the letter as was now her custom, "Emily, Duchess of Wrotherham."

There was no immediate reply, and she found herself suddenly so restless that she could not sit still, and she continually paced the floor until her aching legs and tired back could stand no more. She was not sleeping well either. There seemed to be no position that was comfortable in bed, and the baby was very active, often waking her from a light sleep with his kicking and turning. It must be a boy, she told Darty, for no girl would ever behave so rudely to her mama!

One morning, after an especially restless night, she found herself awake very early, and unable to remain in bed, she went to the window to watch the sun rise. The weather had cleared at last after a week of fog and rain, and it appeared that it was going to be a beautiful day. Suddenly, she knew what she had to do. It was only a hard day's riding to Wantage, and if the coach went slowly and she was well wrapped up, with a hot brick to her feet, and broke her journey somewhere overnight, no harm would come to her or the baby. Yes, she thought, excited by her plans, I will go and visit my mother's grave. I am ashamed I have not done so long before this.

Not only her maid, but Darty and Mrs. Turner as well tried to convince her that taking such a journey was a reckless decision on her part, with the birth only a month or so away, but Emily would not listen to them. She was so determined to go that it was only two days later that she left Reynolds in the carriage at the churchyard in Wantage and walked alone across the small graveyard, holding her sable cloak tightly around her against the chill of the wind. She was glad there was no one else abroad on this blustery winter day, and when she reached her mother's grave, she stood quietly for a moment, her eyes closed in prayer. And then, tired from the jolting of the carriage, she sank down on an olden fallen tombstone nearby to rest.

Her eyes were somber as she stared at her mother's grave. How much trouble Althea Wyndham has brought me, she thought. And yet, considering everything, how brave a woman she had been! Left alone with a small baby to support, she had snapped her fingers at society, held up her head, and done exactly as she pleased. She was stronger than I am, even if what she did was wrong, Emily thought. I cannot approve of her life—in fact, I still deplore it—but even so, I have a reluctant admiration for a lady who went her own way and managed to laugh at all the consequences. She had never whined nor expected special treatment, and she had never railed against her fate. What would she think of a daughter who was so determined to be correct, and so cowardly to boot, that she had turned away a loving husband that she herself adored because of what society might say? Who *were* society, after all, that they were more important than her love for Charles, and his for her?

She seemed to hear her mother's light, disbelieving laugh in the sighing of the wind.

"My dearest Emily, you have been a goose!" her breath-less voice whispered in her ear. "It has been such a long time since you quarreled with your Charles. Ah, his father was not his equal, my dear. Charles *loves* you; he loves you so much he married you. And what do you do, all haughtiness and pride and superiority, but send him away? And it has been four months, Emily. A man like Charles! How long do you think it will be before he is taking up with one of my successors, if he has not done so already?"

"Oh, no," Emily moaned, her hands to her hot cheeks. "He must not . . . I could not bear it."

Again the trill of laughter echoed in her head. "Nor can he, my dear. Do you know nothing of men at all? But come, you say you cannot bear it? Then you must do something about it at once, and pray you have not left it too late. Think, Emily! Is the title 'duchess' enough satisfaction for you that you will let him make love to this lady and that and ignore you? Do you really want to be his wife in name only? If you do not, you must make a push to get him back, my dear daughter. Oh, yes, a definite push. Lady Ackroyd is so very beautiful—and unconventional—even as I was. Can you do it? Have you the courage?"

"Yes, I can—I will!" Emily said through gritted teeth.

"My dear, how like your father you are, after all! He had just the same determination and faith in himself. And if you can find it in your heart to forgive me and remember that the life I led has nothing whatsoever to do with how you choose to live your life, you will win through. Remember, too, that as a Wyndham you are every bit the duke's equal in birth and you can take your place beside him proudly with your head held high.''

Emily waited, but there was only the sound of the wind sighing in the elms, rustling the dead leaves that carpeted the graveyard, and far away, the cawing of the rooks. She sat perfectly still, holding her breath and waiting, and then, very faintly, she heard her mother's voice once more.

''I shall pray for your success, my dearest daughter. Go now and make all right with your Charles, as only you can do. He is so proud, only your complete surrender will suffice. Swallow your own pride; it makes a poor bedfellow, believe me.''

The wind swelled and died away, and then there was a heavy silence that told Emily she would not hear her mother's voice again.

She rose stiffly, putting one hand on Althea Wyndham's tombstone to steady herself, while her other hand supported her distended abdomen where her baby—Charles' baby—slept and waited, and then she felt it move and kick her and it seemed to give her added strength. For *his* sake, too, she thought. Our child deserves to be born to a happy marriage. He will need both of us.

''Thank you, Mother,'' she whispered, her hand caressing the rough tombstone. ''I will not shame you or my father anymore, I promise.''

She made her way back to the gate where her carriage was waiting. ''We will return toward home now, John,'' she told the coachman. ''I do not care to remain in Wantage. Make for the post road and the Green Man at Barret, where we will stay the night.''

''Aye, your Grace,'' he said, touching his hat as one of the grooms helped her to her seat and Reynolds wrapped the fur rug around her. Emily smiled at them. She felt calm and serene and sure of herself and the course she planned to follow. She would write Charles as soon as she reached home and she would tell him how much she loved him and beg him to forgive her for making their marriage such a mockery. Somehow she knew that he would come to her at once, that all her imaginings had been simply that: silly illusions she made up in her head. He loves me, I know he loves me still, she told herself. Didn't he promise he would come as soon as I relented?

She resolved to instruct Charles' steward to forward a draft to her Uncle Gregory as well, repaying him for the money he had given her, and for the price of the cottage at Wantage as well, as she had promised she would do so many months ago. She had never asked for any money before, but now that she was prepared to be Charles' wife in every way, she would authorize this expenditure without a qualm. She decided to have the steward write Lord Wyndham a cold and formal note, saying that Emily, Duchess of Wrotherham, had asked him to conduct this small piece of unfinished business for her. And then she wondered what her aunt thought now of her unsatisfactory yet ducal niece, and she smiled a little.

When she reached Wrotherham Park the following afternoon, it was to find an express had arrived for her from London. Giving her furs to her maid, she went into the library to read it, not even bothering to sit down in her impatience to discover what Charles had to say.

But the duke had not written himself. His secretary, Mr. Watts, apologized, saying that his Grace was in the midst of hasty preparations to travel abroad, and had asked him to inform the duchess of his plans. Robert Stewart, Viscount Castlereagh, had at last requested that he go to Vienna, bringing with him some new plans that had been formulated at the Foreign Office for Wellington, who, along with Prince Klemuns von Metternich of Austria, was busy drawing up the peace treaty. The duke, his secretary explained, did not feel he could refuse the commission, although he hoped to return to England in a few weeks' time. They were to leave immediately.

Emily sank down into a wing chair before the fire, crushing the letter in despair as her face grew pale and her eyes focused on a spot far beyond the cheerful blaze. She had lost her chance, for even now Charles was traveling to Austria and so was out of reach. After a moment she smoothed the letter out to read on, but there remained only a few instructions about estate matters and the usual closing courtesies.

Then, down at the bottom, Emily saw a short postscript in Charles' bold handwriting. "If I should not be able to be with you, know I am thinking of you, Duchess," he wrote. "And if the baby is a girl, please name her Emily. I have always wanted another Emily, just like her mother. If it is a boy, may I suggest Thomas Wyndham Saint Allyn, in memory of your father?''

There was no signature, only the bold initial "C," and Emily felt tears sliding down her face as she put the part of the page where Charles' hand had rested against her cheek. Her husband seemed very far away, for now, having made up her mind to call him back to her, she felt even more lonely and abandoned. She wondered what he was doing right now. Was he thinking of her? Was he standing perhaps in the stern of his ship, staring back at the land he left, as she had done when she left Belgium?

The duke had not arrived at the coast of England, although he was long overdue, for his carriage had lost a wheel and there had been several hours' delay in a small village. The wait had done nothing to sweeten his temper, and now he sat staring moodily at the road, an imperturbable Mr. Greene across from him, tapping his fingers on his knee and cursing the delay. Coming to the end of a particularly pungent sentence that concerned the fate of ignorant postboys, village idiots who claimed they were wheelwrights, and boring depressing hamlets, he looked up to see his valet's steady eyes on his face, and flushed a little.

"I beg your pardon, Greene," he said, trying for a lighter tone. "Not a very amusing journey for you, I'm afraid."

Mr. Greene inclined his head. "It can come as no surprise, your Grace," he said with the familiarity of the old retainer. "Your lack of good humor has been noted not only by myself but by all your servants for several weeks now."

The duke frowned, but undeterred by this warning, Greene continued, "If I may be so bold as to presume to advise you, sir . . . ?" He paused, and the duke waved an impatient hand in permission. "It is not difficult to see that your Grace and the duchess have quarreled, but may I suggest that you do all in your power to make all right as soon as you can? Your state of mind is all too evident, and Mr. Wilkins has informed me that her Grace is also unhappy. The duchess loves you, sir; she loves you very much. I admit that although I was much opposed to your marriage to Miss *Nelson*, I have nothing but profound admiration for the former Miss *Wyndham*. Indeed, I would even go so far as to say that she is respected and admired by all your staff, and we are all distressed to see her unhappiness, especially now.''

He paused again, and the duke, who had been staring at him in some amazement throughout this unprecedented speech, said in quiet tones, "I thank you for your concern, Greene. However, my quarrel with the duchess must be resolved by her. There is nothing I can do to bring it to an end."

Greene nodded, although the duke noted his tiny sniff of disapproval. "When you return from this mission, sir, may I suggest *you* try again? I am sure you can make the lady see reason, for I cannot believe that your famous address will fail you at such an important time. One has only to remember the numerous conquests you have enjoyed in the past. Consider the Princess Garibaldi—Lady Trent—Mrs. Huntington—even the Countess of Brace, where the odds against your storming that citadel were running seven to one in the clubs.''

He stopped, lowering his eyes to the folded hands in his lap, and the duke raised one dark eyebrow as a little smile played at the corners of his mouth.

"Why, Greene," he said in pretended astonishment, "your knowledge of my affairs and your encomiums positively amaze me. I did not realize the extent of your admiration for my prowess with the fair sex. One would think I had only to beckon to have a lady succumb to my charms."

"Just so, your Grace," his valet agreed, unperturbed by this raillery. "We must hope that marriage has not dulled your well-known powers of persuasion in this most delicate and important matter. After all, the Duchess of Wrotherham is not to be compared in any way to those other, er, *ladies*."

The carriage rumbled on to the coast, Mr. Greene once more the silent, obsequious servant. The duke sat and stared out at scenery he did not see, for his mind was busy reviewing this amazing conversation and the possibility that there still might be, as Greene had suggested, something he could do to resolve the problem.

Doctor Randall made one of his regular visits to Wrotherham Park three weeks later and announced he would return to stay in a few days' time, for the duchess was very near her term. Emily smiled at this good news, for the last few days had been especially difficult for her. She had retired to her rooms, having her meals sent up, for it made her so breathless to climb the stairs, even supported by footmen. She told herself there was some good in this final separation from Charles, after all, for although she longed to have him close to her, giving her his love and strength, something in her rebelled at having him see her in these last stages of pregnancy. How much more satisfying to meet him with their baby in her arms, as slim as she had been when they first fell in love.

The third week of March, the doctor was duly established at Wrotherham Park, along with two nurses, and four days after their arrival, Emily awoke in the middle of the night to find herself in labor. It was not until the following afternoon that she was delivered, and although childbirth had been harder and more painful than she had ever imagined it would be, she had not lost her courage, even in the final stages when she felt she was being torn apart.

The labor pains had surprised her, beginning almost as backaches that built up and then ebbed away. Sometimes they ceased completely and she was able to doze for a while, but eventually they grew inexorably into harder and harder contractions, with less time between them for her to catch her breath and try to relax. The most frightening thing of all was to know that there was no way she could influence or stop them, that they would control her until the baby was born, and she held tightly to Darty's hand and the nurse's hands for reassurance.

"Charles!" she cried out whenever the pain threatened to overwhelm her, and his name seemed to give her strength. She lay panting on the bed, her eyes closed in exhaustion, moments after the seventh Duke of Wrotherham entered the world, lustily squalling his indignation at having to leave that safe, warm haven where he had spent the previous nine months.

"A fine boy, your Grace," Doctor Randall said with a smile as he attended his patient. "And you will be fine in a short time as well."

"Oh, let me see him, please," Emily begged, opening her eyes, and the nurse who had washed the baby and wrapped him in a blanket brought her her son. She had no idea what color his eyes were, for he had them tightly closed as he continued to wail, but the top of his little red head was covered with soft black hair. Emily smiled and held out her arms, and as the nurse put the baby into them, she felt a wave of love such as she had never known for this tiny mite that she and Charles had made between them.

"Charles Thomas Wyndham Saint Allyn, how nice to meet you face to face at last," she murmured.

There was great rejoicing among the staff, and Mr. Wilkins took the liberty of writing of the happy event to the servants left in London. Emily slept, waking only to eat and try to nurse the baby. By the time her milk came in, her son was protesting loudly at this enforced famine, in what Emily thought a very ducal, demanding way, and when he finally settled down at her breast, she could not imagine which one of them was happier that it was over.

As soon as she was able, she wrote Charles a short letter, telling him his son had been born and what she planned to name him, but although she longed to write of her love and beg him to come home to England quickly, she did not. Soon after Charles' arrival in Vienna, she had learned from the papers that were sent down from London that the treaty had been delayed by Alexander I of Russia, who wanted it to include a Holy Alliance of European Emperors; a league of allied rulers all sworn to come to one another's aid in times of war, and she knew from what she read that this was causing difficulties among those nations who had no desire to be tied to such an alliance. Since it was clear that England was one of the foremost objectors, there was no chance that Charles would be able to abandon his post until the czar had been brought to reason or England had forged another way.

Emily regained her strength quickly, and as soon as there was no possibility of her contracting childbed fever, Doctor Randall took his leave. She was supposed to remain in bed for two weeks, but she felt so well that she insisted on rising for part of every day. In this she was abetted by Mrs. Dartmouth, who claimed it would help her back to her normal good health that much sooner, although the London nurses could be seen to shake their heads at such folly and disregard for doctor's orders.

The baby, now that he was able to nurse, settled down into a placid routine of feedings, changes, and baths, and endless hours of sleep. His eyes seemed to be turning a very dark gray-green that reminded his mother of the stormy Channel, and he had a steady, unblinking stare and an occasional frown that was very much like his father's. The entire house revolved around him, from the lowliest scullery maid to Mrs. Dartmouth and her attendant nursemaids.

Emily privately thought her son would be so spoiled by all this adoration that he would grow up impossibly proud and self-centered, but there was no way she could stem the flow of love and admiration from the staff for the tiny baby that everyone was calling "the little duke."

13

By the first of April, Emily began to make plans to go up to town. Although she was happy with her son, she could not restrain her eagerness to be in Park Lane when his father came home from abroad so she could welcome him without delay, and in such a manner as to banish this marriage of convenience forever.

Mrs. Turner and Mr. Wilkins advised caution, thinking the move much too precipitate and the air of London dangerous for the little duke, but Darty once again came to her rescue.

"We must let her go, Mrs. Turner," she said one afternoon when she was enjoying a cup of tea in the housekeeper's rooms. "She'll only fret herself to death down here, and that would be the worst thing a nursing mother could do. I'll keep the baby as safe in town as he is here, and I imagine when the duke comes home, he'll soon have them back here at the park, you mark my words."

Mrs. Turner agreed, but remembering the stiffness that had grown up between the duke and duchess, she could not help but feel apprehensive, and she confided her worries to the old nurse.

"Yes, I know there is something wrong, but what it can be, I have no idea, for the duchess has not confided in me. Perhaps that is why she is so eager to be in London when her husband returns. But never fear! I'll see she travels in easy stages and doesn't overtax herself."

Emily laughed out loud the morning she came down the steps dressed for traveling to find the entourage that waited to take her to town. There was the coach for her and her maid; another large coach for Darty, the baby, and two nursemaids;

a huge fourgon loaded with luggage and furniture; and several grooms to serve as outriders, as well as the coachmen and their attendants.

"Even the queen would not require so much," she scolded Mrs. Turner, knowing full well that Mr. Wilkins and several other servants had already gone ahead to make all ready for her arrival in town. "To think that all this—this pomp!—is for a tiny baby who barely weighs ten pounds!"

When Emily saw the housekeeper's worried look that she had displeased her, she went to kiss her. "Thank you, dear Mrs. Turner," she said as that good lady flushed with pleasure at the gesture. "I was only teasing, you know. You are too good to me. I know you will see that the park is run as smoothly as ever while I am gone, and I promise to let you know when we plan to return."

She settled herself in the lead coach and waved to all the assembled servants as the cavalcade set off at a decorous pace down the drive.

It was three days later before they turned into Park Lane and she was helped down by a beaming Mr. Wilkins. How long it has been since I was here last, she thought as she preceded Darty and the baby into the imposing town house, and the servants began to unpack the coaches.

The baby was taken upstairs to the nursery, and Emily wandered around the rooms where she and Charles had begun their marriage. She remembered Charles had not made love to her here because of her loss of memory, and smiled. *That* will soon be remedied, she promised herself as she went up to her rooms. She felt a lightness and happiness to be here, almost as if she were that much closer to him now she was in London instead of at Wrotherham Park. Surely it could not be much longer before he returned! She had had a short reply to her letter that, although formal in tone, could not hide his impatience to see his son.

While she waited for him, she decided to begin to brave London society by herself. She marveled that she felt so strong and sure of this decision after all the time she had feared the *haut ton*'s disapproval. It was almost as if her son's birth had caused her to be reborn herself, so that the straightlaced, insecure girl that she had been once had been replaced by a mature, confident woman.

She sent a note to the Countess of Gant, informing her of

her arrival and begging her to call, and she wrote to Lady Staunton. Emily might not like Charles' cold, proud aunt, but she was determined to use every weapon in her arsenal to gain acceptance to society, and she knew Lady Staunton would be an invaluable ally.

Whether it was the correct, restrained formality of her note, or the fact that she asked the lady's help with the baby's christening, she did not know, but Lady Staunton called that very afternoon.

Emily instructed Wilkins to bring her guest to the most formal drawing room, and she rose to her feet as Lady Staunton swept in.

"Thank you for coming, m'lady," Emily said, graciously extending her hand to forestall the necessity of the ritual curtsy she was sure the older woman resented. "So kind of you to give me the benefit of your advice."

Lady Staunton inclined her head an inch as she took a seat on the stiffest sofa, and Emily continued as if she had just been greeted with the warmest expression of affection. "You see, the baby has not been christened, for I did so much want Charles to be here for the ceremony. You see my quandary!"

Lady Staunton drew herself up even straighter. "By no means must you wait," she ordered. "It is of course unfortunate that the duke is absent—so like a man to be abroad when he is needed!—but the heir must be christened as soon as it can be arranged."

She paused, and Emily noticed the two red spots that appeared in her thin cheeks. "I would be happy to arrange the ceremony for you, your Grace," she said in her tight, toneless voice. "I think it safe to say that my knowledge of the correct procedure to be followed for such a momentous event surpasses yours."

"What a kind offer!" Emily replied, knowing she had won a major skirmish. "Would you care to see your great-nephew, ma'am?"

Lady Staunton professed herself to be all eagerness to do so, and Emily rang the bell. She talked lightly of her journey and affairs at Wrotherham Park, and asked after Lord Staunton until the seventh duke was borne in proudly by a smiling Mrs. Dartmouth.

Fortunately he was fast asleep, so his behavior could not be faulted, and by a lucky chance, Darty had dressed him in one of Charles' baby gowns, little knowing that Lady Staunton had embroidered those tiny rosettes with her own hands some thirty years before.

Even her frigidity could not survive that coincidence, and she pronounced the baby the handsomest infant she had ever seen. She spent several minutes holding him in her thin arms, all the while pointing out the Saint Allyn nose, chin, ears, mouth, and general bearing, and when Emily did not contradict her, she began to think the new duchess not as impossible for her exalted post as she had at first feared. Besides, much could be forgiven the girl who had so promptly produced the heir, and the baby had arrived only a little early and could be considered perfectly respectable.

As she took her leave, she gave Emily the first smile she had ever seen on that cold face. Lady Staunton foresaw little difficulty in manipulating the new duchess, and the chance to have a hand in the molding of the next Duke of Wrotherham—and hopefully with more satisfactory results than she had achieved with his father!—gained her complete capitulation.

Promising to call again soon, she invited Emily to come to her home on Mount Street for tea the following afternoon so she might be introduced to a few of the more select people of the *ton*, and then she swept away to visit Westminster Abbey to arrange the christening before calling on such of her friends as could be expected to appreciate the marvelous qualities of the newest Saint Allyn.

Emily allowed her the victory, well aware she had also been victorious.

Jessica Cathcart was not long in making an appearance either, and after assuring Emily that her son was the most perfect, well-behaved, and undoubtedly intelligent baby she had ever seen—second only to her own children, of course—she began to talk about the balls and parties and dinners and receptions that the duchess might now look forward to attending.

"But, Jessy," Emily said as they sat over their teacups in the drawing room, "I really think I should wait until Charles returns before I begin to jaunter about quite as much as you propose. To go to a formal party without my husband . . . no, no! I will be thought bold, and you are well aware that, with my background, it is necessary for me to exercise considerable restraint."

"Rather you will be thought an antidote if you insist on

such antiquated fustian! Why, when Nigel had to return to the country for a month, I did not cancel a single engagement. Come, my dear, trust me! I know why you speak as you do, but courage, my friend. We will beard the lion in his den together, and all will be well.''

Finally Emily agreed that there was no harm in riding in the countess' carriage that same afternoon in the park, and going shopping and then on to a luncheon the next day, but she refused to consider balls and the more formal evenings until she could attend them on Charles' arm.

"But in three weeks I am giving the most divine ball," the countess mourned. "I shall be so disappointed if you are not there. Well, we shall see."

Her blue eyes sparkled and she looked so confident that Emily had to laugh. "Yes, you think that in three weeks you will have time to cajole me into attending, do you not? We shall see indeed, Jessy," Emily told her as they parted. "Besides, I am nursing the baby and my schedule most certainly must take second place to his. He is a *very* demanding young man!"

"Aren't all men, no matter what their age?" the countess asked before she went out to her carriage.

All through the next days, London was treated to the sight of the beautiful new Duchess of Wrotherham, here, there, and everywhere, and if there were some high sticklers who thought to turn up their noses at Althea Wyndham's daughter, it was not long before they could see they would be much in the minority. To be sponsored by the dashing Countess of Gant was one thing, but a lady approved by the correct and proper Lady Amelia Staunton as well must be acceptable anywhere.

Emily was aware that there were some who still looked askance at her and sniffed and turned away, especially among the older ladies who remembered her mother only too well and had never forgiven her her defection from their ranks, but she held her head high and ignored their stares and whispers. There were plenty of others who seemed to be delighted to greet her, include her in their parties, and introduce her to their friends.

But the final seal on her acceptance came from Lady Merks, an august dowager and friend of Lady Staunton's, who had the reputation of being society's most severe disciplinarian.

Emily had gone to drink tea with Mrs. Whyte, a friend of Jessy's, and was dismayed to find Mr. Edward Willoughby among the party. Teddy, as he was known to all his friends, was by no means needle-witted, but even he recognized the new duchess as the most beautiful woman he had ever seen in all his twenty-four years, and he had become quite a nuisance whenever they chanced to meet. In Mrs. Whyte's drawing room, he hovered over Emily, a vacuous smile never leaving his face as he gazed reverently into her eyes. He insisted on fetching her teacup and all but knelt at her feet in his obvious admiration as he presented it, making, as Lady Merks observed from across the room, a "perfect cake of himself."

Emily was polite yet cool, and not even his most extravagant compliment or most heartfelt sigh caused her to blush or lose her composure. As she was leaving, Lady Merks close behind her, the young man so far forgot himself as to make her a passionate declaration in Mrs. Whyte's deserted front hall.

"Assure you, my queen, slain by Cupid's dart at first sight," he exclaimed, clasping her hand in his and pressing it to his heart. "Pledge you undying devotion! Eternal love! Say you will be kind to me!"

Lady Merks paused just inside the drawing-room door to shamelessly eavesdrop, as Emily replied, in a cold voice dripping with icicles, "You not only forget yourself, sir, you insult me! However, if I can be assured this distasteful incident will not be repeated, I will not inform my husband of it. He would be most displeased to learn the Duchess of Wrotherham was being bothered in such a way."

Lady Merks almost applauded, for even if there was no harm in silly, foppish Teddy Willoughby, the duchess had handled him beautifully. She went away to confide in Mrs. Jordan-Holms that, for herself, although of course she must deplore the lady's mother, she found the new duchess to be not only beautiful but well-bred as well, and that her demeanor and manners were such that they could not give anyone a disgust of her. She especially commended her refusal to attend formal parties without her husband and the delicacy with which Emily had remained secluded in the country during her

pregnancy, and she wished other young wives among the
haut ton would emulate such a fastidious example.

"I shall *know* her," Lady Merks announced in a voice that
brooked no opposition, and in short order almost all of London
followed her lead.

Even so, Emily was glad that Lady Quentin was not to be
found in London this particular Season and that Lord Andrews
acted as if he had never set eyes on her before in his
life.

After the lonely days in the country and the quiet life she
had led there, and the months prior to that when she had
toiled as a lowly lady's maid, this success and all the gaiety
of the Season went to Emily's head, and she bloomed with
new beauty and confidence. Motherhood had removed the
last traces of her girlhood, but in its place had come a mature,
calm graciousness of manner, an elegant roundness to her slim
figure, and a glow to her face and eyes that caused many a
gentleman to wish he had had Charles Saint Allyn's good
luck. The only thing that was missing from Emily's life was
her husband, and not a day went by that she did not pray for
his quick return and wish he was beside her. All the gentlemen
were chagrined to discover that the beautiful duchess
was not at all interested in even the lightest, most innocent
flirtation while she waited for the duke's return.

As it turned out in the end, she was not at home to
welcome him when at last his mud-bespattered traveling coach
pulled up in Park Lane one afternoon in early May. The duke
climbed down a little stiffly, for he had been traveling at a
fast pace for days. Between his dark eyes was the tiny frown
that Mr. Greene was afraid would become a permanent feature,
as he gave instructions to have the coach unloaded before he
strode up the steps to give the knocker a mighty crash.

"Your Grace!" Wilkins exclaimed as he opened the door.
"We had no idea . . . I mean there has been no word of your
arrival . . ."

"Must I go away, then?" the duke asked with a little
smile. "And why are you here, Wilkins? I thought to find
you still in the country with the duchess and planned to travel
there tomorrow."

He looked around the hall as he spoke, and it was plain to
see that instead of the skeleton staff he had left here, the
house was alive with servants and activity. One footman was

bearing a large bouquet that had just arrived into the drawing room, and on the hall table he could see what appeared to be an inordinate amount of gilt-edged cards of invitation. He turned back to his butler, one eyebrow raised in inquiry, and then, from some floor above him, he heard a baby cry, and he whirled toward the sound.

"Just so, your Grace," Mr. Wilkins beamed, coming to take his hat and gloves. "Her Grace and the little duke are both in residence."

"Where is the duchess?" Charles demanded, still staring up to where his son seemed to be calling for him. He started forward and then paused as Wilkins replied, "She has gone to drive with the Countess of Gant, Sir Philip Maynard, and Mr. Robert Day, your Grace."

"Those rattles!" Charles exclaimed, the frown deepening on his face.

"The duchess is very popular, but I expect her to return at any moment, sir," Wilkins continued, as if he had not noticed the duke's disgust. "As you can hear, your son can be most impatient and demanding. It is generally remarked that he takes after his father in that respect."

Remembering that Wilkins had dandled him on his knee more than once when he was a child, and slipped him sweets, made the duke forebear to comment on this assessment of his character. Besides, he was distracted by the baby's wails, which seemed to be growing in volume, and he was becoming very angry. How dare she go out with those worthless fribbles when her baby needed her? He clenched his fists and prepared to mount the stairs two at a time just as the knocker sounded and Wilkins went to admit the duchess, who ran in, closely followed by Jessica Cathcart. Charles stood very still at the bottom of the stairs, watching his wife as she removed her dashing bonnet of chip straw and velvet ribbons, saying as she did so, "Just listen, Jessy! Did you ever hear anyone so imperious? And all for a few minutes' delay . . ."

Her voice died away as she caught sight of the duke standing behind his butler, his weary face grim and furious.

"Charles!" she exclaimed, dropping her bonnet and taking two impulsive steps toward him.

"Good day to you, madam," he said in icy tones, folding his arms and leaning against the newel post. Emily stopped as if she had been struck and the puzzled countess looked from one to the other as the duke continued, "I trust our child has come to no harm while you have been flitting about amusing yourself?"

"Well, I like that," Jessica said, unable to control herself. "Charles, you are being a bear." She glanced again at Emily's set white face and added, "I daresay the baby has just now awakened, for Emily is a wonderful mother, you may ask anyone you like."

The duchess seemed to recall herself, and now she dragged her eyes from her husband's face and took a deep breath.

"Thank you for your support, Jessy, but both of you must excuse me now. Go home, my dear friend, and I will speak to you later. And Charles"—here she turned to the stern figure of the duke—"I shall hope to see you again soon, so I might introduce you to your son. Perhaps in half an hour's time?"

Her voice was calm as she nodded to them both and moved regally to the stairs, her back ramrod-straight and her head held high. There was a heavy silence in the hall until she disappeared and they heard a door closing above them, and then in a few moments, the baby's wailing ceased. The sudden silence seemed to wake the duke from his frozen state and he came forward, holding out his hands and trying to smile.

"Jessy, your pardon. I am indeed a bear not to greet you more cordially. Say you forgive me."

He took her hands, but the lady was having none of such formality and stood on tiptoes to kiss him. "Bad Charles! But I will forgive you this time in honor of your homecoming, for you do not look as if you have slept for days. I will go away immediately, and hope to see you later, when you are more yourself."

She moved to the door, which Wilkins hurried to open for her, and added, "Remind Emily, if you please, that there can be no impediment now for her to attend our ball. She would not go to any formal parties without you, Charles, even though I told her she was being positively gothic! But now Nigel and I will be expecting you both."

Waving her hand in farewell, she left the house. As Wilkins closed the door behind her, he saw the duke frowning down at the floor, one hand rubbing his chin, his eyes bleak with his thoughts.

"If I may suggest it, your Grace," his butler said with all the insouciance of the old, privileged retainer, "Lady Cathcart is right. You will feel better after you have washed and changed and had something to eat. By then, the baby will be ready to receive you."

The duke shook himself and started slowly for the stairs. "Thank you, Wilkins. Send Greene to me as soon as he has seen to the baggage, for I would not meet my son for the first time in all my dirt. No food, though; just a glass of sherry if you will."

It was well over half an hour later that the duke knocked on his wife's door. Emily was sitting in a low chair near the window, holding a sleepy, replete baby in her arms, and he caught his breath as he entered at the picture she presented. How often had he dreamed of her just this way!

"Thank you, Betty," she said to the nursemaid waiting to remove her charge. "You may go. I will call you when I wish you to take the baby."

"Very good, your Grace," the girl said, bobbing a curtsy and smiling shyly at the duke.

"Come in, Charles," Emily said, trying to ignore her rapidly beating heart. As the duke tiptoed forward, she added, "There is no need to be so cautious. He won't cry again, not now."

She rose and held out the baby. "May I present your son, your Grace?"

"Is he all right? He is so tiny!" the duke said, looking more than a little panicked, and Emily wished she felt more like laughing, for his expression was so comical. He took the baby gingerly in his arms and stared down at that rosy little face, and then he smoothed the blanket back. For a moment there was silence and then he said, "I see he has black hair, madam."

"I never doubted he would for a moment, Charles," Emily replied. The duke raised his rapt eyes to her face as she continued, "He does not have your eyes, though, not yet at any rate. His frown, however, is the exact duplicate of yours; everyone has remarked it. Here, sit down in this chair for you look tired."

Stop babbling, Emily, she told herself as the duke obeyed. "Was the birth hard?" he asked, his face frowning again.

"Hard enough, and long, although Doctor Randall said it

went well and everything was normal. He assures me the next one will be easier.''

The duke's head snapped up, but before he could question that last statement, little Charles opened his eyes and stared up at his father. One tiny hand fluttered for a moment, and then he yawned widely and seemed to grin before he fell fast asleep.

"Did you see, Emily?" the duke asked in an excited whisper. "He smiled at me."

The duchess wisely did not mention gas or burps or full stomachs, as she nodded, but she could not help but say, "Of course he yawned as well. Not very awestruck by his papa or the occasion, is he? Aunt Amelia says he is the most ducal baby she has ever seen."

As she went to sit across from him, Charles raised his head again. It seemed to take a visible effort for him to look away from the baby's face, and Emily was glad she was not in the least offended by this treatment after their long separation.

"You call Lady Staunton 'aunt'?" he asked in a bemused tone.

"She asked me to. There was some unpleasantness when we first met, but the baby has brought her around. And she arranged the christening. I am sorry you were not here, but Aunt Amelia would not let me wait. The Cathcarts stood godparents; I was sure you would approve. And Aunt has been so helpful in introducing me to society, as has the countess as well."

Charles frowned a little. "I see. Of course, it is an object with you to stand well there, for I can see you mean to cut quite a dash among the *haut ton*, but I beg you, Duchess, to consider your *cicisbeos*. Sir Philip, Mr. Day, bah!"

Now Emily's brows rose. "You have some objection, Charles? I see no reason why the Duchess of Wrotherham should not take her proper place in society. I am not little Emily Wyndham or Margaret Nelson, lady's maid, now. Of course, I plan to be in the first ranks as the wife of a premier duke."

What the duke might have replied to this startling statement was lost, for just then the baby's hand closed around one of his father's large fingers.

"See here, what a grip he has!" the duke exclaimed, the

warm smile she loved so well coming to his dark face. "I do believe he likes me."

Emily rose and rang the bell. "Of course he does, but now he must go back to the nursery and sleep, Charles. He sleeps most of the time, it seems, but Darty tells me he will soon be better company. Let me take him."

The duke gave up the precious bundle with reluctance. "When will he wake again?" he asked, and Emily smiled.

"Probably right in the middle of dinner. He has no thought of anyone else's convenience at all. I am so glad I named him Charles. Ah, Betty, there you are. You may take the baby now."

The duke rose and stared at his wife. She looked so beautiful holding their child, so dear and familiar, and yet there was something different about her. When was the last time she had teased him like that? She seemed to have gained a great deal of poise as well, and the smile that he had so seldom seen in the last months now lit her face with almost every sentence. In her smart driving dress and stylish London hairdo, she did not look at all like the young servant he had made love to in Belgium.

She came toward him now as the nursemaid shut the door behind her. "You must rest, Charles. I have never seen you look so tired. Shall we meet at dinner, or do you dine out?"

"I have no plans for the evening, Emily," he said. "I shall be happy to join you."

Emily's eyes darkened in dismay. "Oh, dear, I had forgotten! Lady Jersey has asked me to join her party for dinner and the theater. I shall send my excuses at once . . ."

"By no means!" the duke snarled. "Do not let my unexpected presence curtail your engagements, madam! I shall be happy to dine at my club. And now, if you will excuse me, I am indeed weary."

Emily curtsied as the duke, his face a black thundercloud, bowed and went away. She sank down into her chair again and stared out the window. It had not gone at all as she had planned. Why was Charles so angry with her? And how was she to tell him she wanted to end this make-believe marriage, to be his wife again, if he would not let her talk to him and be with him? Why, the only time he had spoken kindly to her since he entered the house was when the baby was with them. Whatever could be wrong?

In the next few days, it seemed to a confused Emily that the Duke and Duchess of Wrotherham met only by chance. Sometimes she would find Charles in the breakfast room when she came down, and he would ask after her engagements for the day before he told her the schedule he himself planned to follow. He was always polite, but so cold that she felt the distance between them was wider than it had ever been before.

The truth was that the duke, for the first time in his life, was ridden with jealousy, an emotion his wife never even suspected. She had been so sure Charles would be pleased by her acceptance into the *ton,* and so proud of her for behaving at last as the Duchess of Wrotherham should, that she was quick to accept invitations to drive or walk, to go to the theater or the opera, or to attend a card party or reception, and she never hesitated to tell him everything she did. She did not notice how angry this made him, nor how often he flung himself out of the house to take refuge in his clubs. The only time they found themselves at all in accord was when the baby was with them, but since the little duke still slept most of the time, these occasions were few and far between. Greene shook his head over both of them and went about his duties almost as tight-lipped as his master.

They did attend a soirée given by Lady Merks together. Emily had asked rather diffidently if Charles would care to escort her, and he had replied formally that nothing would give him more pleasure. Emily dressed with care that evening, and Charles, seeing her come down the stairs in her diamonds and white silk, caught his breath at her beauty. He resolved to try to win her back by any means it took to do so, but by the time Sir Philip Maynard, whose arrival coincided with theirs, helped his wife down from the carriage and begged for a dance, and Robert Day asked for the second waltz as they all went up the stairs to greet their hostess, and he saw other men hurrying to Emily's side as they entered the ballroom, the duke's resolutions disappeared in a new flood of anger. As he took her in his arms for the first dance, and probably the last he would be allowed to have with her, he thought in fury, the evening was ruined for him. Emily, who had been glowing with happiness to have him at her side, could not fail to notice the hard white lines around his mouth, nor the anger in his black eyes, and her enjoyment in the first waltz she had ever danced with her husband was gone. When it was over, he left her very much to her own devices for the remainder of the party, and the evening could not be said to have been a success for either of them.

On the way home, she tried to ask him what was wrong, but after observing that he wondered why she needed his escort when she was cutting such a swath in society, and begging her to watch what she was about to be encouraging all the worst fops and pinks of the *ton*, the duke changed the subject and refused to discuss the soirée further. They both retired for the night to their own bedrooms—Emily bewildered and Charles in a rage—to spend a sleepless night, each staring up at their dark ceilings.

Charles was absent all the next day, gone with friends on a riding expedition to Richmond, and so they did not meet again until dinner. The light conversation that they engaged in in front of the servants gave Emily no clue as to how she was to proceed, but when the duke excused himself the minute the covers of the last course were removed, saying he rather thought he would look in at Brooks if the duchess had no objection, she decided she had quite enough.

She signaled Wilkins that she was through, and went alone into the drawing room. She had no engagement herself, for the Cathcart ball was the following evening, and she wanted to rest so she would look her best for it, for Charles had promised he would not fail to attend with her.

She sat for a long time in front of the drawing-room fire, her eyes sad and bewildered. Instead of the dancing flames, she saw only his beloved face: those intent eyes and lean cheeks, the crispness of his black hair, and that dear remembered mouth she longed to feel possessing hers once again.

Suddenly his image faded, and Althea Wyndham's face, floating in a cloud of blond hair, appeared among the flames. Emily could not hear her voice, but it seemed from the sad way she shook her head that her mother was trying to tell her something. After only a moment, the vision was gone and Emily was left alone. Mother, she begged silently, come back! I need you to tell me what to do! But there was no sound except the crackling of the fire on the hearth, and eventually Emily went to bed in despair.

When she woke the next morning, she had her answer, although where it had come from, she did not know. Very well, she thought as she lay in bed waiting for the baby to be brought to her, Charles seemed satisfied to continue this marriage of convenience, for he had never shown by the smallest sign that he was still in love with her or longed to be with her, but she would not give up without a fight. She owed that much to herself and to her mother's memory. Tonight, she thought, her eyes glowing in anticipation, before we go to the ball I will confront Charles as I meant to do when he first came home, and I will insist he tell me his true feelings. And I will confess that I love him even if he does not love me anymore. If he does not want me, as much as that would hurt, at least I will know where I stand, and the situation cannot be any worse than this limbo I live in now.

That evening, after she had nursed the baby, Emily stood before the pier glass. She was dressed in a new gown of pale-green silk that showed off her supple waist. It was cut low on her shoulders and exposed half her creamy breasts, and with it she wore the Saint Allyn emeralds on her hands and wrist and at her throat, as well as a delicate tiara of emeralds and diamonds on her high dressed golden hair. As Reynolds fussed around, adjusting her skirts, she stared at her reflection, assessing herself and her toilette coldly and without conceit. Yes, I am beautiful, she thought, as beautiful as Althea Wyndham had ever been, and for the first time she was proud she looked so much like her mother. Suddenly she knew she would never have any more visions of her mother, never hear her voice again, for there was no further need for it when this reincarnation stared back at her from the glass. She knew she was standing on the brink of a turning point in her life, and she felt serenely confident that she could deal with whatever was in store for her. She nodded a little at the mirror, a smile curling her lips as she silently thanked her mother once again for showing her the way. Then she took her gloves and fan and went down to join her husband.

The duke, in faultless evening dress, bowed low as she entered the drawing room, and held out his arm to escort her to the table for dinner. "A beautiful gown, madam," he said, hoping she did not notice how hard it was for him to appear nonchalant now she was so close to him, so beautiful and desirable. There was that delicate perfume she wore that he remembered, and it made his senses swim. "I see by all your new gowns that you have been busy acquiring some town polish while I was toiling so hard amid the allies.''

"I hope you are home for good, sir," she replied, smiling up at him as he seated her beside him, and then she added softly for his ears alone, "I do not believe I told you that you were sorely missed."

"We shall see," was all the duke could find to answer as he signaled Wilkins that they were ready to begin.

Talk at dinner was light and general, but when the last course had been removed and the decanter placed beside the duke, Emily signaled for the servants to leave the room. Charles looked at her, his dark eyes intent on her pale, composed face.

"Do you mind, Charles?" she asked. "It seems we have so little time to talk, I thought I would remain with you instead of retiring this evening to the drawing room."

"As you wish, of course," he said, mystified by this unusual behavior.

He watched her look down at her hands, which she had clasped before her on the table, and bite her lip as if she were uncertain how to proceed, but just as he was about to speak and break the sudden silence, she raised her eyes to his and he caught his breath. Those pools of emerald held him in her spell as they had always done, and he stared into their velvety depths as she said, "Once, a long time ago, Charles, you said that you could see I did not trust you, but you hoped that I would do so one day. It was the afternoon at the farm when you saved me from the French soldier and questioned me about my background."

"I will never forget anything that happened that afternoon," he said quietly.

Emily did not take her eyes from his. "Well, believe me when I tell you I do trust you now. I have trusted you for a very long time."

She paused again, and Charles felt himself stiffening, almost as if he could not bear to hear what she was about to say next. Was she going to trust him to give her her freedom? Was she about to say she did not want a marriage of any kind with him? He knew he could not hold her against her will, not now when she had given him his heir.

With a conscious effort he said through stiff lips, "I am, of course, honored, madam. Trust, at the very least, we must have between us.''

Suddenly she rose from the table, almost tipping over her chair in her haste and throwing out her hands in revulsion. "No," she cried, "no more! I cannot bear it!"

The duke stood up to put his hands on her arms to steady her. "Cannot bear what? I do not understand . . .''

Those emerald eyes were flashing now and delicate color flooded her cheeks as she said in a low, intense voice, "I cannot bear to have you treat me this way, so cold and formally. Charles, I love you! Please say you forgive me for refusing your love and sending you away, for forcing us into this marriage of convenience, and take me back into your life. I do not think I can live if you do not love me, and most certainly not like—''

But she was allowed to say no more, for the duke swept her into his arms to kiss her, and even as she gave herself up to the myriad sensations his kiss evoked, there was a singing in her heart that she had succeeded. It was not too late! He loved her still. A long time later when he raised his head, she saw a suspicion of tears in his eyes that she knew was duplicated in her own.

"My golden Lorelei," he whispered, "how I have longed to hear you speak those words! When I came home, I meant to try once more to make you care for me, but when I saw the other men around you, when you were always busy going to this party and that, I despaired because I thought your love for me was gone forever, and you were content to maintain only the facade of marriage. And I was so angry, so jealous every time you smiled at another man, or danced with him—''

"So that was what was wrong the evening of Lady Merks' party," Emily exclaimed, leaning back against strong arms so she could see his face. "Oh, Charles, how foolish of you, how foolish of both of us! I entered society to make you proud of me, to show you that I meant to be truly your duchess at last. I intended to tell you how much I loved you the minute you came home from Vienna, but there was no way I could approach you when you held aloof and were so stiff and lordly.''

They smiled at each other for their folly, and then Charles drew her close to kiss her again. Emily did not remember him ever holding her quite like this, so near to him it seemed he feared she might change her mind and disappear even yet; nor had he ever kissed her with quite so much demanding hunger, as if he were starving for her. She did not protest his crushing embrace, for she felt as he did and she knew that after the arid desert of their long estrangement, they would always want each other just this way.

At last he took his lips from hers, but so reluctantly it was as if he could not bear even this tiny interruption of their passion, and as she looked into his eyes again, she saw the sparkling, intent look she remembered from their brief time of happiness at Wrotherham Park. He raised one black eyebrow, and staring back at him, her eyes glowing with a light that dimmed the magnificence of the jewels she wore, she nodded.

Together they walked from the dining room, across the wide hall, and up the stairs. Emily was acutely conscious of Charles' iron-hard arm around her waist, clasping her tightly against his long, muscular body, which kept pace beside her, and she did not even notice Wilkins' bow, nor the stiffening to attention of the footmen as they passed them, for to her at that moment there were only the two of them in all the world.

They went into her room, and as he closed the door, she turned to him and waited, never taking her eyes from his face. For a moment they stood in silence, and then he removed her tiara with hands that trembled a little, dropping it on a chair beside them before he took the pins from her hair and let it tumble down in shining golden waves, to run his fingers through it as he had dreamed of doing all those long, empty weeks just past.

And still they did not speak as he undressed her, the new silk gown falling in a shimmering heap to the floor, and her jewels and lacy underthings flung aside in reckless haste. When he lifted her in his arms and carried her to the bed, Emily shivered as she felt her whole body throbbing with her need for his love. As he undressed, she watched through half-closed eyes those broad shoulders and narrow hips, the curly black hair that covered his chest, and his long, powerfully muscled legs, and then he was beside her, with only the glow of the firelight to illumine the room, and she was able to give herself up at last to his impatient, fervent lovemaking with the ecstatic abandon she remembered so well.

Some time later as they lay wrapped in each other's arms, she suddenly remembered the ball and chuckled to herself.

She had thought Charles almost asleep, but at the sound of her laughter, he moved away a little and raised himself on one elbow so he could see her face.

"Charles," she whispered, "we have forgotten the ball! Whatever will Nigel and Jessica, indeed everyone, think of us? Perhaps we should dress again—it is not so very late after all . . ."

The duke looked around lazily at the disordered room, and then he turned to admire the satin smoothness of cream and rose and gold that was his wife's nude body in the flickering light of the fire. As he smiled down at her, her emerald eyes sparkled with impish teasing. Her golden hair was spread on the pillows behind her, and one long tress curled over her shoulder and came to rest against a rose nippled breast, and slowly he traced its route with a gentle hand as he said, "Do you remember saying once that what we two deem proper carried enough credit to overset any of the world's opinions? It is a sentiment I concur with completely."

Emily caught his tracing hand and held it to her breast as he added, "The Cathcart ball may be the social event of the Season, and you, my love, as the shining star of that Season, will no doubt be sorely missed by scores of your admirers, but I rather think that this evening, the Duke and Duchess of Wrotherham are going to be otherwise engaged. Oh, yes, most definitely, mm, otherwise engaged."

About the Author

Barbara Hazard was born, raised, and educated in New England, and although she has lived in New York for the past twenty years, she still considers herself a Yankee. She has studied music for many years, in addition to her formal training in art. She added the writing of Regencies to her many talents in 1978, but her other hobbies include listening to classical music, reading, quilting, cross-country skiing, and paddle tennis. Her previous Regencies, THE DISOBEDIENT DAUGHTER, A SURFEIT OF SUITORS, THE CALICO COUNTESS, THE SINGULAR MISS CARRINGTON and THE ENCHANTING STRANGER, are available in Signet editions.

JOIN THE *REGENCY ROMANCE* READERS' PANEL

Help us bring you more of the books you like by filling out this survey and mailing it in today.

1. Book Title: _____

   Book #: _____

2. Using the scale below, how would you rate this book on the following features? Please write in one rating from 0-10 for each feature in the spaces provided.

POOR		NOT SO GOOD			O.K.			GOOD		EXCEL-LENT
0	1	2	3	4	5	6	7	8	9	10

RATING

Overall opinion of book .... _____
Plot/Story .... _____
Setting/Location .... _____
Writing Style .... _____
Character Development .... _____
Conclusion/Ending .... _____
Scene on Front Cover .... _____

3. About how many romance books do you buy for yourself each month? _____

4. How would you classify yourself as a reader of Regency romances?
   I am a ( ) light ( ) medium ( ) heavy reader.

5. What is your education?
   ( ) High School (or less) ( ) 4 yrs. college
   ( ) 2 yrs. college ( ) Post Graduate

6. Age _____ 7. Sex: ( ) Male ( ) Female

Please Print Name_____

Address_____

City _____ State _____ Zip _____

Phone # ( )_____

Thank you. Please send to New American Library, Research Dept., 1633 Broadway, New York, NY 10019.